UNDONE

BOOK 3 OF THE LOCKWOOD TRILOGY

MELISSA CASSERA

Book Cover by Damonza
Editing: Dawn Ius, Jessica McKelden

2023 Edition

Print ISBN: 979-8-9873878-3-2

Published in the United States of America

PLAYLIST

"Just a Girl" - Florence + The Machine

"I Walk the Line" - Halsey

"Breathe Me" - Sia

"Secrets and Lies" - Ruelle

"Shameless" - Sofia Karlberg

"No Turning Back" - City Wolf, Royal Crimson, Hollywood Black

"Honour" - Black Hydra

DEAR READER

UNDONE IS THE third installment in the Lockwood Trilogy, a dark, upper YA paranormal romance series. This book is not a stand-alone and is meant to be read after *Control* and *Unravel*.

It's also a good idea (though not required) to read the *Black Sea* novella prior to this book.

Undone is told from the POV of both Natalie and Henry and will conclude their love story. While their story and perspective may be ending "for now," this won't be the last you'll see of these characters.

In some ways, things are just getting started.

Enjoy the ride.

THE RESET

NATALIE

(The ending of *Unravel…* to jog your memory)

Nausea.

That's all I feel in this moment, like I'm about to barf up ten pails of puke. It takes me a second to register where I am.

Oh, right. I'm backstage at Jack—my boyfriend's—inauguration. And by that, I mean he's about to become class president of Lockwood, the way-too-expensive school we attend on a private island in Washington state. 175 rich kids smashed into posh purgatory for our senior year of high school.

My stomach sloshes and churns. I must have eaten something earlier that didn't agree with me. I probe my memory. I had tea. Oatmeal. The normal stuff. Maybe it's just nerves or general annoyance because Jack is being a level-ten douche today.

As I look out from backstage at this ridiculous spectacle, I knock my head against a twelve-foot flower tunnel of white roses and wisteria. Petals shower to the ground. My eyes scan the room and I scoop up the stray petals, wanting to barf again as I shake a few from my hair.

Frankly, everyone is so distracted with their own drama at Lockwood, I don't think they'd even notice these petals mixed with puke.

A strange image claws its way into my brain, like someone's plugged a USB cable into my forehead and started playing a movie—starring me.

I see myself in a darkened corner of a hallway, my back pressed against a stone wall. I'm wearing a silky red dress and a Venetian mask and there's some guy caging me in that spot. He rips off his mask, looming over me. I definitely don't recognize him. He says in a raspy whisper, "You're in danger."

The image disappears and I'm once again looking at the inauguration— students shuffling into their seats. A live orchestra readying in the corner.

What the hell was that? It felt like a daydream, but certainly not one that I conjured on purpose. My wool uniform jacket suddenly feels itchier, hotter than normal.

"You look like a ghost," Jack says, surveying my appearance. "What's the matter?"

"I don't know. I feel sick," I reply, nausea creeping into my chest again.

"Well, I'm about to go on. Can you pull yourself together?"

Oh, Jack. Always so understanding. How I wish I was ballsy enough to slap him right here in the hallway, watching the shock and embarrassment on his face.

Suddenly, another image fires into my brain.

It's the same guy that was in the last one. *We're in the hallway at Lockwood. He grabs Jack by the shirt and shoves him—sending his body clear across the hall like some superhero. Or supervillain. Jack's body smashes into the lockers so hard, one of them springs open from its lock.*

The image dissolves and I'm left staring at Jack, perfectly fine and unharmed. Pinpricks of nerves climb all over my skin.

"What is going on with you?" Jack shoots me a pissy look, like I'm ruining his big day.

I don't know why it's such a big deal that I'm on that stage with him when he accepts the class presidency. It's not like "first lady" is something I aspire to be. No shade to first ladies.

Jack's voice snaps me from my thoughts. "Why don't you go to the bathroom and splash water on your face? And maybe do something with your hair. They're going to take our picture when I swear in."

His annoying demands jumble into one giant blur as my head clouds and bile rises in my throat.

❧

After spending five minutes puking in a stall, I find my friend Ciel by the sink area, touching up her already-perfect lip gloss.

"You ready for today, Jackie Kennedy?" she says in a singsong voice, then immediately abandons that tone when she clocks my appearance. "Natty, oh my god, are you hungover?"

"No." But it sure feels like I am.

I notice that Ciel seems to have constructed a flower crown from the rose petals on stage. It looks great, just like she always does. I glance at my reflection in the mirror. My skin is pasty and my eyes are rimmed with heavy, dark circles, as if I've been turned into a zombie. I yank out my clip and my hair puffs out in a hopeless cloud of curls.

"Did you see the new guy?" Ciel says, while tousling her beachy waves.

"Huh? What? I don't know." I'm only half-listening as anxiety swirls in my gut, traveling up to my throat.

"The new guy. Scholarship kid. He's hot. Probably poor, but hot. And kinda weird."

Before she can say another word, another image floats into my brain.

It's Ciel, standing on a balcony with some woman I don't recognize. They're arguing. No, maybe they're about to kiss? The woman leans closer to Ciel… and shoves her off the balcony.

The image vanishes and I'm staring right at Ciel, her eyes dancing over my face. Unease weaves around my limbs, and I'm frozen at the sink, trying to process these weird vignettes that keep haunting my mind.

"Natty? Is everything okay? You want some lip gloss? Lip gloss always makes me feel better." Ciel holds out the tube.

No, things are most definitely not okay. Bizarre images keep scrambling my brain, and the worst part is that they all feel real, like fragmented memories ready to swallow me whole.

∾

My shoes clack down the empty hallway as I head backstage, dread coiling at the base of my spine. I need to find some way to stop these images, daydreams, whatever the hell they are.

My friend Adip's voice rings out behind me. "Natty, wait up!"

Adip is someone I always enjoy talking to, in a very platonic, sibling-like way. But right now, I just want to get through Jack's speech, then spend the rest of the day in bed, sleeping off whatever's glitching inside my brain.

Adip falls into step next to me. "Hey, I had a crazy dream about you last night."

"Oh yeah?" I say, not really paying attention, nor slowing down. Adip keeps up with me as I round the corner, heading backstage to get this whole spectacle over with.

"I was in bed, in my dream, and some dude was sitting on the edge. He woke me up and said he was your dad."

"What?" A laugh bubbles up out of my throat, which feels somewhat relieving after barfing up my guts.

"I'm serious! It was freezing cold, and there was frost on my sheets, like he brought winter inside my room or something."

"Well, my dad is pretty icy, so that tracks."

"It wasn't your dad, like, not the dad I've met. This was some other guy I've never seen. He had these weird blue eyes that didn't look real, if that makes sense."

I pause, turning to face Adip. "None of that makes sense, but it was a dream. It's not supposed to."

"No, I'm telling you Natty, this felt so real. The dude told me I had to watch over you, like some guardian angel. I don't know. I must have been really high."

"Apparently."

"But get this. When I woke up, my window was open. Just flapping in the breeze like someone left and forgot to close it."

As much as I'd like to entertain Adip's weed-induced dreams, I can hear Headmaster Rochester making an announcement inside the auditorium.

"I've gotta get in there. Let's talk later."

As I twist away from Adip, he grabs my hand and gives it a friendly squeeze. "I know you think it sounds crazy, but I swear that wasn't a dream. I feel weird. Do you feel weird?"

Oh boy. Adip must have been smoking some really interesting stuff last night.

"I feel like I have food poisoning, and Jack is going to have my head if I don't get in there with him. We'll talk later, okay?"

Tugging my hand from his, I move down the hall. I don't make it far when another one of those damn images sneaks into my brain.

I'm sitting across from my father at a restaurant on campus. Some guy about my age sits next to me, another person I don't recognize.

"You're not my child. When your mother came to me, she was eight weeks pregnant with you and completely terrified," my father says.

The image vanishes and I'm sick again. Adip just shared some crazy dream, and now I'm having a flash of my father telling me he's not my father? That familiar sense of nausea spikes through my core, followed by a wave of anxious goosebumps.

I manage to get backstage just before Jack goes on stage.

Headmaster Rochester announces, "Let's give a Lockwood chant for our class president, Jack Carter!"

Jack looks back at me and his expression immediately morphs into horror when he sees my appearance. In other circumstances, this might delight me—tossing this act of rebellion in his face. But right now, my mind is vibrating with confusion and pure nausea.

As I step onto the stage behind Jack, I'm immediately blinded by a camera flash. The deafening roars and cheers rippling through the student body make my head want to burst from my neck.

Another flash in my face, and I snap at the photographer. "Stop, I can't see."

The photographer shoots me an annoyed look and backs away. "You look terrible anyway," he says.

When I finally regain my eyesight from the blinding flash, I spot Jack at the podium in all his glory. He raises his hand with a powerful wave and the crowd erupts into even louder tremors of excitement and applause. My body wobbles with dizziness as I take my place behind him, to the right. Attempting to squelch all this mess inside my brain and body, I focus on the crowd—a sea of beautiful faces in designer uniforms.

My eyes latch on to one student, and my stomach tightens as I realize it's the guy I saw in my mind, the one sitting next to me when my father revealed he wasn't, in fact, my father. I'm rendered paralytic as the student grins at me from the audience.

I suck in a deep breath to try and settle down my nerves, averting my gaze from the grinning stranger who somehow managed to claw into my brain.

Then, my eyes land on another strange thing. A line of guards blocks the back of the concert hall, holding rifles. I've never seen them before. As far as I know, we don't have guards at Lockwood.

The guards stare ahead with stone-faced expressions—all except one, whose eyes seem fixed on me. Nerves claw into my bones and spider through the rest of my body as yet another image enters my mind.

I'm outside, wearing that red dress again, but this time, I'm on my knees on the pavement, like I've taken an unfortunate spill. The guard extends his white-gloved hand in what appears to be a kind gesture, and I clasp it. Within seconds, I yank my hand away, scrambling to my feet, racing away from him, terror plastered on my face.

I blink away the image as Jack continues his speech. Fear prickles the back of my neck. Why was I running away from that guard, the one standing across from me right now, staring at me? Are these images some kind of weird premonitions?

I squeeze my eyes closed, trying to steady my breathing, and tune back in to Jack's speech, hoping it will calm me down. I know his speech so well, I can recite it myself. I repeat the words in my mind. Maybe that will halt these horrific slices of a movie I don't want playing in my head.

Suddenly, Jack's words trail off and a loud gasp erupts from the audience, followed closely by several shrieks. I pop open my eyes, noticing the guards pointing their rifles at the commotion.

I crane my neck to try and see what's going on. Shoes screech against the hard floor as students scurry from their seats. Jack whips his gaze around the room, annoyed by the interruption.

As the crowd parts, I'm finally able to get a clear view of what's happening.

It's a student—the other one I saw in my head. The one who was issuing me a warning. He's standing up, clutching his chest, having trouble breathing. He staggers backward, eyes popped wide, a look of sheer terror on his face. No one is helping him. Why is no one helping him?

My heart clenches as another image pops into my brain—

I'm pinned to the ground in the middle of the woods, desperately trying to fight off the guard. I smash my fists into him when suddenly, his body slumps down over mine. The weight of him lifts and I crawl away, noticing the student standing there. The same student having a panic attack right here in this auditorium… saving my life.

The image disappears, and without thinking, I rush to the edge of the stage, heart thundering in my chest. I can hear Jack shouting after me. My shoes smack to the ground and I bolt ahead, shoving my way through Lockwood's elite, and get to the student just as he crashes to the floor.

I lean over him and grab on to his arms. His eyes are squeezed shut, like he never wants to open them again. I give his arms a squeeze and he stirs. His eyes flutter open and clash with mine—deep green with flecks of gold. His eyes, his face, is familiar. Not just from the images in my head, but I have a deep sense that we're somehow connected.

His breathing accelerates, then his fingers snap around my wrists, his nails digging into my flesh as his gaze darkens. His jaw clenches, nostrils flared—the savage pounding of his pulse strumming against my skin.

For what feels like eternity, I can't move. I can't think.

Until finally, a few words escape my throat.

"How do I know you?"

CHAPTER ONE

NATALIE

HIS GRIP FEELS familiar.

This stranger lying on the ground in the middle of the Lockwood auditorium, squeezing my hand as if I'm his lifeline.

The orchestra stops playing. The other students are dead silent—watching me on the ground with this student I've never seen before except inside my head. I can even feel my boyfriend's eyes from the stage, burning a hole into my back. Jack must be livid I ruined his big moment.

"Who are you?" I whisper to the stranger on the ground.

His body trembles, sending an electric bolt pulsing up my arm, making me flinch, but not enough to let go of him.

I search his eyes for any truth, noticing the rise and fall of his chest as his breath quickens, like he's about to have another panic attack.

As if he can't take it anymore, he shoves me away, sending me crashing against the ground.

"Natty, oh my god." Ciel rushes over, crouching down to help.

But I can't take my eyes off this stranger. He's kneeling now, with a tortured, confused, yet apologetic look in his eyes. He breaks our gaze, scanning the room, seemingly terrified. I follow his eyeline, noticing those strange guards, their rifles pointed at him, like he's some kind of animal. Fortunately, they point their rifles up in unison, now aimed away.

I hear commotion behind me, turning just in time to see Jack flying off the stage, going right for the stranger.

A sharp protectiveness takes over my body as I press to stand, blocking his way. "Stop," I command, which Jack clearly doesn't like, as evidenced by him staring daggers at me. "Just leave it alone."

"This is *my* day," Jack says, fire practically spitting from his mouth.

Out of the corner of my eye, I notice the stranger shoving his way through the guards and fleeing out the exit.

"Are you okay, Natty?" Ciel asks as Adip curls his arm around her.

"She's fine. Let her go," Adip says, as if he knows something I don't.

That same electricity spirals through my body, and I come unglued from the floor, from my pissed-off boyfriend, from all of it—taking off after the stranger. I ignore Jack as he barks orders in the background, demanding that I not leave.

As I move past the guards, that same creepy one casts a glance in my direction. It's quick but noticeable, sending an uneasy shiver down my legs. My hands smack into the heavy metal door, shoving it open into the crisp fall air.

It takes me a moment once I'm outside to find him. He's already several paces ahead, but standing still, like he's frozen in place.

"Hey," I call out, but he doesn't seem to hear me.

I approach him, cautious, noticing his eyes are squeezed shut and he's counting backwards.

"Ten…nine…eight…seven…"

"Are you okay?"

He stops counting and his lashes flutter for a second before he blinks opens his eyes.

Swallowing my anxiety, I try to speak to him again. The sleeve of his uniform jacket is bunched up around his elbow, and on instinct, I reach out my hand to touch him in what's meant to be a comforting gesture. As soon as my finger grazes the bare part of his arm, another shock ricochets through my skin. He yanks away from me and I notice a tattoo on his forearm, some Greek symbol, I think.

"Do I know you?" I ask.

He shakes his head, casting an anxious glance around the campus.

"Because this is going to sound crazy, but I saw you."

"What do you mean you *saw*?" These are the first words he utters, and it's jarring to hear his voice. It sounds so familiar.

"I had these weird flashes in my head, and you were in them."

His eyes narrow and his body is visibly shaking, as if he's trying to control himself. He grabs my arm and yanks me to him as the breath whooshes from my lungs. There's no electric shock this time, just frantic energy.

"What the hell are you doing?"

I attempt to wriggle out of his strong grip as he pushes up my uniform jacket sleeve to reveal the underside of my forearm. He casts a glance of relief before he lets me go.

"What was that about?"

"I was looking for something," he says.

"On my arm?"

He doesn't answer, and I get the distinct feeling he's about to run.

"Look, I saw you, in my head. You told me I was in danger. You saved my life."

His entire body visibly stiffens as he leans into me. "We shouldn't talk about this here. There are cameras everywhere on this campus."

"They don't work. The school said they turned them off last year."

"And you really believe that?"

My skin pulsates with nerves. I hadn't considered the school was lying and I suppose he makes a good point. Maybe they only said they turned them off so they can catch us doing something illicit. Although, they pretty much let us do whatever we want here, so I'm not sure what they're trying to do.

"I have a place we can talk," he says, motioning for me to follow.

⌘

We don't speak a word to each other as he leads me up the steps inside one of the dormitory buildings, onto a maintenance floor. He shoves open a door and leads me inside a private bathroom.

"Is this yours? You have your own bathroom here?"

"Perks of arriving at Lockwood late, I guess."

"I didn't even get your name," I say.

"Henry. Henry Thorne." He leans back against the sink, piercing me with his stare.

"Aren't you going to ask mine?"

"You're Natalie Covington," he says.

How does he know my name? Suddenly, another one of those images enters my mind.

I'm in this bathroom with him, but he has me in the shower, my forearms pinned above my head against the cold tile. Through clenched teeth, he tells me that he saw what was going to happen to me, that he can see the future.

The image dissolves as horror and disbelief sinks in.

"We know each other, don't we? I keep seeing these things, and I feel like they're memories. You told me you can see the future."

Henry doesn't breathe a word, but I can sense his pain—that there's some truth to the images flipping through my mind.

"*Can* you see the future?" I ask.

A shiver seeps into my bones as he stares at me, still not uttering a word. It drives me crazy that I can't tell what he's thinking.

"We were right here in this bathroom, in *that* shower, when you told me. I saw it. I *remembered* it." My words sound crazed, even to me, as they burst from my throat.

The silence stretches on between us as Henry lowers his gaze. My patience loses the battle and I grab at his hands, tugging him into the shower. I spin to face him, pressing my back against the tile, reenacting the image in my mind.

"You were in front of me, you had my hands pinned above my head." I play this out for him, clasping onto his hands and holding them above my head, letting him cage me in.

He squeezes his eyes closed, as if this is all too much to handle.

"You turned on the water, I don't know why. Maybe to drown out any sound? And then you told me you could see the future."

The corners of his mouth twitch as he opens his eyes again. His gaze sears into mine. "Your eyes. They were just brown, but now they're green, like mine," he says.

My heart smashes into my throat. My mom's eyes turned from brown to green, and I always thought that was a strange story— secretly wishing I'd have the same fate. And now it happens, right in this very moment? There's something going on, something I don't understand, but desperately need to.

"Turn on the water," I say.

Henry doesn't make any moves, doesn't even remove his gaze from mine. So I crank the handle, letting freezing cold water pummel down on our clothed bodies.

As the water warms and heats, cascading over us, soaking through our clothes, Henry begins to fray. Time stretches on as our breathing accelerates, locked in the unknown.

Panic seeps through his words as he presses his forehead against mine. "I'm starting to see it now. I remember," he says.

And so do I. Memories flood into my brain like a torrent, our minds melding under the water.

Henry saving my life. Our first kiss. Him leaving. Me searching for him. Killing Oliver. A fight between him and the guy who was smirking at me from the crowd—Wes. Killing Amelia. Waking up on a boat with Henry. Running through the streets with him. Being trapped with him. Standing in a room, Henry, Ciel, and Wes encased in glass—my mom lying dead on the ground. Learning this is all an experiment. Amelia saying that I won't remember, none of us will. Amelia crawling toward a glass object, reaching for the lever. I try to stop her and everything goes blank.

Realization unfurls through Henry and I at the same time. We clutch on to each other, letting the water rain down over us while fear stretches around our bodies like tentacles.

"I remember everything," I say, feeling relieved to be here with Henry, yet terrified of all the danger that awaits outside of these walls.

Henry releases my hands and cups my face, planting a kiss on my lips. I sink into his embrace, letting the heat from the water and our bodies consume me.

"Thank god I found my way back to you," he says.

Amelia reset our world and now we're back here at Lockwood, a second round—day one of her twisted experiment.

Except *we remember*. We outsmarted her, out-powered her.

And we need to stop her for good.

CHAPTER TWO

HENRY

NATALIE FUCKING COVINGTON.

Thank god I found her, that we found each other. Water pours down over us, seeping through my uniform shirt and into my skin. But all I see is Natalie. Her eyes. Her lips. *Her.*

Her hand reaches up, fingers trailing over my cheek, but it feels like she's touching every inch of me.

I clasp her hand, gripping it with mine, taking it to my mouth. "God, I fucking love you." The words blurt from my throat, like a missing piece slotting into place.

"I love you too." Her voice is barely audible over the water, but all that matters is that I heard it.

Every second, every moment, every terrible fucking memory that led us to this point feels worth it. Because it brought me here, back to her.

She sinks back against the cold, tiled wall, her gaze locked onto mine. I press closer, my hand reaching to twist off the faucet, silencing the drumming water.

Her uniform blouse is soaked through and clinging to her like a second skin. Water droplets hang on her dark lashes, tracing a path down her cheeks. The sight is so goddamn mesmerizing—her tousled hair sticking to her face in wet strands, her vibrant eyes now a muted green, almost vulnerable.

As the last drops of water drip down from the showerhead, the room is filled with a charged silence. The only sound is the harsh rasp of our breathing, echoing off the tiles. The air is dense, heavy with the steam, a cocoon I never want to escape.

The chill of the room pricks at my bones, but the heat radiating from our bodies negates it. Water glistens on her bottom lip, a drop about to fall. The sight sends a jolt through me, a raw, primal urge that nearly knocks me off balance.

My body reacts to her, an instinctive pull that has me groaning in the back of my throat. Her breath hitches in response and I crash my lips onto hers, drunk with need, two people who've been starved for far too long. She moans against my lips as they move with hers, stirring every inch of me.

A sudden knocking echoes from the hallway, sobering our moment.

Knock, knock, knock.

Who the hell is that?

Knock, knock, knock.

The sharp rap on the door echoes through the silence like a gunshot. The sound isn't forceful enough to be on the bathroom door. It must be coming from outside my dorm room.

"Hey man, you in there?"

A familiar voice cuts through the fog of our heated moment, cold reality smashing into us. *Wes.* His voice is unmistakable, a sound I remember all too well.

Panic flutters in Natalie's eyes, mirroring my own. We huddle closer in the shower, pressing together, shivering.

"Do you think he remembers everything?" Natalie's whisper

brushes against my ear, her question hanging heavy in the air. I wish I had an answer.

"Maybe I should talk to him," I murmur, attempting to pull away, but Natalie's grip on me tightens, fear swimming in her eyes.

"No, don't. It's too dangerous."

Wes's voice continues to echo through the hallway, his words becoming more insistent.

The bathroom door isn't locked, a fact that hits us both like a punch to the gut. Any moment, he could come in and find us, soaked, shivering… together.

There's no time for us to argue, no time to reassure Natalie. I make a snap decision. With a quick, apologetic glance at her, I begin to shed my wet clothes, the damp fabric clinging to my skin as I strip down.

Natalie retreats further into the shower, her gaze fixed on me. I grab a towel from the rack, hastily wrapping it around my waist.

Her eyes linger on me, wide and worried, but she doesn't say anything.

I offer her a small nod, trying to convey a confidence I don't exactly feel. I pull her back into my arms, her wet body chilling against my skin. "I've got this," I whisper into her hair. The lie sits heavy on my tongue, but it's a necessary one. Right now, she needs to believe that I can handle this, even if I'm not entirely sure myself.

I cup her face in my hands, forcing her to look at me. Unable to resist, I lean down and kiss her again, more intense this time.

Every touch feels as if it could be our last.

Reluctantly, I pull away, the taste of her still on my lips. "I'll be back."

With a final glance, I step into the hallway, leaving Natalie hiding in the shower.

I'm instantly met with Wes's scrutinizing gaze. His eyes rake over my towel-clad form. "Hey man, I didn't mean to get you out of the shower. I'm Wes. Just wanted to make sure you were okay. That was pretty crazy back there."

His presence claws up my spine as I study his face, searching for any hint of recognition, any clue as to what he's really up to. "You followed me here?"

"No," he replies too quickly.

"Then how'd you know where my dorm was?"

"Mr. Fiore gave me your name the other day, told me to come find you. Said you could help with me with pre-calc. Math is not my strong suit." It's a flimsy excuse. I can't believe I bought it the first time around.

Wes's gaze drops to my forearm, his eyes narrowing at the sight of my marking, the psi symbol. "Where'd you get that?"

Fuck. How do I play this? He's going to immediately know I'm lying if I don't fess up about being a precog, but maybe that's exactly the way to coax the bullshit right out of him.

I shrug, forcing a casual smile. "Stupid decision one drunken summer. I'm sure you know how it is."

Wes pulls up his own sleeve, revealing his identical tattoo.

I maintain my composure, refusing to give him the satisfaction of surprise.

"You're not shocked that another precog is standing before you?" Wes says, his voice full of amusement.

"I've run into precogs before," I say, my tone flat. "What are you really doing here?"

"Relax, man. We need to stick together." His voice turns serious. "I'm not bullshitting, I came to make sure you were okay."

"I'm fine. Just not feeling well," I say, deflecting. "I'm gonna lie down for a bit. We can talk about the whole tutoring thing another time."

Of course, he doesn't budge—because he's the fucking worst. "Was it a vision? Is that why you had a panic attack back there?"

My patience wears thin and I snap. "It wasn't because of that. I really need to chill for bit. I'll catch up with you some other time."

Wes's hand shifts in his pocket, wrapping around something. A glint of metal catches my eye, and my nerves claw into my throat. Is he really about to fucking stab me?

It's Wes, so likely the answer is… *yes*.

I steel myself, ready for a fight as the hallway falls silent, tension winding tighter and tighter.

Wes seems to sense my unease, removing his hand from his pocket without the dagger. He gives me a reluctant nod, stepping away from the door. "Find me when you're ready to talk."

I watch him leave, making sure he's not lingering around the corner, watching us. Whatever Wes is up to, we need to be ready, because I know this is just the beginning of whatever hell he has planned.

CHAPTER THREE

NATALIE

MY BODY TREMBLES from the water cooling on my skin.

Cold tiles seep through the fabric of my clothes as a knot of dread tightens in my stomach. Each second stretches into an eternity. I strain and fail to hear Henry and Wes's muffled conversation in the hallway.

The sound of footsteps sends a jolt of adrenaline coursing through my veins, my breath hitching in anticipation.

Suddenly, the footsteps grow louder, the familiar creak of the bathroom door. A rush of relief winds through me when Henry steps into the room, the towel still wrapped around his waist.

In an instant, I'm out of the shower and in his arms, desperate for the heat of his skin, a stark contrast to the chill of my wet clothes.

"What happened?" I say, my voice barely a whisper.

Henry clings to me with a troubled gaze. "I couldn't tell if he knew anything or not, but I sensed that he did. We need to leave Lockwood. Now."

The urgency in his voice sends a jolt of fear through me and I clasp onto his forearms with trembling fingers. "We can't just leave. What about Ciel? Amelia knows I care about her. And Adip?"

"If we're back in the original timeline, that means Wes and his uncle were sent to kill you. It's only a matter of time—"

I cut him off. "Amelia said herself she doesn't want me dead. This is all some twisted experiment. We're just lab rats in her game."

Henry cups my face, tipping it up to his. "We can't wait around to see what happens next. What if she changed her mind? What if she wants you dead this time? I can't—"

"My father—my *real* father—he's apparently immortal. I'm not sure if that means I am too."

Henry swallows hard, clenching onto me tighter. "I won't take that risk. I can't. I won't lose you."

His words tug at my heart and I have a rabid need to kiss him, our lips meeting in a desperate, heated clash. It's not long before my lungs scream for air, the lack of oxygen making my head spin. I cling to the feeling, letting it simmer, intensify, before finally, I have to break away.

I murmur into his lips, "We can't leave Ciel and Adip here. Amelia will absolutely go after them." My senses return and I'm shivering, the chill of the room and my drenched clothes finally catching up with me.

"You need to get out of these wet clothes."

As I start to peel them off, he steps back, creating a respectful distance, but he doesn't turn away. His gaze sticks on me, watching as each layer of wet fabric falls to the cold floor. The weight of his stare tugs at my core. I take my time, acutely aware of his watching eyes as I peel off my blouse, my skirt, my tights, my bra, my under-wear, the wet clothes pooling around my feet.

I reach out for the towel he offers, our fingers brushing against each other. Electricity zips up my spine and I see the echo of it in his wild green eyes.

We stay like this, our hands lingering, our eyes locked. The fear of everything we're up against fades momentarily into the background, replaced by the fire between us.

With a deep shiver, I wrap the towel around my body, and the sudden change in temperature snaps us both back to the reality we face. We need to put this—*us*—on the back burner. Just for now.

"We need a plan," I say, clutching the towel tighter around me. "We have to find a way to keep Ciel and Adip safe while we figure out how to rescue my mom and take Amelia down."

Henry nods, his gaze thoughtful. "She must have a weak spot. Something or someone she cares about."

I suck in a deep breath, steeling myself for what I'm about to reveal. "Amelia said something about knowing my father." I watch as Henry's eyebrows knit together in confusion. "The man I *thought* was my father isn't my biological dad. It was all a lie."

His eyes widen. "What does that mean?"

"I don't know. There wasn't enough time to ask my mom all the questions I wanted to in that place. And Amelia certainly wasn't going to spill the truth. But Adip said… he said my dad came to see him. He thought he was dreaming, but what if he wasn't? What if that *was* my real dad? And if it was, why would he go to Adip and not to me?"

There's a moment of silence as the weight of everything sinks in. If my father is alive, and if he did visit Adip, maybe we have another ally.

Or is this another part of Amelia's twisted experiment?

Dread coils in my stomach and I think I'm going to be sick. Queasiness swells inside me, my mind reeling with uncertainty.

"I need to lie down for a minute."

Henry leads me to his dorm and we lie side by side on his bed, his arm gently wrapping around my shoulders. I rest my head against him, feeling the steady warmth of his presence. The rhythmic beat of his heart helps ease my tension. Our bodies are still wrapped in towels, the heat of our skin seeping through the thin fabric and sending an altogether different kind of shiver down my spine.

His hand begins to trace soothing patterns on my back.

"We need to figure out what the hell to do," I say, my voice muffled against his chest. "What if we go back to the precog headquarters, where Amelia is?"

Henry is silent for a moment, his fingers pausing on my back.

"I don't have the physical map because, well, that hasn't technically happened yet. But the directions…they're burned into my memory."

"But that's exactly what Amelia wants. She wants to draw us back there. So is it really the best move to go?" His voice is heavy with a resignation I understand all too well.

I swallow hard, the gravity of our situation sinking in. "It's dangerous to go there, but it's also dangerous to stay here at Lockwood."

It's an impossible situation. We have to face Amelia, we have to find my mom, and we have to win. But how the hell do we do that?

"We need to come up with a way to destroy that device she uses to reset time, so we're not just looping in this horror show 24/7."

"We need to destroy *her* too." Henry echoes my thoughts, a grim determination settling in his eyes. "She's the root of all this. If we take her out, we take out the problem."

His words hang in the air between us. "Why is Amelia doing this to me? Is it all about power and control? Or is there something more? It feels like she's got some personal vendetta."

"The only way we'll know is by figuring out who Amelia Collins really is. Who else knows her? Who can we get information from?"

"Wes does," I say reluctantly, my mind whirling. "But we don't know what he remembers, and we can't trust him anyway." A memory lodges in my brain, a sharp detail that may be important, giving me a spark of hope. "There *is* someone else. Back when all this happened last time, and you were kidnapped by the authority, I found something inside a framed photo my mom gave me. It was a note mentioning the Nine O'Clock Gun. I went there with Wes."

"I know, I saw you two. It was a vision—or rather, a nightmare—for me."

My stomach clenches and drops, forgetting how warped all of this is—Wes is a sensitive topic for us. I'd do anything to erase everything that happened with him, my choices at the time, but I can't.

"I'm sorry. I wish I'd never gotten involved with him."

"I know." Henry pulls me tighter. "Forget it. What happened when you went to the Nine O'Clock Gun?"

"I met this guy Ray and he gave me a box of my mom's things. But my mom said she never left that for me, didn't know him at all, so it was obviously a set up by Amelia. Ray must have been working for her. Maybe we can go see him, try to get information out of him? It's worth a shot."

Henry nods, but worry still gnaws at me.

"But we can't just leave Ciel and Adip here alone. Maybe I can suggest a night out together in Vancouver? We'll take a walk at the seawall, I'll go see Ray. It's not the best plan, but it's something."

"It's something." Henry kisses me before tossing me some sweats to change into.

We reluctantly get dressed, our gazes tracing over each other's bodies, desire still pulsing between us. With a final, lingering look, we leave the fleeting safety of his dorm room.

Our movements are careful, calculated, as we move through the hallways. We step out into the open campus, the crisp air brushing against our skin.

The campus is dead quiet, with students still inside the inauguration, the orchestra music muted by the distance. As we cross the campus, every corner feels like a threat, and we're straining for any sign of trouble.

We round a corner, and suddenly, he's there.

Jack.

My boyfriend. A fact I totally forgot about in this current timeline.

His gaze is like a physical blow, stormy and incensed. He takes in my attire—Henry's oversized sweats hanging loosely off my frame. He studies the damp tendrils of hair curling against my neck, his eyebrow arching up in silent accusation.

"Where the hell were you, Natalie?" His eyes dart between Henry and me before fixing them solely on Henry with a raged gleam. "And what the hell are you doing with my girl?"

CHAPTER FOUR

HENRY

THE GLARING REALITY that Natalie is still Jack's girlfriend in this timeline crashes down on me like a bitter, cold shower.

Jack stands just a few feet away, his eyes narrowing to lethal slits. He's clearly hell-bent on beating me to a pulp. I could easily take him—given that the last time I punched him, he went flying across a hallway—but making a scene right now, with the whirlpool of chaos we're already trapped in, seems pretty fucking stupid.

"Look, we should talk." Natalie's eyes are soft and pleading as she tries to pull Jack aside.

His face flushes a ridiculous shade of crimson as he volleys his eyes between the two of us. "Talk about what? How you left me standing all alone on that stage to chase after this asshole?"

"Watch yourself," I threaten, my voice low.

Jack sneers, his anger rising. "Don't tell me to watch myself. You royally fucked my inauguration."

"Get over yourself, man. The world doesn't revolve around you."

An arrogant huff escapes his throat. "At Lockwood it does. I own this school. I'm the class president."

Natalie leads him a few paces away, raising her voice to be heard over our tension. "Jack, enough. Look, there's no good time to do this, so I'm just going to rip off the Band-Aid. We're over."

His reaction is immediate and intense, a wild glare, as though he might strike her. My blood boils at the thought, and I'm two seconds from smashing his face in.

"What did you just say to me?" he says, his voice ice cold.

"It's over. We're done." Natalie is calm but firm.

Jack reels back in disbelief, a mix of shock and wounded pride on his face. I'm not sure if it's the breakup that has him so rattled or the blow to his ego.

"You are seriously ending our relationship at my *inauguration*, the most important day of my life? Are you out of your mind?"

Natalie tries reasoning, keeping her voice steady. "No, I'm very, very sane, and I know for sure that we don't belong together. So let's just go our separate ways. I know you're into Josephine. Go be with her."

Fury and confusion play across Jack's face but he doesn't budge. He opens his mouth to protest, and I do my best to close it.

"Look man, why don't you just walk away, yeah? She told you, it's over."

His gaze snaps to mine, disbelief flooding over his expression, then cuts his eyes back to Natalie. "You can't be serious, Nat. You're breaking up with me for *this* guy? Isn't he just a scholarship kid?"

"What the fuck does that matter?" I say, my patience wearing thin.

"Because you're getting a free ride here, and now you're trying to ride my girl," he says, eyes glinting with rage.

His pathetic remark pushes me beyond my limit. I stalk over to him. "If she says it's over, then it's over. Now back the fuck off before I make you regret it."

In a sad attempt to appear imposing, Jack puffs up his chest and tries to reach my height. He's not short by any means, but he's no match for me. "How about *you* back off, scholarship boy?"

He smacks his hands into my chest and shoves me. It's a weak attempt, and I barely move. It doesn't deter him, though, and he tries to push me again, a bit more forcefully this time.

"Jack, that's enough," Natalie says.

He ignores her, shoving me once again, tripping my fuse. I retaliate before my rational mind kicks in, pushing him back with enough force to send him sprawling in the mud. He lands with a thud, ruining his immaculate uniform. There's a beat of silence as he scrambles to get back on his feet, splattering more mud on his clothes in the process.

"I'm going to kill you," he seethes, his threat barely a whisper.

Before either of us can make another move, Adip storms over and steps in, forming a barrier between us. He confronts Jack. "Hey, man, she said it's over. You need to respect that." His voice is calm and level.

Jack cuts an icy glare to Adip. "How the hell would you know what Nat said? You weren't even standing here."

Adip gulps down a breath, clearly uncomfortable with the accusation. I hate to admit it, but Jack is right—how *did* he know what Natalie just said?

"Just leave it, man. Go back to your dorm, chill out."

Jack's gaze swivels back to Natalie. "You told Adip before me? Does the entire school know about your plan to dump me on *my* day?" As Jack gives up and backs away, his eyes shift to mine one last time, filled with defiance. "This isn't over, asshole, not by a long shot."

Adip tries to placate him as he retreats. "Jack, take it easy, man."

With one last scowl, Jack turns and storms off, leaving us in an uneasy silence. Natalie sucks in a deep breath, her shoulders drooping slightly, while Adip appears as if he's just diffused a bomb.

Natalie pipes up, her eyebrows knitted together in confusion. "Adip, how *did* you know I was breaking up with Jack?"

"I don't know, I just… overheard. I wasn't even supposed to be in this part of campus. I took a wrong turn and somehow ended up here." He points off to a spot in the distance, a location so far away it seems impossible that he could have heard our conversation.

My pulse skitters. "You heard from all the way over *there*?" I ask, skeptical. "You sure you didn't just assume what was happening?"

Adip raises his hands in defense. "I swear, I heard Natalie clear as day. Maybe my senses are really sharp? That weed I smoked last night… Man, I don't know what it was laced with, but I'm feeling some type of way."

Natalie's eyes narrow slightly. "Did you smoke something different?"

"Nope." Adip laughs. "Same old stuff." With an easygoing grin, he extends his hand in my direction. "We haven't even met, but I feel like I know you somehow. I'm Adip. You new here?"

I accept his handshake, his grip firm yet warm. "Yeah, I'm Henry."

Adip darts a curious glance between Natalie and myself, an unasked question dancing in his eyes before he voices it. "How exactly do you two know each other?"

Natalie responds with a slight shrug. "It's complicated."

Adip raises his hands in a nonchalant surrender. "Fair enough, I'll take your word for it." His acceptance of our vagueness comes with surprising ease.

Thinking back to Adip's strange dream Natalie shared with me, I prompt him for more details. "Natalie mentioned a dream you had last night. Can you tell us more about that?"

Adip squints as if he's replaying the dream in his head, his voice trembling slightly as he speaks. "I was in bed, in my dream, and this guy was sitting next to me. He woke me up and said he was Natalie's dad, but not the one I've met. Another guy. It was so cold

in my room, like freezing. I noticed frost on my sheets, and he…
he said I needed to protect Natalie, like I was her guardian angel or
something. When I woke up, my window was open. It was flapping
in the wind as if someone had left and didn't bother to close it."

He seems like he's telling the truth. He's either a fantastic liar or
this really happened to him.

Natalie presses for more details. "What did the man look like?"

Adip's gaze drifts away as he describes the man who claimed
to be Natalie's father. "Tall, built like a swimmer… really broad
shoulders. His hair was sandy brown, almost blond. And his eyes…
they were really blue, like the sea. Kind of creepy, but mesmerizing
at the same time. I don't know how to explain it. And there was this
faint scar on his cheek, too, I guess he'd been burned. Oh, and there
was water on the floor of my room when I woke up, like he'd walked
in with wet shoes. Which is messed up. My sheets were all damp. It
felt so real, but it must have been the weed, right? Did I sleepwalk
outside and drag back the rain? I wasn't wet though…" He trails off,
confused.

His description sends a chill down my spine. It doesn't feel like
the musings of a drug-addled mind, but something more.

Something we can't ignore.

CHAPTER FIVE

NATALIE

JUST AS ADIP finishes relaying his dream, Ciel saunters over to us. Her eyes glitter with curiosity, reflecting the sunlight. "Hey, you guys." She snakes her arm through Adip's and nestles against him.

"Hey, babe," Adip murmurs in response, leaning in to kiss her.

Ciel sighs softly into his lips, deepening their kiss. A group of students walks by, turning their heads to watch and whistle.

Ciel pulls away, her fingers tracing the front of Adip's shirt in a clear invitation. "Blow off the rest of the day with me."

Adip looks tempted—I can see the gears working behind his eyes—but he shakes his head. "Wish I could, but I should go check on Jack."

"Why, what happened?" Ciel's curiosity is piqued. "He still pissed about the inauguration?"

"I'll let Natalie fill you in. Raincheck for later?" Adip places one more lingering kiss on Ciel's lips before jogging off towards the main campus.

She turns her attention to Henry and me. "So, are you going to introduce me to your friend?" She gives Henry an evaluative once-over.

"This is Henry," I say.

Henry manages a short, guarded wave.

Folding her arms over her chest, Ciel's demeanor changes, her previously playful expression turning serious. "You shoved my friend in the auditorium. I should be pissed at you. That's abuse, you know."

Henry's eyes flash, ready to defend himself, but I intervene. "Ciel, calm down. It was an accident."

"That's what abuse victims say. I heard it on a podcast." She rakes her eyes over Henry for a moment longer before dropping the subject. Turning her attention back to me, Ciel says, "Okay, fine, Natty, spill. What's the deal with you and Jack?"

Henry steps back. "I'll give you two a moment alone." He moves a few paces away, settling on a nearby stone bench among Lockwood's beautifully manicured bushes, keeping us within his line of sight.

Ciel's eyes widen in disbelief as I confirm my breakup with Jack. She takes a moment, seeming to weigh the news, before a slow grin spreads across her face. "You know what? I'm into this. You've been tied to Jack for too long. This is a new school, a new year, time for a fresh start." Her gaze shifts over to Henry, curiosity swimming in her eyes. "So the guy who pushed you, you want to mess with him now? I don't judge, if you like things a little rough. I do, too, sometimes."

"Ciel, it's not like that."

Her eyes wander over to Henry again. "Who is he anyway? He's super hot."

"He's the scholarship kid," I say, repeating her words back to her.

"Huh." She blinks in surprise.

"You said it earlier in the bathroom. You asked me earlier today if I had seen the scholarship kid yet."

She seems lost in thought for a moment. "I didn't mean that guy. Scholarship kid is…" She cranes her neck, scanning the campus, before a sly grin crosses her face. "That guy over there." She points behind me, and I follow her gaze.

Leaning against a nearby building is Wes, wreathed in a cloud of smoke, his gaze wandering towards us.

Henry follows our eyeline and rises from the bench, protective.

I shoot him a warning glance to stay put, then look back at Ciel. "You know him?" I say, cautious, trying to steady my reaction.

Ciel gives a nonchalant shrug, her eyes dancing with intrigue. "We haven't officially met…not yet anyway. I'm still figuring out the Adip situation. I mean, I like Adip, sure, but with that guy…" She pauses, tilting her head towards Wes. "There's a vibe. I can feel it."

My heart plummets into my stomach. *Holy shit.* Is it possible that Ciel is still bound to Wes? That's…no, that's impossible. Their bond was severed when I brought him back to life. That was a different timeline, a different reality.

Or was it all an illusion? Another one of Amelia's cruel, twisted games? Perhaps Wes and I were never truly bonded. A tidal wave of relief washes over me, followed closely by a surge of anxiety. If Ciel *is* still bonded to Wes…

"I think I'll go introduce myself," Ciel says, already beginning to drift towards him.

"No, wait, Ciel!"

My protest falls on deaf ears as she weaves her way through the courtyard. I can't risk letting Wes get his claws into her. If he's retained his memories from before, he won't hesitate to use Ciel as a pawn—bonded or not.

Motioning for Henry to join me, I quickly fill him in. "This isn't good," I say, my words barely audible. "Ciel is drawn to Wes for some reason, and it seems like there may still be some kind of bond between them."

"I thought he supposedly bonded to you," Henry says, his expression contorted in both confusion and disgust.

I shake my head, my heart knocking against my ribs. "I don't have all the answers, but we need to find them."

Henry and I approach Wes and Ciel. His surprise at seeing us is almost comical, the fleeting look of pleasure that crosses his face only adding to my mounting unease.

Ciel, oblivious to the tension, winds a strand of her hair around her finger, lost in Wes. "I was just getting to know our new friend," Ciel says. "This is Wes."

Wes grins at Ciel but his gaze shifts to me, like a jagged knife cutting through my defenses. I study him, sizing him up, silently analyzing his every breath. *What do you remember, Wes?*

"And this is Natalie."

"Natalie." Wes repeats my name as if it's unfamiliar. "Nice to meet you."

His act may convince Ciel, but not me. *You know my name, asshole. And I'm on to you. I just need to know what else you remember.* Even if he has no memory of what happened, things were reset, and that means he's here on campus, tracking me. His job is to make sure his uncle has a direct line to my death—or kidnapping, since Amelia wants me alive on a constant torture loop.

I shoot him an innocent smile. "Nice to meet you too."

"And Henry, we've met," Wes says with a jovial grin.

Henry manages a nod.

Wes acknowledges Henry with a nod back. He raises a cigarette to his lips, puffing out a cloud of smoke. His uniform jacket is cuffed on his forearm, revealing his psi symbol branding that appears like a tattoo for those who don't know better.

Ciel's eyes are immediately drawn to it. "Oh, I love your tattoo. What's it mean?" She grabs his arm, tracing the symbol with her fingers.

"It's the twenty-third letter of the Greek alphabet," Wes says, feeding Ciel's curiosity. "It has several meanings, one of which is psychic phenomena, like premonitions or precognition."

My heart leaps into my throat. What the hell? Is he purposely inviting suspicion?

"I just thought it looked cool, though. No deeper meaning for me." Wes shrugs nonchalantly, taking another drag from his cigarette.

"It looks a bit like a pitchfork or a trident," Ciel muses, leaning a bit closer to Wes.

He glances at it. "Yeah, I can see that." His eyes shift from Ciel to me, sending a chill racing up my spine. "What are you up to later?" he asks Ciel, but his gaze is still locked onto mine.

"Are you asking me out?" Ciel teases.

"We have plans," I blurt out, my tone clipped.

Ciel gives me a puzzled look. "We do?"

"Yep, was planning to surprise you but it seems like the surprise is out now."

"What plans?" Wes says, finishing his cigarette with a final puff.

I swallow the nerves coiling up my throat. *Make something up.* "Girls' night."

"Sounds fun. Mind if I drop by?" Wes asks.

I notice Henry's hand balls into a fist.

Ciel grins. "Not at all. We'd love to have you, right, Natty?"

"Uh, maybe," I say, trying to conceal my real feelings. There is no fucking way Wes is coming to girls' night...or anywhere near us.

Ciel shrieks, glancing at her watch. "Damn, I'm late for class. I was going to skip, but I'd rather save that for a better occasion. Can't wait for tonight." She casts one more flirtatious glance in Wes's direction.

He smirks as she rushes off, leaving the three of us in an uneasy silence.

"So, how'd you two meet?" Wes says, his eyes bouncing between me and Henry.

"We go to the same school," Henry says, not playing Wes's games.

"Sure, but how *exactly* did you meet? Was it in the auditorium just now? Or before?"

"Why do you want to know?" Henry's voice is sharp, his protective instinct showing.

"I'm just a curious guy. It'll probably be the death of me someday," Wes says casually.

All of his words sound so familiar, lines he's delivered to me before, in a different timeline. Only now, everything he says hits like a fresh scratch on an old scar.

Wes steps away from the wall, lingering near me for a moment. "I'll see you and your friend tonight."

As he stalks away, anxiety squeezes my chest. Wes remembers something. I'm sure of it.

CHAPTER SIX

HENRY

I HATE THE way Wes was looking at Natalie—like a predator locking onto its prey. I noticed every one of his sickening glances.

"He remembers, I know it." Natalie echoes my thoughts, her voice tinged with fear.

My mind churns. "If he *does* remember, then his intentions are different. He wouldn't be here to track you. So what's his real plan?"

"Maybe he's still working with Amelia. But that means he would know where to find her. Maybe we can use that," Natalie says, threading her fingers together, picking at the skin around her fingernails.

"What are you thinking?"

"Before things went south, before he was a student here, he shacked up in a room in the building called the treehouse. It used to be the bioscience building. He must be staying there now. We could break in, look around. There must be something—notes, clues. It's worth a shot."

Nerves twist around my gut as Natalie leads the way to a deserted part of campus with a building that doesn't look anything like a treehouse.

I push open the heavy metallic door, clasping her hand as we enter. The door swings shut behind us with a loud thud.

We move through the silent corridor, the clacking of our shoes against the worn hardwood echoing off the walls. A small stairway at the end leads down to a more secluded part, housing a single door with a small window.

I peer into the window, but the room looks completely abandoned, discarded wood and a thin layer of sawdust covering the floor.

"Doesn't look like he's staying here."

Natalie releases my hand and twists the knob, opening the unlocked door. We step inside the room, scanning it for any sign that Wes was here.

"So where the hell is he staying? He's not officially a student here, so he can't be in a dorm," Natalie says.

My mind coils over the possibilities and unease crawls over my skin. "Maybe Amelia is altering things," I say. "It's all an experiment to her, right?"

Realization washes over me, dousing me in anger. I scan the room for cameras, half expecting Amelia to be observing us right now. *Probably is.*

I move toward the far corner of the room, Natalie threading her arm through mine. "I don't see any cameras, but that doesn't mean Amelia's not watching."

Suddenly, the door to the room slams shut. The sudden snap of the lock cuts through the air. My nerves spike into my throat as I rush towards the door, unable to twist the knob open.

We're trapped.

"Who just locked us in here?" Natalie's question pierces the silence like an arrow. Her voice trembles, setting off the alarm in the back of my mind. The room feels like it's closing in on us, the walls pressing closer as if conspiring to keep us trapped.

Through the door's window, I search the deserted hallway for any signs of movement. Dread coils up my spine when I see nothing…no one.

"There's no one out here."

"What the hell is going on?" Natalie says, fear chopping into her words.

Suddenly, smoke billows into the room from the baseboards.

"What's happening?" I stammer out, watching the ominous cloud grow.

The smoke pours faster, like lava erupting from a volcano. It swirls around us, a menacing fog invading our lungs. Natalie coughs violently.

With no other windows in this room, our only exit is the one on the door.

"We need to break the window," Natalie chokes out, desperation pooling in her eyes.

I seize a wooden plank from the floor, its worn texture splintering into my palms. With every ounce of strength I have, I smash it into the window, waiting for the shattering sound of breaking glass.

It never comes.

The plank ricochets off the glass as if it's made of something else…something unbreakable. I attack the window again and again, the impact rattling through my body with each futile attempt. Natalie joins in, her attempts also failing, the impenetrable glass mocking our desperation.

The room grows smaller as the thick smoke obscures our vision and robs us of oxygen. I toss the plank down on the ground, my lungs heavy and close to seizing. There has to be a way out of this fucking room.

Natalie's voice emerges from the smoke. "We have to try and use our collective powers. We've done it before."

Neither of us know how to wield our powers yet, but we've been thrown into chaos before, and yet managed to find a way out and back to each other.

I counter with my concerns, smoke wrapping us in a sinister blanket. "But our powers haven't unlocked, right? That didn't happen until I changed my vision."

Her muffled response cuts through the thick cloud of smoke. "I think we both have powers that have been suppressed. It doesn't matter whether you've changed your vision yet or not."

Her belief in our untapped abilities calms the panic gnawing at my insides. There's no time to weigh options while trapped in this endless torture chamber. It must be Amelia's doing, all part of her twisted experiment.

"Hold my hands," Natalie says.

I go along with her suggestion, our palms clasping, fingers intertwined, just like we did that day on campus when we kissed for the first time. Haunting memories of the precog authority building—of falling into that bottomless black hole, what happened a different time we tried using our collective powers—lunges into my brain.

As the smoke whirls around us, I focus on the surging energy between us. Slowly, I can feel it stir in a vortex of power. The floor convulses beneath us and water begins to gush from the ceiling. A rush of oxygen fills my lungs as the smoke recedes and water floods into the room, nipping at our thighs.

Suddenly, the water picks up speed, crashing into the room with a force that nearly knocks us off our feet.

"What the hell is happening?" I shout, my words drowned out by the deafening rush of water.

Before I can process anything, a massive wave slams into us, knocking us down and separating our hands.

The water drags me away from Natalie, and my body crashes against the wall as the wave pulls me under.

In the murky depths, I spot Natalie in the distance, her figure blurry in the rocky water. I swim over to her and we collide in a desperate embrace. Our heads resurface, gasping for air in the tiny pocket that remains.

The water level nearly touches the ceiling and we're submerged again, locking eyes beneath the surface. Fear grips my chest, fisting my heart. There's only one way for me to die—a dagger. But Natalie? Her fate is uncertain, and the possibility of her drowning to death before my eyes is unbearable.

Fighting the current, I pull us towards the last sliver of breathable air. "Look at me," I command, holding her face in my hands. "We have to try and merge our powers again."

Her eyes flicker, an electrifying green. Then, her eye color changes again, this time to an otherworldly blue. The color is so vivid, so odd, it's as though she's been taken over by something—or someone—else.

I shout her name, but she doesn't respond. Her gaze is vacant as we gasp for the last breath of air before the water engulfs us completely.

"Natalie!" My words are distorted, swallowed by the water, bleeding into nothingness.

Natalie appears catatonic, possessed even. I'm no longer staring at Natalie—at least, not the one I know.

Suddenly, the water recedes with punishing force. We're hurled onto the cold, hard floor as the room empties, water vanishing into the walls and ceiling.

My body throbs but I push through the pain, rushing to Natalie, who lays sprawled on the floor, unconscious.

Dread soaks through my skin as I peer down at her eyes, still an eerie, luminous blue, staring blankly at nothing. I give her a frantic shake. "Natalie, Natalie, c'mon."

Memories from a CPR class I took during an ocean cleanup mission in Istanbul flicker in my mind. I tear open her shirt and lean in, placing my lips onto hers, forcing air into her waterlogged lungs.

A violent cough erupts from her throat, and water spills from her mouth.

Relief sweeps through me… temporary relief from the chilling reality of what just happened.

Her eyes squeeze shut as she continues to cough.

"Take it easy."

When her eyes reopen, they're no longer blue—reverting to green. Was it a hallucination brought on by the lack of oxygen? Or was this Amelia's doing? Or something else?

"What the hell just happened?" she croaks, her gaze darting around the empty room. "I blacked out. Now all the water is gone."

A shiver passes through me as I attempt to explain. "I don't know. Your eyes turned blue—bright blue—and then the water… it just drained out of the room. It was like something else took control of your body."

She trembles in my arms at the revelation. "You said my eyes turned blue?"

"Yeah," I say, the memory tattooed in my mind. "It was so vivid. Unreal. Like the sea."

A moment of silence hangs between us before she speaks again, her voice barely above a whisper. "That's what Adip said in his dream…the color of my dad's eyes. Blue, like the sea."

CHAPTER SEVEN
NATALIE

The room around us shifts from a water-filled death trap to a bone-dry box. I can't escape the lingering thought that this was all Amelia's sick experiment to gauge our powers, to push us into a corner until they erupted. And it seems she's getting exactly what she wants, considering Henry thinks I was possessed—manifesting a devastating flood, drowning this entire room… and nearly drowning us.

My eyes, blue like the sea.

That's what Henry said. Adip's vivid dream crashes into my mind. If this is all my real father's doing, why doesn't he come to me? Why hasn't he before?

I shake off my tangled thoughts. "We have to get out of here."

Adrenaline surges through my bones as I clamber to my feet and hurry towards the door. I grip the cold metal knob, giving it a twist. To my surprise, the door is unlocked, opening easily. *Too easily.*

Fear crystallizes within my veins. I know this is Amelia's influence—I can feel it.

Henry and I bolt from the room and charge down the hall that seems strangely untouched despite the terror that unfolded just moments ago. We escape the building, bursting out into the open air, fleeing Amelia's puppetry. At least, momentarily.

Our feet smack onto the cold ground outside and we both gulp down air. The building itself bears no signs of the chaos. The campus hums with its usual rhythm, completely oblivious to our struggle. Lockwood is strangely good for that.

"We need to find Amelia," I gasp out, my chest still heaving from the ordeal. "She keeps messing with us, and she isn't going to stop."

"Do you still want to go to Vancouver to confront that guy, Ray?" Henry's question cuts through the residual panic, grounding me in reality.

"Yes. And if my father *is* really visiting Adip while he's sleeping, I want to be there."

"What if that's just Amelia playing tricks?"

Henry's words stir around the base of my neck, crawling down my back. Of course that would make the most sense. She's warping everything. It's going to be nearly impossible to find her, stop her.

But we have to try.

A terrible idea crosses my mind. "I hate to say this, but I think our best way to get to Amelia is through Wes." I grimace as his name spills from my lips.

Henry's gaze lances through me and I can sense his objection. Truthfully, I share it too. Wes is the last person I want to deal with, but his fixation on me could be a twisted advantage.

"So what… you're planning to spend time with him alone? Over my dead body."

"That's not what I meant," I say. "But if I spend time with him *and* Ciel, he might let something slip, or at least we could find out where he's rooming on campus. Continue our search."

"I hate this plan, you know that." Yep. It's written all over his face. "I want to be there."

"I think he'd be too cautious around you," I say. "He might still think we've lost our memories, that he has a chance with me."

"I don't want you feeding his sick obsession."

"I know, but right now, it's the best lead we have," I say, trying to sound confident. The reality is, I'm terrified of what Wes knows… what he might do…what his greater plan is. Wes is a wild card and I don't yet know how to play him in this timeline.

"I was hoping I'd have more visions, some kind of a clue of how things might shake out this round, but nothing. It's almost like they've been sliced off," Henry says.

"My mom said Amelia implanted your visions of me last time. Maybe she stopped because she realizes we're on to her already."

A shiver races over my skin as my gaze sweeps over to a bank of trees, catching an odd flicker of movement. I squint to make out the details, noticing a figure with a shaved head, clad in long-sleeved black coveralls, tattoos snaking out from the neckline.

"Do you see that person over there?" I whisper to Henry, pointing towards the figure.

His gaze follows my direction, eyes widening in recognition before he breaks into a run, charging towards the mysterious watcher. I'm hot on his heels, struggling to keep up, as the person turns around, revealing piercing green eyes that glitter with defiance.

"Iva!" Henry's shout echoes through the still air. *He knows her?*

She leads us deeper into the forest, so far that we can no longer see the building. Henry finally catches up to her, barreling into her and forcing her to the ground.

"Get off me," she says with a snarl, her words laced with a thick French accent.

"Why are you here?" Henry says, holding her down.

She struggles against his grip, spitting defiantly. "You think I'm going to tell a stranger?" Why did she call him a stranger when he knows her name?

"You were watching us. Why?" he persists, undeterred.

"I wasn't watching you two. I was looking for someone," she says, her gaze darting between us.

"Who?" I say.

Her expression softens a touch. "My sister."

"Why would your sister be here?" Henry probes, releasing his hold.

She quickly regains her footing. "Because she sent me a letter," Iva says.

"She's a student here at Lockwood?" I ask, skeptical.

"No, she's in her twenties. She said she works here."

Henry and I exchange bewildered glances. Something about her story doesn't ring true.

Henry turns to her. "Look, this might sound crazy, but we've met before. In a different timeline," Henry says, his words tightening against my stomach.

Iva shoots him a peculiar look.

He continues. "I was locked up in the place where you said you were raised."

"What place?" she says, brows knitting.

I mirror her confusion, wondering how this new twist ties into our already convoluted situation.

"The place doesn't have a name, it's like a… rehab for precogs. Our birthplace and our torture chamber when we break our rules," Henry says.

She pierces him with an unblinking stare. "What is a precog?"

Henry pales, abruptly snatching at Iva's arm to find her psi symbol branding—the one all precogs have. She is covered in tattoos, but there is no psi symbol.

As she yanks her arm free, something glints in her pocket—a dagger. Without a second thought, a surge of adrenaline slicks over my body, propelling me forward. Iva grips the handle of the dagger and I knock Henry out of the way.

My hand clenches around Iva's wrist, my strength skyrocketing.

She grins at me and laughs. The oddness of her reaction coils in my gut like a snake ready to strike. She manages to free herself from my grip and draw her dagger, shoving me down to the ground.

My limbs flail and crash, but I scramble back onto my feet in a split second. Henry is already on the move, rushing towards us, but Iva raises her hand and somehow creates an invisible forcefield around him. He's trapped, helplessly pounding against the unseen barrier.

I brace myself as she turns to me, hand raised, likely to cage me off as well. But she fails… Nothing happens.

"Interesting," she says.

She races at me, but I don't back down, trying to wrench the dagger from her grip.

"Did Amelia send you?" I say through gritted teeth.

She gives no answer, just shoves into my body, knocking us both off balance. We crash to the ground, but she recovers quickly, flipping over and pinning me down. She holds the dagger above my neck, its sharp tip teasing my throat.

Another surge of raw power swells within me. Electricity pulses through my body. *I've felt this before.* Light begins to emanate from my palms as a sea of miniature stars bursts forth from my grip.

Iva's scream rings through the forest as her dagger starts to melt, the molten metal spreading up her arm, bleeding over her flesh. Another constellation pours from my grip, encasing her entire body in a metal shield.

Then, with a resounding crack, the shield fractures and explodes into metal shards, flying everywhere. I brace myself as the fragments pierce the forcefield trapping Henry, causing him to stumble back as it dissolves.

I slowly rise, fixating on my palms. The stars wink out, leaving me in stunned silence. Iva's body seems to have vanished into thin air. Panic knots in my stomach as my mind struggles to grasp the reality of what just happened.

Henry rushes to my side. "What was that? How did you... do that?"

My hands tremble as I study them. "I think I unlocked a new power."

My revelation is cut short by the sound of slow, deliberate clapping echoing through the trees. Our heads whip around, locking onto the source of the interruption.

There, in the clearing, stands Wes.

His lips split into a chilling grin as he claps, his presence casting a grim shadow. "Now that? *That* was a good show."

CHAPTER EIGHT

HENRY

MY HEAD'S STILL spinning, piecing together what just unfolded—
the sight of Natalie wielding a new power. Iva, reduced to nothing
more than a memory and shards of metal.

If that even really happened. It's not clear if it was real or just
some illusion… another sick part of Amelia's experiment.

But there's no time to make sense of any of it, not when the devil
himself is in the details… and standing right in front of us.

Wes.

His applause taints the air as he grins with perverse satisfaction, staring right at Natalie, gleaming with some twisted sort
of recognition.

A violent rush of protection surges through me and I step
between them.

What does Wes remember, if anything? What's his plan? The
questions gnaw at my edges, eating away at me. It's not as if he'd tell
us the truth, even if we asked.

Cold dread laces my veins as I share a tense glance with Natalie before turning my gaze back to Wes. "What the hell are you doing all the way back here in this part of campus?"

Wes shrugs, making my fists clench. "I could ask the two of you the same thing."

Neither of us tell him that we were looking for his makeshift dorm room, the one that apparently doesn't exist in this timeline.

"Did you lock us in that room?" I ask.

"What room?" He looks genuinely confounded, but like everything Wes says, it's probably bullshit. "I'm just impressed, that's all." He locks his eyes on Natalie, dragging out his words. "What... *are*... you?"

Wes takes a step towards her and, without a second thought, I shove him away. He stumbles slightly but quickly regains his footing.

He throws his hands up, chuckling. "Easy. No need for violence."

Fury clenches my stomach. "What's your deal, man? Do you even really go to this school?"

A flicker of confusion crosses his face, quickly replaced by a wry grin. "Yeah, I'm here on a scholarship."

"Who sent you?" I cut in.

He evades my question, deflecting. "Look, it seems like we're all on the same side here. Natalie is clearly not... human. Neither are we. No reason to turn on each other." He smirks again, turning his gaze to Natalie. "Besides, she *did* invite me to hang out later."

Natalie steps forward, her eyes flashing defiantly. "You invited yourself."

Wes simply shrugs, the glint in his eye becoming more pronounced. "I remember it differently."

Anxiety corrodes my veins.

Natalie squares her shoulders, her gaze unwavering as she challenges him. "What else do you remember... or not remember?"

The glint in Wes's eyes intensifies as he evades more questions. "Well, it seems you two are deep in some couple's crisis and I'm feeling like a third wheel, which is not a good look for me." With a dramatic, mocking bow that makes me want to punch him even harder, he steps backward. "Enjoy the rest of your day." He tosses the statement at Natalie, taking a few more steps back. Giving her a wink that makes my jaw clench, he adds, "I'll see you later, Natalie."

The way he addresses her directly, as though they share some unspoken understanding, fans my rage.

He turns on his heel, disappearing through the trees, leaving us in an unsettling silence. A prickling sensation of vigilance rises in me. His nonchalant attitude, his coy grin—makes me want to kill him even more.

"We have to follow him," Natalie says, grabbing my hand.

I hesitate, apprehension coiling around my limbs. "That's exactly what he wants. It's a trap."

"We can't just sit back and wait for him to make the next move," she argues. "We have to be proactive. I obviously unlocked some crazy new power just now."

Her confidence fuels my own. Whatever Wes has up his sleeve, we're in this fight together. "Okay."

We track Wes from a safe distance, heading back onto the main artery of campus, blending into the sea of students. Wes strolls ahead, unbothered, which stokes my nerves even more.

As we pass clusters of students, I notice various whispers directed at us. Great, the Lockwood gossip mill gone wild.

The gothic architecture of the campus library looms ahead. Wes approaches the towering building made of weathered stone, disappearing into the entrance.

Natalie and I exchange a look before trailing behind him, the massive double doors swinging shut behind us. The atmosphere changes as we step inside, the air becoming hushed and weighted with the scent of books and aged wood.

As we tread across the marble floors, hushed whispers ripple through the space. Natalie walks beside me, her hand intertwined with mine.

The deeper we move into the library, the more furtive glances and annoying giggles buzz like a swarm of bees. Eyes watch us from behind stacks of books and laptop screens. Undoubtedly, rumors of Natalie's breakup with Jack and her sudden appearance with me— the new guy who made a spectacle earlier today at the inauguration—have already traveled at lightning speed. Fortunately, Wes seems oblivious to our pursuit. Or at least, he's pretending to be.

Realizing we're the subject of everyone's curiosity, I let go of Natalie's hand.

She clasps it again with hers. "I don't care what everyone thinks," she says.

I look at her then, *really look at her*. God, I fucking love this girl. There's nothing more I'd like to do than kiss her right now, but our attention snaps back to our task when we see Wes enter the rickety library elevator. We duck into the shelves as the elevator doors creak closed behind him.

Determined not to lose him, we race to the elevator and study the worn-out digital panel above the doors, the numbers increasing with a low ding until it stops at the twenty-third floor.

"I didn't know this place even had a twenty-third floor," Natalie says, her brows twisting in confusion. It's not something I've noticed, but I'll take her word for it.

As the elevator descends back to the ground floor and opens with a chime, we step inside, the heavy doors clattering closed behind us. The interior is just as antique as the exterior, lined with polished wood paneling that echoes the library's dark, gothic mood.

The elevator buttons are lined in two columns, the highest floor being eighteen. She was right. So how did Wes manage to go up to the twenty-third floor?

Natalie presses the button for the eighteenth floor. "Maybe there's another way up there."

As the elevator begins its slow climb, tension knots tighter in my stomach. If Wes has vanished onto a non-existent twenty-third floor, then what exactly are we walking into?

Suddenly, the elevator jerks to a vicious halt. Natalie stumbles into me, gripping onto my arms, while I steady myself against the elevator wall. My gut twists as I realize this enclosed box has suddenly transformed into a cage, and we're locked inside.

Natalie's hand trembles as she punches the button to open the doors, but the elevator responds with stubborn silence. Again and again, her finger stabs at the button, each press spiking my nerves. I hit the emergency button but it offers no relief, its red light mocking us.

"We're trapped," I says, voicing what I know we're both thinking, the words leaving a bitter taste in my mouth.

The claustrophobic elevator feels smaller by the second.

A wave of panic washes over Natalie's face and I hate that I can't fix this. Hate that we're trapped, prey to someone else's plan yet again.

"We've got to find a way out of here," I say, scanning the confined space, searching for any sign of an escape route. "What if we try to use our powers again?"

Natalie, a hopeless expression on her face, leans against the wall. "I don't know how my powers work. Neither do you. We just keep… trying things and making a mess."

"So we keep trying," I say, attempting to instill some hope while we untangle this fucked-up web of powers, secrets, and lies.

My attempt to help seems to only add to Natalie's overwhelm. "I don't know. I don't know anything," she says, her voice a whispered cry. "How am I supposed to fix all of this? Why is this happening?" Her eyes well up with tears.

I pull her into my arms, holding her tight as panic begins to consume her. I let the world outside this elevator, our whole predicament, drift away for just a moment. "Look at me." I cup her chin, tilting it up so our gazes lock.

Her frantic eyes search mine for reassurance.

"We've gotten through things before. And we'll keep doing it, together. That's all that matters."

Her eyes flicker with desire, that deep hunger that neither one of us can deny, no matter how bad things are. The world blurs around us as our lips meet, drowning out our fears.

The taste of her is so fucking intoxicating. Natalie's back hits the elevator wall as my hands find her hips, lifting her with an ease that sends heat throbbing through my core. Her legs curl around my waist as I drag my lips down her neck, teeth grazing her skin, drawing a soft moan from her.

Her hands slide through my hair, anchoring me to her as I move back to her lips. I barely notice the air growing thin around her until Natalie breaks away, chest heaving as she gasps.

Giving her the space to breathe, I set her legs down, allowing her body to steady against the elevator wall. My lips trail down her body, sinking down until I'm kneeling in front of her, pressing my forehead against the apex of her thighs, my hands tracing the curve of her hips, then squeezing as she presses into me.

It…this…*she* feels so fucking good, I don't even hear the elevator doors gliding open. It isn't until a familiar voice cuts through the tension that we snap back into reality.

"Looking for me?" Wes's voice carries a hint of rage, but his face is unreadable, pulling us back to the harsh reality.

Raw anger flares in my chest. I rise, my hands clenched into fists at my sides.

"Stay down on your knees." His words drip with disdain.

"Isn't that what you are? Just some subservient twat vying for Natalie's affection?"

A rage unlike any I've felt before consumes me. *What did this asshole just say to me?* I press to stand, moving to punch him, but I find myself jerked back by some invisible force and slammed against the cold elevator wall.

Something holds me there, my feet dangling above the floor. I fight against the invisible bonds, but they're unrelenting—a cruel mockery.

Wes turns his attention to Natalie. He raises his hand, and like a puppet on strings, she's yanked towards him. She fights, flailing her limbs, but she's no match for whatever he's wielding. My heart lodges in my throat as Wes grabs her arm, yanking her from the elevator.

"Let her go! Natalie!" I scream her name, but it's swallowed by the echoing slam of the elevator doors.

A cold emptiness shocks my bones as I'm left suspended, help-less, my heart pounding against my ribs as the number at the top of the elevator door turns to twenty-three.

CHAPTER NINE

NATALIE

A SENSE OF dread twists my stomach as the elevator door slides closed, leaving Henry behind. *Trapped.*

I glance up. The number twenty-three illuminated above the door burns into my vision. I twist to face Wes, noticing we're on what looks like an abandoned floor. Rows of dust-laden shelves filled with tattered, forgotten books stretch out before me, their musty scent hanging in the air. The place seems untouched, lost in time, like a secret floor concealed from the rest of campus below. The yellowed, stained-glass windows do nothing to illuminate the space.

"Having fun in there with your new boyfriend? You move on fast. That's not a judgment. Your ex seems like a douche," Wes says, smirking at me.

His flippant comment hits a nerve, like everything he does. "Cut the shit," I say, and then start pummeling him with questions. "What's going on? What do you know? How did you pull me out of the elevator? Where's Henry?"

"Whoa, you have a lot of questions. And so do I," he says with a smug, amused expression. "Want to play a game?"

A chill races down my spine as he takes a few confident steps toward me, and I instinctively retreat, ducking into the maze of bookshelves.

"I'm not interested in playing games with you."

The aisle is dank, deserted, like a final resting place for abandoned knowledge. Wes steps closer, his looming shadow seeping over me, stretching across the rows of forgotten books. A knot of fear tightens in my gut, but I force myself not to back down. As I edge back, I bump into a pile of books and one tumbles onto the hard floor, the thud echoing throughout the silent room.

Swallowing down my panic, I throw him a question. "Where are we?"

"A library," he says, smugness dripping from his words.

"I know it's a library," I snap back, my voice echoing off the walls. "I'm talking about this floor. Number twenty-three. The elevator doesn't go up that high."

The corners of his lips twitch into a grin. "Yes, it does."

He moves closer as I retreat further into the maze of aisles, his steps shadowing mine.

"No, it doesn't."

Turning a corner, I tuck behind a set of shelves, using them as a makeshift barrier between us. "Stop following me."

Surprisingly, he listens, pausing on the other side of the bookcase that goes two ways, his gaze fixed on me through a small gap in the books. He slides a stray book aside, the sound grating against the shelf, and our eyes lock.

Seeing an opportunity to gain some control over this situation, I press on. "Why is no one else up here?"

He shrugs with nonchalance. "Probably because it's a rotting mess. Can't imagine these books are the latest editions."

My patience wears thin, questions pressing against my lips. "So why are *you* up here?"

"If you'd stop using that bookshelf as a barricade, I'd show you."

We engage in a silent duel, locked in a tense standoff.

"What do you want to show me?"

He moves in the opposite direction, slipping away into the labyrinth of bookshelves. "Follow me."

And I do, cautiously trailing behind him. He guides me to the rear of the library, to a hidden alcove among the maze of books. He motions to the corner, and my eyes land on a mattress, a hot plate, and a small lamp—identical to the setup I saw before. *So this is where he's been staying.*

"Why are you showing me this?" I say, my gaze still fixed on the makeshift dwelling.

His answer is as cryptic as ever. "Because it's a secret. Trying to even the playing field since I found out about your… that little gift you have. Stars shooting from your palms, melting someone into a metal inferno and exploding their body? Impressive, Covington."

Covington. How does he know my last name? Maybe he *does* remember after all. The thought makes my skin crawl, but I keep my expression steady. "So you find out about my powers, and in exchange, you show me a mattress? Seems fair." I nod, sizing him up, calculating the possibilities of what he remembers, how I can navigate this whole fucking mess. "How do you know my last name?"

He ignores my question, gesturing to the mattress. "You want to lie down? Get comfortable?"

A surge of disgust curls in my stomach at the thought of sharing a bed with Wes, ever again. "I'll pass." I force the repulsive memories aside, prying a bit more into what he knows or *remembers.* "What are you doing at this school? And don't feed me that scholarship line. If that were true, you wouldn't be living in here."

With a cocky smirk, he leans against the nearest bookcase. "That would be another secret. What are you going to give me for an answer?"

I've never wanted to slap someone more. "What, exactly, are you implying when you say 'give you something'?"

He chuckles at that, a sound that makes my stomach churn. "This might sound a little crazy, but you could put in a good word for me with your friend, Ciel?"

His revelation hits me like a wave. Is he toying with me, playing a game, trying to figure out what I know? Or is he truly clueless? Or still bound to Ciel?

I push back on his proposition. "One minute you're inviting me into your bed, and the next you want to be with my friend?"

He shoots me an innocent look. "I just asked if you wanted to lie down, seemed like you had a rough day. I wasn't trying to... *be inside of you.*"

His crude comment further sparks my repulsion. How did he manage to become even more vile in this new timeline?

My patience wears thin. "You lure us up here, trap us in an elevator, talk about being 'inside of me' as if I'd ever let that happen, and then expect me to talk you up to my friend?"

"Lured? You two followed me."

He has a point, but I refuse to give him the satisfaction of admitting it. Instead, I steer the conversation back to what's been bothering me. "What did you do to us back there? To Henry and me? Was that... magic?"

Wes eyes me thoughtfully, a spark of interest in his gaze. "Like you, I have other... abilities."

"Right," I say, my tone biting.

No asshole, you're wielding magic. And lying. And I want to know your fucking plan.

I match his lies, hoping to extract some information. "Fine. I'll talk to Ciel. Now, why are you here at Lockwood?"

"I'm on a job."

Yeah, a job to kill me.

"What kind of job?" I push further.

"That, I can't tell you. Not now, anyway."

His evasive responses push me to my limit, and before I can stop myself, the words tumble out. "You were sent here to kill me, right? Or to keep track of me until your uncle pulls off the job."

Wes's face drains of color, a stark contrast to the asshole swagger I'm used to. His body shudders as though struck by a sudden, invisible blow, his hands clawing at his head. What game is he playing now?

"Your uncle will approach me outside of a school dance, drag me into the woods, where you will happen to be."

Let's see how good of a liar you are in this timeline.

"What are you talking about?" His confusion at my words is strangely palpable, but I'm not buying it.

"Oh, are we still pretending? Fine. You were sent here to track me down. The same way you tracked down my mother."

Horror flickers across Wes's features. "I don't—"

"I see it, right there in your eyes," I say, cutting him off as impatience curdles my words. "You can cut the bullshit."

He responds with a tortured grunt, clutching his head tighter, his knees buckling beneath him. It's quite a spectacle, almost deserving of applause. So I give it to him, just like he did for me earlier, my hands clapping together at his budget indie-film of a performance.

"No more games," I say. "*I know.* You're here for me."

He stares ahead, his gaze vacant, devoid of any coherent response.

Irritation gnaws at my patience and I drop to my knees, waving a hand in front of his glazed eyes. "What is this pathetic act? Just be straight with me."

A flicker of awareness sparks in his eyes and he lunges at me, grabbing my face and crashing his lips down on mine.

Startled, I fight against him, clawing at his arms until I manage to break free. Anger snaps against my veins and I lash out, smacking him across the face. "Don't *ever* touch me again."

He sits there holding his cheek, bewildered, then clutches his head again as if he's a robot glitching.

It sinks in. Is he having visions? Or memories? Or both?

His silence stretches, tension prickling along my skin. He hauls in a ragged breath, pushes himself upright, and then strides over to a bookshelf.

"Where are you going?"

Ignoring me, Wes continues ahead into the maze of books.

"Answer me!" My voice rings out into the silence as he traces his finger along a few books, pulling one out and letting it thud onto the ground.

"Oops," he says with a vague air. And then he walks away, disappearing around the corner.

I scramble to retrieve the discarded book as the elevator creaks open in the distance. I race in that direction just as Henry charges out.

Wes is nowhere to be found.

Henry gathers me into his arms. "What the hell just happened? Where is he? Did he hurt you?"

I shake my head, heart thumping into my throat. "No, but I think he wanted me to have this book."

CHAPTER TEN

HENRY

MY GAZE SWEEPS over Natalie, searching for any harm, even though she just confirmed Wes didn't cause any. I glance at the book she clutches like a lifeline, the book he wanted her to have. As much as I want to know why he's here lending out library books, there's no time to dwell on some piece of literature. Not when he's still somewhere on this floor. Not when I want answers about more important things than a fucking book.

"Where is he?" I move through the aisles, prowling through the tall bookshelves, straining for any sight of him. "Come out and talk to me, asshole."

There's an unsettling emptiness that bounces back, the silence gnawing at my nerves.

We comb through the entire floor, every damn aisle, but it's as if Wes has been swallowed by the musky air in this place. Dread lodges in my stomach as each passing second chips away any hope of finding him… of confronting him.

"It's like he just disappeared," Natalie says.

"That's impossible. There's only one elevator. One way out."

The empty room and oppressive silence seem to mock my conviction. If there's anything I should know by now, it's that anything's possible when you're not the one pulling the strings.

"He's staying in here. Let's go through his things." Natalie white-knuckles my hand, leading me over to a worn mattress, a lamp, and a hot plate—his makeshift dorm.

I dig under the mattress, finding nothing.

Natalie grabs for his backpack in the corner, pulling out a small, tattered notebook. Her hands tremble as she flips it open. She reads through the pages, her eyes wide with horror.

"What is it?"

The color drains from her face. "It's all about me. He's tracking me—I know that already—but it's just… reading about it…"

A seething fury takes root within me and I grab the notebook, combing over his notes about her—her routines, her whereabouts on campus. Stalking her, watching her, treating her like his prey.

And then I find the most disturbing passage—his recounting of Natalie undressing while hiding in her closet.

My hand crumples the page, nails biting into my palm, as the growl of rage swells in my chest. "I'm going to kill him." I didn't mean to say it out loud, but here we are. "He was hiding in your dorm room."

Natalie's head snaps up to meet my gaze, her eyes widening. She shakes her head quickly. "Just ignore that for now… If he remembers, then we need him. He could lead us back to Amelia."

She's right, as much as the thought of keeping him around makes my stomach turn.

"Let's get out of here. We can go back to my room, look through this book he gave me," she says.

We make our way back to the elevator, the silence between us thickening with every step. Inside the elevator, the glowing numbers on the panel seem to mock us, jumping from twenty-three to eighteen.… then counting down from there.

We manage to make it across campus unscathed. Back in Natalie's dorm room, we settle down on her bed, the worn book that Wes discarded in the library lying between us. It's filled with nonsensical poems, meaningless to our situation, and yet it feels like an intrusion, another piece of him that's wormed its way into our existence.

We thumb through the pages, but the words just spiral into a dizzying whirl of frustration. "I don't know what to make of this," Natalie says. "Maybe he's trying to keep us distracted, to throw us off track."

"What did he say to you? Does he remember anything?"

"I don't know. Everything he said was so blatantly weird. But he *is* tracking me—we found his notebook. So maybe he doesn't remember anything. He's supposed to come over tonight, for girls' night. Do we just wait for him?"

"You know my answer to that," I say, frustrated. I don't want to stick around here waiting for Wes, playing his game, trying to figure out what he knows or doesn't.

Natalie pauses on one of the pages. "Hang on, this page is half torn out." Natalie shows me the text that remains—a poem.

> *Beware the pull of the cosmic tides,*
> *Where time and space in harmony resides,*
> *A dance with the stars, where magic hides,*
> *In the whisper of the cosmos, time confides.*

I make an attempt to work out the meaning. "Stars… tides… magic… Is this in relation to your abilities? What you are?"

Natalie shrugs, unsure. "Wes purposely dropped this book on the ground. He obviously wanted me to take it. Is it a clue? A trick?"

Natalie leans back on the bed, exhausted. "Maybe he's trying to help. Or maybe he's hoping we'll become more and more tangled up in each other's lives until I can't escape him."

"That won't happen." I fold my arms around her. She will escape him—I'll do whatever it takes to make sure of it.

"If he gave this book to me, he must remember something, right?"

My mind wanders over the unknowns. "Or he saw what happened out in the woods with Iva. Maybe the reference to stars and the cosmos has to do with that."

With a heavy sigh, she sinks deeper into my arms, her leg draping over my hips, head nuzzling against my chest. "I just want it all to go away for a few minutes. Just all of it."

I wish that too. She has no idea how fucking bad I want that.

She peers up at me, the longing in her eyes clear. "Don't you wish we could go back?"

I tease her. "We did. Time was reset."

Her laughter fills the room—a sound I've missed. She pinches my arm and in return, I pin her down, rolling on top of her, our bodies sinking into the mattress.

"That's not what I meant," she says. "I just wish we were back to things being slightly more normal, like the night we studied in your room."

My hand traces along her cheek, grazing down to her neck. "Normal? I was haunted by visions of you. And you couldn't stand the sight of me."

"That's not true. I just didn't know why you balled up a note and threw it at me. You were always so hot and cold."

"I was frustrated. I didn't know how to deal." I continue tracing my hand along her neck, down to her chest, grazing over her hip. "I wanted to save you, but I didn't know how. And I couldn't for the life of me stop thinking about you." I nuzzle into her neck, taking my time to drink in her scent, dragging my lips along her skin.

Her voice breaks through the silence. "That's because you were having visions of my death."

I gaze back into her eyes. "It wasn't just the visions. I couldn't squeeze you from my mind even if I tried. I still can't. I don't want to."

A fire burns in her eyes as her lips meet mine, stirring a familiar hunger in me. I press into her, making her whimper. One thing that certainly hasn't changed in this new timeline is how hungry—fucking *starved*—I am for her.

My forehead meets hers. "How does it feel when I kiss you… when I touch you?"

She inhales sharply, breathing me in, her eyes fluttering shut. "Like my life is slipping away… but I don't care. Because when I'm with you, everything is alive." She hooks her leg around my hip, winding her hips into mine, increasing the friction, driving me mad. She whispers into my mouth. "Why did you leave? That night when we came to find you at that prison. When you got into the fight with Wes. Why did you leave?"

Him. That's why.

The memory makes my stomach churn, coldness bleeding between us. I push away from her but she grips my shirt, yanking me closer.

"Tell me. Don't run away."

"Because you were with him. I thought you… I assumed you chose him over me," I say.

"But I *wasn't* with him. I never chose him. I was just using him after you left, and that was a mistake. I wish I could take it back. But I choose you… it's always been you. And I will choose you again and again. I don't care how many times things are reset."

Our lips meet again in a fierce collision, the urgency, the possession erasing any residue of Wes. I growl into her mouth, my heart jackhammering as she undulates her hips into mine. I reach my hands under the band of her sweatpants, dipping down between her legs—marking her, claiming her, ridding his fucking memory from her forever.

I pull my face back at her groan, staring into those gorgeous fucking eyes.

"Don't stop," she says, urging me on.

Her hands yank off my shirt, exposing my back, and she sinks her nails into my shoulder blades. I spread her thighs apart, sliding my hand down further, her body jerking under my touch. My fingers curl inside of her as her eyes roll back, lips parted open, sucking in air.

"Look at me."

I know neither one of us wants to stop, but I can't risk her losing consciousness. Her back bows off the mattress as I shift to the side, deepening my fingers inside of her, my entire body throbbing, dying for her.

She keeps her eyes fixed on me, moaning, sinking her teeth into her bottom lip as her eyes flutter.

"We should stop," I say, waiting for her to make the call.

"We should, but..." She reaches her hand down to hold mine in place, adrenaline and arousal ripping through my veins.

I keep going, touching her, drinking in her expressions as she responds to me.

Then a distant scream from the hallway pierces the air, shattering the moment, making the decision for us.

"What the hell was that?" Natalie says as we spring to our feet, adjusting our clothes and running out of her dorm toward the source of the sound...

Ciel's room.

CHAPTER ELEVEN

NATALIE

MY ENTIRE BODY is throbbing, pulsing, dizzy from desire—and from fear.

I bang on Ciel's door. "Ciel, you okay in there?" My voice echoes against the hardwood door.

The unsettling silence that follows sends anxiety winding up my throat. There's a faint rustling sound inside the room.

Henry bangs on the door. "Ciel, open up or we're coming in." His gaze finds mine. "I'll break this door if I have to."

After what seems like an eternity, the door finally creaks open. Ciel stands there, her hair a wild mess, face flushed, dressed in a half-buttoned uniform shirt and lace underwear.

"Are you okay? We heard you scream."

The blush on Ciel's cheeks deepens. "You heard that? Oh god, sorry. I didn't realize I was that loud. Shit."

Momentarily relieved, I don't bother to ask what's going on. I'm crystal clear, assuming Adip must be lingering in the background, frantically throwing on his clothes.

But the sight that greets me next freezes the blood in my veins.

From behind the partially opened door, Wes emerges, shirtless, his hands working to zip up his pants. His cocky grin feels like a slap to the face. His smile widens as he takes us in. "Hey, you two. Sorry for the noise. I tried to keep her mouth covered."

Ciel's carefree giggle makes my stomach churn. This is the last thing I expected to see. A sickening knot twists in my stomach as she leans into him.

Henry grabs my hand, tightening his grip. "We'll leave you two alone."

"Don't go on my behalf. I was just on my way out," Wes says, unable to wipe that shit-eating grin off his face.

Ciel chimes in. "Yeah, you guys can stick around. We're finished getting acquainted." She giggles again.

"We're good, thanks." Henry drags my speechless body back to my dorm room, the sound of the lock clicking into place echoing through the silence.

The moment we're alone, I blurt out my confusion. "What the hell was that?"

Henry sinks onto my bed, his face mirroring my shock.

Questions tumble out of my mouth in a rush. "He's got to be using her to mess with us, right? Or is he still bonded to her somehow?"

"Amelia thought she wiped our memories. Maybe other things went upside down, like their bond."

I attempt to make sense of the madness, the thoughts in my mind whirling like a violent storm. I have no idea what Wes's motives are, what he knows or doesn't know. Once again, he's taking up too much real estate in my mind.

Henry's voice breaks through my chaotic thoughts. "He's probably doing this to get to you. Purposely confusing things. You know how he operates."

Realization bubbles in my mind. "To distract us from whatever is *really* going on…" My thoughts trail off as I attempt to process our warped reality.

"This is crazy. Forget Wes and his games, we just need to get to Amelia."

"I know, but we need that map. That's if she's even in the same place. Maybe we can just try to retrace our steps." A surge of anxiety winds up my middle, scratching against my throat, knowing how flawed that idea is.

Henry's face darkens, as if a shadow has swept across it. "I don't remember how to get there at all. The memories came back, everything but that. Do you remember?"

With a heavy sigh, I shake my head. "No." I swallow the lump in my throat. "We have to try. If we can get to Amelia and I can destroy that mechanism, she won't be able to manipulate time anymore. Maybe that will strip her of some other powers too." A sudden thought ignites in my mind. Not necessarily a smart idea… but an idea. "Can we go to the Armory? Sneak in like you did before, steal the map again?"

"That's way too dangerous. Impossible, even. You don't know what I went through when I joined them, or pretended to."

Ignoring the anxiety gnawing at me, I move closer to Henry on the bed. There's so much that's been left unsaid, stories untold, buried under the constant weight of our circumstances.

I clasp his hand, feeling a bit of relief from his touch. "Tell me what happened there."

He hesitates, his gaze turning distant. "No, it doesn't matter. Nothing good will come from telling you about that."

I tug his face to mine. "Please, I want to know."

Just as the wall around him starts to crumble, a knock at the door shatters the moment.

"It's probably Wes. Or Ciel. Or both," I say.

Henry crosses the room to answer the door, finding Ms. Whitney, my guidance counselor and our French teacher, standing there.

"I'm looking for Natalie. You're the new student, Henry, right? I believe you'll be in my French class. I'm Madame Whitney."

Henry nods politely, maintaining the charade, like we haven't already lived this once before. "Nice to meet you."

Something flickers in Ms. Whitney's eyes as she glances between us. "Natalie, your father is here. There's been an emergency, I'm afraid."

My father? My heart stutters and freezes at the mention of his name. "What kind of emergency?"

"It's not something I'm at liberty to share. If you could just come with me, he's waiting for you."

It feels odd to think of my father as being alive, considering I watched him die by Amelia's hand. And apparently, he's not my real father anyway. I wonder what kind of bullshit emergency he made up in this timeline. A sinking feeling of dread seeps through my stomach.

I challenge Ms. Whitney. "Why can't he just come to my room?"

"All parental meetings are required to happen in the designated area. Lockwood policy."

My voice rings with disbelief. "Even in an emergency?"

Ms. Whitney's eyes soften slightly. "Natalie, I understand that there might be some issues between you and your father, but this is a conversation you need to have with him."

I cross my arms defensively. "What if I refuse?"

"Look, I'm not supposed to get involved in family affairs, but…" Ms. Whitney's voice falters, trailing off as if she's on the verge of tears. "It's your mother. Natalie, there was an accident."

The world seems to tilt on its axis and anxiety swells my throat, nearly choking me. *My mother?* That doesn't make any sense. She died when I was sixteen, yet now I know that was a lie. She's alive, held captive by Amelia under some arbitrary agreement.

"I… I don't understand. My mother died in a car accident two years ago." I feed her the lie that was fed to me.

Ms. Whitney stares at me, confusion and concern mingling on her face. "Natalie, I met your mother. She was with your father during orientation. That was only a few weeks ago."

Dread pools in my stomach. How is that possible? Did Amelia change history? Does that mean my mom really *is* dead, or is this another part of Amelia's sadistic game?

There's only one person who could possibly shed light on this, as untrustworthy as he is—my father. But this time, I'll demand proof. I'll ask to see my mom's body.

"I'm coming with you," Henry says as I follow Ms. Whitney out of the room.

Ms. Whitney's rule comes out like a reflex. "We really don't allow other students in without their parent, Henry."

"I don't care. She's not going there alone."

The walk across the campus is a silent one. Chaotic thoughts whir through my mind as I plot my confrontation with my father.

Ms. Whitney leads us to a familiar building—the one designated for family phone calls. She pauses at the door. "Your father is inside. I'll give you two some privacy."

I step inside the building, glancing back to make sure Henry is behind me. He moves forward to join me, but two guards curl around the building and seize his body.

"No!" The scream tears itself from my throat. I lunge towards him, but Ms. Whitney shoves me further inside, slamming the door behind me. The ominous click of the lock echoes through the room.

Desperation floods through my skin as I wrench at the handle, hammering against the door, my screams echoing in the empty room. This has to be part of their game, a trick to separate us. How could I have let this happen?

Suddenly, the scent of cigarette smoke invades my nostrils. I whip around to find Wes standing there, exhaling.

Venom spreads through my bones and my hands itch with the urge to strangle him. "Was this all you? Did you plan this? You did, didn't you?"

"You want a drag?" He extends the cigarette towards me.

With a swift motion, I snatch it from his grasp, grinding it under my shoe.

"That wasn't nice. It was my last cigarette. Are you mad because I fucked your friend? I didn't mean anything by it. I thought about you the entire time."

His words confirm my suspicions. "So you *do* remember everything."

A smirk plays on his lips. "Now I do… yes. Things were kind of foggy until our little meeting earlier in the library. Then all the memories came rushing back, crystal clear." He rakes his eyes over me. "Every one of them."

A wave of nausea hits me. Being trapped here with him feels like a twisted nightmare.

"Why did Ms. Whitney help you?"

Wes offers a casual shrug, his eyes never leaving mine. "She works for Amelia."

I challenge him, refusing to believe that everyone around me could be complicit in this hell. "How do you know that?"

"When we were at the authority last time and you were busy playing house with Henry, I went ahead and got the information you wanted." He smirks again, clearly loving that he's one-upped me.

A shudder of revulsion runs through my bones. "So you made up that story about my mom to get me here alone?"

His nod confirms it, and he seems all too pleased with himself.

"How else could I separate you from the golden boy? Time was reset and you're still running to him. How many takes do we need before you get it right?"

"I will *always* choose him."

"That doesn't really suit my plans."

"Wes, stop fucking around. I don't want you. I never did and I never will. I don't care if we're bonded or you use magic or whatever you try. It will *never* be you."

His gaze darkens, a twisted blend of pain and madness. He steps closer, bridging the gap between us. His hand reaches for my cheek, but I swat it away.

"Tell me, does his touch feel better than mine?"

"Stop." Cornered, I retreat until my back hits the wall.

He pulls out his dagger, pressing it against my neck, the cold blade gliding along my skin.

"You're trying to intimidate me. It won't work. I know you won't kill me."

"You're right," he says.

In a swift movement, he draws the blade across my skin, leaving a shallow cut on my collarbone.

Shocked, I clutch the wound, staring at him in disbelief as he licks the blood from his blade.

"You taste exactly how I remember."

Disgusted and shaken, I shove past him, heading for the door, twisting the locked knob in desperation. "Let me out of here."

"It's no use. It won't open."

"Then I'll break it down." I begin to kick at the door, each thud clattering against the walls.

"Natalie, you can't escape."

As if I'd believe anything he says. I continue my assault on the door, desperately trying to summon my powers. Why can't I unlock them now when I need them most?

"Natalie, you won't be able to break the door. Besides, it's not going to lead you where you want to go… back to your precious little Henry."

His words stop me in my tracks. I spin around, suddenly noticing very different surroundings—a brand new room, a space that strangely feels very far away from Lockwood.

And I'm trapped here… with Wes.

CHAPTER TWELVE

HENRY

My **shoes scrape** against the concrete as the guards haul me away from the building… from Natalie.

I wrench my arms, trying to break free from their iron grip, desperate to summon my fucking powers but I can't seem to do it at all.

Darkness presses in as the last bit of light slips away. The campus, usually packed with students at this hour, is strangely quiet. Ms. Whitney stands ahead, following as the two guards tug me further away from the building.

"You won't get away with this," I say, attempting to threaten Ms. Whitney, but she seems maddeningly calm.

My eyes dart upwards as we grow closer to the front gate of the campus, catching a flickering red light. The surveillance camera.

I draw in a deep breath, the air sharp in my lungs, yelling up at it. "You think you've got us, Amelia? We will find you. We will end this. You won't win."

As the guards thrust me against the gate, a figure emerges from the shadows. Great, someone else joining the torture chorus.

As they step into the slice of light from the streetlamp, I'm shocked to see that it's Adip.

He strides over to us, his face full of confusion. "What's happening here?" His eyes dart from me to Ms. Whitney to the guards.

Ms. Whitney manages a weak explanation. "Henry has some behavioral infractions and will be temporarily removed from campus. Please head back to your dorm, Adip."

Fuck her and her web of lies.

I cut through her deception. "Don't listen to her, Adip. Natalie's trapped in the building where they do the family phone calls. You have to get her out of there."

Ms. Whitney scoffs. "Henry is clearly not of sound mind. Please, Adip, just go back to your dorm."

Before she can continue to paint me as unhinged, Adip blurs into motion. He covers the distance between us and the gate in a heartbeat, his speed unimaginable… *inhuman.*

"You're not taking him off campus." He presses his trembling body against the gate, covering the lock.

One of the guards releases my arm and lunges at Adip. They scuffle a split second until the guard goes limp, collapsing onto the ground.

In Adip's hand is a long, gleaming, silver blade that seems to have materialized out of nowhere. His eyes widen in horror as they land on it. "Oh my god, where did this come from? What…what did I just do?" He drops the weapon as if it's burned him, backing away from the guard's lifeless body.

Fear seizes Ms. Whitney and the remaining guard, and he lets me go. They exchange a panicked glance before bolting out of the Lockwood gate, leaving me, Adip, and the fallen guard standing in the unforgiving light of the gate's overhead lamps.

Adip stammers, his words bleeding out in a panic. "What am I gonna do? He's dead. I killed him. I killed someone."

He's reeling, and I can't blame him, but I can't deal with his emotional fallout right now. "Adip, we have to get Natalie."

I can see the fear in his eyes. He's caught in a mess he doesn't understand, and I feel a pang of guilt. Adip didn't ask for any of this.

"I promise, I'll fill you in. But right now, we have to find Natalie."

Thankfully, he pulls his shit together, enough that we can race through campus, to the building where Natalie is trapped.

I unlock the door and we rush inside. The building is an eerie mass of silence.

"Natalie?" I yell out, my voice echoing back as I turn to Adip. "You go that way. We can cover more ground."

We split up, scouring every inch of the building, but there's no sign of her. My heart pounds like a war drum in my chest as we search. The seconds drag out, torturous and slow, causing even more dread to seep over my bones.

Back in the lobby where we started, I notice a stubbed-out cigarette on the floor. I reach down to pick it up, realizing it was freshly put out, causing my heart to lurch. *Wes.* I know it. That piece of shit was here. The thought of Natalie being with Wes, that he lured her here, makes me want to rip down these walls.

Adip rushes into the lobby. "I don't see her anywhere."

"We need to get to Amelia."

"Who is Amelia?" Adip sinks to his knees as if he's about to pass out. He begins to ramble, on the edge of hysteria. "I'm seriously struggling to handle all this right now. I was in my room taking a nap and that guy—Natalie's real dad or whatever—was there in my dream again and then suddenly, I was at the front gate. And you were being dragged away. And then I killed someone? Was that even real? Holy shit, man!"

"I know this all seems crazy, but there's an explanation. Just come with me."

Adip follows, speechless, clutching his stomach like he's about to vomit, as we make our way back to the gate, only to find that the guard's body is now gone… and so is the weapon Adip used to kill him.

I look up at the blinking camera light. She's watching us. *Fucking Amelia.*

A hard knot of determination winds in my gut. "Adip, I'm going to tell you everything. But I need you to do something for me. You said Natalie's father visits you in dreams, right?"

He nods, grimacing like this is all too painful to process. "I don't know. It's just a dream, right?"

"I'm coming with you back to your dorm. I need you to try and go to sleep. Maybe we can summon him."

He whirls on me, eyes wide in disbelief. "How the hell am I supposed to sleep now?" His words are incredulous, almost comical, but there's nothing funny about this situation.

We're running out of time, and I'm running out of options.

Natalie needs us.

❦

Adip is under his covers, peeking his eyes over the blanket like I just told him a scary story. That's valid, because this must be fucking frightening to take in.

"So let me get this straight. You thought you were a precog but then found out you're a half-demon, and so is that other guy, Wes, and Natalie's some sort of celestial goddess?"

I give him a terse nod. My mind is still consumed by Natalie, wherever she might be, whatever's happened to her. "Something like that."

Adip lets out a slow breath, pulling the blanket tighter around his neck. "And we've lived this before because that Amelia woman keeps hitting the rewind button?"

I make a feeble attempt to explain, trying to keep the weariness out of my voice. This conversation is the last thing I want to be having right now, but I need Adip's help. "We think it's the first time she's reset things, but we don't know for sure."

"But why is this Amelia woman like this? Why is she so evil?" he asks, a note of genuine curiosity in his voice. It's a good question, one we've been trying to answer ourselves.

I offer up the one explanation we have. "Power... control."

Adip looks thoughtful for a moment. "Seems kinda over the top, don't you think? This woman is doing the most, and for what?"

"People have done far crazier things for power."

He considers this for a moment, nodding slowly. "And what about me? Am I some kind of demon or a constellation or something? How am I mixed up in all this?"

I rub the tension out of the back of my neck. "I don't know. It's possible. Did you ever feel like there was something... different about you?"

A smile forms on his face. "Well, yeah. I spin some sick beats. You wanna hear?"

I shake my head. This isn't the time to entertain Adip's musical aspirations.

He meets my rejection with a frown. "Maybe it's stupid, but I thought I'd be a DJ one day. Travel the world. Play festivals. Concerts. But now that I've killed someone, I guess that dream is shot to hell."

As I watch Adip try to lighten the situation, I'm reminded of how normal our lives used to be. It feels like a lifetime ago. I've never been normal, but at least back when I was having visions, before I came to Lockwood, things were somewhat bearable. Although, I didn't have Natalie, and I'd trade all the normalcy in the world to have her back with me.

Adip yawns, his eyes growing heavy. "Man, I took an edible and it's really hitting me."

"Good, that's good," I say, not even bothering to hide the relief in my voice.

Now, all we can do is wait and hope that Natalie's father can help—if that's even who he is. Maybe he's just part of some fever dream, or Amelia fucking with us.

My stomach tightens as Adip drifts off to sleep.

Please, please let this work.

CHAPTER THIRTEEN

NATALIE

WES SINKS AGAINST the wall with a pleased smirk as Amelia enters the room, the steady click of her heels echoing off the walls, her emerald-green dress as immaculately tailored as her hair. Guess she has plenty of time for primping while she fucks with our lives.

She regards me like a cat toying with its prey, a tiny, sadistic smile playing on her lips.

Panic bubbles in my gut, warring with determination. I refuse to be a pawn in this sick game of hers again. "Where am I? Why do you keep doing this? It can't just be about power or control. There's got to be some other reason you're targeting me."

She arches an eyebrow, her smile not wavering. "You should ask your father about that."

The mention of my father sends a jolt of surprise through me. "My father? You mean the guy pretending to be or—"

"No," Amelia interrupts, her smile now a smug smirk. "Your *real* father. Sadly, it's not possible to reach him. But if you want someone to blame."

Confusion sweeps over me. "What did *he* do? Did he do something to you?"

Her smile fades. "You could say that."

My heartbeat swells faster, frustration twisting my bones until they crunch. "So you've designed an entire torture chamber around me because of some guy I never met? Is this really how you want to spend your life?"

Her icy laugh echoes in the room. "Oh, don't worry about me. I'm happier now than I've been in years."

Her revelation sends nerves trickling through me. She's not opening up about my father, so I try a different approach. "Where is my mom?"

A flicker of something crosses her face. "She died in a car accident."

I call her bluff. "Bullshit."

Amelia tries again. "She died in the last timeline. I couldn't bring her back."

Refusing to accept her words, I press further. "I don't believe you. Are you jealous of her? Huh? Did you have a *thing* with my dad or something?"

A darkness descends over Amelia's expression, her eyes blazing with fury. Harnessing her powers, she propels me against the wall, and a painful shock jolts through me. "Don't talk about things you don't understand."

Wes finally budges from his cozy place against the wall and steps between us. "Take your hands off of her, Amelia."

I hiss, glaring at him, trying to ignore the throbbing pain in my back. "I don't need your help."

Amelia steps away, her demeanor slipping back into her trademark icy calmness. "You should play nice with him, Natalie. He is your soulmate after all."

I scoff at her repulsive words. "No, he's not."

Ignoring my denial, Amelia glides over to the door she came in from, opening it to reveal a bedroom. "Your room is ready for you." She cuts her gaze to Wes. "Part of our deal."

Disgust burns its way through my insides as I peer through the doorway. The room is aesthetically beautiful, with a single bed stationed in the middle. But the idea of sharing that bed, this room, with Wes is revolting.

"You two should make yourselves comfortable. We'll have dinner soon and maybe I can answer some of your questions." Amelia traces her eyes over me. "I picked out some things for you. Much more flattering than those bloodstained sweats you're wearing."

My eyes flick down to the small wound Wes caused, a trickle of blood on the white Lockwood sweatshirt Henry lent to me. Amelia leaves out a different door, one that seems to have magically materialized—an indication that she's warping things once again.

Wes watches me, clearly relishing in my discomfort. I swallow the lump of fear in my throat, forcing myself to stand tall. I won't give them the satisfaction of seeing me break.

I won't break—period.

I step inside the absurdly extravagant bedroom that I'm expected to share with Wes. I sneak a glance at him and see his face split into a delighted smile, which only heightens my revulsion. The walls are cloaked in a deep shade of red, casting a haunting glow over the space. An antique chandelier dangles from the ceiling, its crystals glittering in the dim candlelight. The grandeur of it all screams Amelia's style.

Wes flops down onto the bed, stretching his arms out like he's just checked in to a five-star hotel. It's a plush, king-sized bed, adorned with satin sheets and an abundance of pillows. The contrast between his careless pose and this entire situation sends ice through my veins.

"Nice place," he says, the corner of his mouth twitching in a self-satisfied smirk.

Disgust curdles in my stomach. I cross my arms over my chest, building a feeble barrier between us. "What did you do? Where the hell are we? What deal did you make with her?"

Wes shrugs lazily. "Why don't you join me over here on the bed? We can discuss it."

"Never." The word tastes like venom on my tongue. I glance around the room, my gaze lingering on the heavy, gold-trimmed door. "Answer me."

Wes tosses another pillow under his head, taking a moment to get more cozy. "After my memories came back. Earlier, in the library at Lockwood, Amelia was waiting for me. We had a great conversation."

My heart clenches at his casual revelation. "So she knew that your memories came back?"

"Guess so." His words hang heavy in the air between us.

A pang of fear slices through me. "Do you know if my mom is here?"

Wes hesitates for a moment, a shadow crossing his face. "I'm not supposed to tell you, but yes."

A chill skates down my spine. "Isn't Amelia going to get mad that you broke her rules?"

He shrugs, a dangerous glint in his eyes. "I don't care. We both have things we want."

My pulse quickens. "And what's that?"

"I can't speak for her, but what I want is standing right there." He points at me, turning my stomach.

He starts to toy with his dagger, twirling it absently in his hand. The flicker of candlelight bounces off the blade. My mind keeps flashing back to Henry's face. Where is he now? Is he here? Where did they take him?

Wes carves through my thoughts. "The blood on your shirt looks good on you."

"You're disgusting."

"I'm really sorry I slept with your friend." His voice drips with insincerity, as if I care about his actions one way or the other. The only thing that bothers me about that situation is how it might affect Ciel.

"I don't care what you do or who you sleep with."

His smirk widens, a cruel twist of his lips. "It's your fault, really. I'm frustrated… all this wanting, waiting. Over different timelines. Maybe now that we're finally alone, we can resume our *practice*."

"You will never lay a hand on me again."

His smile, painfully slow and deliberate, carries a sinister promise as he rises from the bed. As he moves in my direction, the room seems to shrink, and I feel like a cornered animal.

"We both have things we want, Natalie. You've used me before, right? You act like I'm so repulsive, but your body says otherwise. I can see you shivering."

His words settle on me like an icy cloak. A glance down confirms his observation. I am quaking, but not for the reasons he believes. "I'm shaking because I hate you."

"Listen, I have the information you want. We're stuck here. So why don't we play nice, yeah?" His words are a thinly veiled threat, their cold implication making my skin erupt in goosebumps.

He lets his eyes travel down to my forearm. "See? Your body betrays you every time. I know how I make you feel, Natalie. I see it."

His arrogance is nauseating. "You're misreading things, as usual. The only thing I feel for you is disgust."

"We'll see about that. In this room, alone, for as long as I want. We'll see how long your resolve lasts."

He might think he has me cornered, but I refuse to be his puppet. The battle is far from over, and I'm not about to wave my white flag.

An ache gnaws through the center of my gut. "Where is Henry? Is Amelia holding him here?"

Wes's demeanor shifts rapidly, his calculated coyness melting into raw rage. "You always have to bring him up, don't you?"

"Yes, I do. I love him."

Wes releases a hollow laugh as he turns away from me. "Oh, I'm looking forward to the day that's not true… when you finally forget all about him."

I swallow hard. "What's that supposed to mean?"

He spins to face me, his smirk replaced by a grimace. "The deal I made with Amelia is that *you* will be *mine*. Henry's not coming back, and you're not leaving."

"No, that's not happening. You can't force me to do anything."

Ignoring my protest, he swoops in, pinning me against the wall.

I push against his chest, but it's like trying to move steel. "Move out of my way. Let me go."

"Where are you going to run, huh? Nowhere. You're here, safe, with me. Your mom is here, alive, and it will stay that way as long as you behave."

I shudder as he paints a grotesque picture of our future. "What does that even mean… behave?"

"Your mom lived at authority headquarters before, unscathed, right?"

"No, they imprisoned her."

"No, Natalie, they treated her well as long as she stayed in line. Yes, there was the whole incident with the drowning, but that's been reset. And your mom's memory is wiped so she doesn't even know that happened. You can live here, with her… *with me…* as long as you behave. Just do what Amelia says and everything will be fine."

"You didn't want Amelia to reset things before. Why are you on her side now?"

"Because she made me a better offer this time, something I'd be a fool to turn down." His delusion clouds my mind as his finger traces a path along my quivering lip. He leans in, his breath dusting against my skin. "Think of it like an arranged marriage. Lots of people have that situation and they're happy. I can make you happy." Disgust unfurls within me as he slips his finger between my lips. "Good girl."

I lash out, biting down hard, and he rips his hand away.

"You bit me." His voice carries an edge of excitement, not pain. The predatory gleam in his eyes is even brighter now.

Summoning my strength, I shove past him, breaking free from his grasp. "I won't live like this. If you think I'm ever going to be happy with you, you have another thing coming."

"We'll see," he says, his words dropping like a lead weight.

My heart lurches at his audacity, but beneath the churn of disgust pooling in my stomach, I feel a spark—a spark of determination. I square my shoulders and lift my chin, glaring daggers at his retreating back. If he thinks I'm going to play nice, he's grossly mistaken.

I will destroy Amelia… and him.

That's when I'll be happy.

CHAPTER FOURTEEN

HENRY

AN OPPRESSIVE SILENCE covers the room as Adip snores away in his bed. Meanwhile, I'm wide awake, mind racing, pulsing with a desperate urgency for Natalie's father to show the hell up and hopefully help me find her.

A jolt of anger sears through me at the thought that she's with Wes. He stole her from me, right from under my nose, *again*. His smug fucking face flashes in my mind, goading me, and my fists clench involuntarily, aching for the satisfaction of colliding with his jaw.

Adip's room is a pressure cooker, every tick of the clock a physical blow, each second wasted increasing the chance that I may never see Natalie again.

The air in the room suddenly cools, like a gust of winter wind just blew in. The sensation ripples through my bones and I squint in the dim light, focusing on the window.

The latch on the window clicks, a sound that's deafening in the near silence, and water begins to seep in, droplets glistening in the faint light, forming a puddle on the hardwood floor. Nerves ride against my skin like static.

From the pool of water, a figure begins to emerge. He's tall, broad-shouldered, with an athletic posture that reminds me of an Olympic swimmer. His light-brown hair is damp, sticking to his forehead, and his eyes are a crazy shade of blue, so deep and bright, it's like looking into the ocean. Hauntingly familiar to Natalie's eyes when they shifted color earlier today.

He doesn't look at me, oblivious to my presence, even though I'm right fucking here.

I stand, trying to get his attention. "Are you Natalie's father?"

His response to me is silence.

He's there, but not there—a watery illusion I can see, but not touch. I attempt to tap his shoulder, but my hand passes through him like vapor, chills running up my arm from the sudden frigid temperature.

Panic surges through me. *Can he see me? Hear me?*

He moves, floating towards the sleeping Adip, and takes a seat on the edge of his bed. His gaze lingers on Adip's slumbering form, a strange kind of sorrow etching lines on his face.

A low groan pulls me back to reality as Adip stirs, his eyes fluttering open. My pulse quickens, each beat hammering against my veins, as Adip focuses on this guy. They exchange words, their mouths moving, but it's muffled, like I'm hearing them from underwater.

"Adip, what's going on?"

But he doesn't react. My words seem to dissipate in the air, swallowed by some invisible barrier.

The world spins. It's as if I'm trapped in some odd dimension while everything moves on around me. My desperation mounts—a guttural scream trapped in my throat. I need answers. I need to get Natalie back. But right now, I'm powerless, nothing more than a silent, invisible observer.

The man reaches out, grabbing Adip's notebook from the night-stand and starts to sketch with startling precision, as if he's done this a thousand times before.

Adip talks again and I strain to make out what he's saying. "Who are you really? Why do you keep coming to me?" His words blubber in the invisible, water-filled barrier.

"I'm Natalie's father," he says, his voice echoing like a ripple on a calm lake. "Cy."

Adip looks around the room in wide-eyed confusion, as if searching for something—or someone. "Henry, where'd you go?" That confirms he can't see me at all.

Cy shakes his head, a droplet of water falling from his hair and disappearing into the bedspread. "I'm only able to communicate with you, not your friend."

Adip presses him. "Why?"

"I'm attempting to cross over into your plane of existence." Cy returns to the notebook, sketching out what appears to be some kind of map.

A chill rolls into the room again, making the hairs on my neck stand on end.

"Your dad made that possible. He and I…were once friends."

Adip looks taken aback, his face contorting with confusion. "You know my dad?"

"We go way back," Cy says.

A hint of distrust flickers in Adip's gaze. "Bullshit. Why wouldn't he give me the heads-up you were coming?"

"Because you haven't spoken to him in years."

The accusation hangs in the air. Adip seems pissed as the silence stretches between them. Cy's mention of his dad clearly hit a nerve.

Cy studies Adip, his gaze thoughtful. "He's watching over you." His cryptic words hang in the room like a fog, raising more ques-tions than they answer.

Rage coats Adip's expression. "You can let my dad know I don't need his protection."

Family is a sore spot for most of us. Guess we have that in common.

"If Natalie's really your daughter, why don't you just go to her?"

Cy looks away, a ripple of tension passing over his face. "Because I haven't been able to reach her. I tried… but I was shut out."

My heart wrenches for Natalie, being torn away from both her mom and real father. I guess we also have that in common. I never knew my real parents either.

Cy glances at the clock, as if the passing minutes are a tangible enemy, closing in on him. "I've got to go." He hands the damp notebook to Adip, pointing at the map he's sketched out. "This is the only way to get to Natalie."

Adip stares down at the map. "Wait—"

A sudden deafening boom erupts from outside, jolting us all.

Cy looks up, his blue eyes widening in alarm. He moves with fluid grace, slipping back out through the window in a blur of motion.

I dart over to the window and watch as he leaps from the building in a perfect swan dive before being swallowed by the night, his form dissolving into the inky darkness below.

I turn to the notebook in Adip's hand, grabbing at the edges, pulling at the page.

Adip widens his eyes, and I realize he can finally see me again. "Where were you? Her dad was just here."

"I was right here the whole time. He couldn't see me. Neither could you. It was like I was in some other dimension. Or the two of you were."

"Are you serious? Who… or *what* the hell is that guy? Is he able to bend time or something?"

"I don't know, but he just swan-dived off a roof into nothing."

My eyes drift to the window, where the memory of Natalie's father still lingers.

Adip's wide-eyed incredulity is palpable, but I don't respond, my attention snagged by the drawing Cy left behind. The pages are damp, almost slick, a remnant of Cy's presence. It's a map, a detailed depiction of a piece of Lockwood's campus.

My fingers trace the lines, landing on a spot I've never been. "I don't know this part of the campus." The unknown section stares back at me, a silent challenge.

Adip squints at the marked location, shaking his head. "This doesn't make sense. It's the woods, all overgrown back there. I don't even think we could get through."

I rub my temples, fighting the throbbing headache that's started to build. "We have to figure it out."

The map leads to a spot off a cliff, beneath a body of water, an enigma that makes no fucking sense to either of us.

"This can't be. Unless Natalie is being held underwater."

Adip sighs in frustration. "Or maybe it's a metaphor. Like she's sinking or drowning? I don't know."

We sit in silence. The weight of the task feels like it's drowning me. Natalie is in danger, and we are the only ones who can save her.

As I look down at the map, I can't help but think about Natalie. Is she scared? Is she alone? Is she sinking into something even worse?

The thought of her held captive with Wes and Amelia sends waves of dread crashing over me. This has to end, and soon. I need to find her, and I need to do it now.

CHAPTER FIFTEEN

NATALIE

WES SITS IN a chair across from the bed, a small lamp casting sinister shadows across his face, making him seem even more treacherous than normal. He's absorbed in his journal, his pen scratching away against the paper with a disturbing intensity. I shudder to think of what horrific things he's documenting in those pages.

I'm still in the clothes I was brought here in, Henry's oversized sweats clinging to my skin. Wes notices as I tuck the hood over my head, wanting to disappear.

He waves his hand toward a closet door. "There's a closet full of clothes for you to change into."

"I'm happy wearing this." My words spit back at him.

Wes smirks and scribbles more notes in that fucking journal, likely memories of me. I can't wait until I'm alone so I can shred that thing into tiny pieces.

"Amelia said we're having dinner soon. I'm starving. Just get changed." He stands and faces away from me like he's doing me a favor. "I'll be a gentleman. I won't even look. Not this time, anyway."

"I'd rather starve." I cross my arms over my chest, a protective shield against his revolting suggestions.

He shrugs, nonchalant, and faces me again. "You could at least play along if you want information. Amelia appreciates cooperation. Trust me."

I scoff. "And I should trust you, because?"

His eyes flicker up to meet mine. "Because I love you, Natalie."

I might throw up.

He sits back down on the bed and returns his gaze to that stupid journal.

"What are you writing in that thing?" I ask.

"Thoughts, mostly. It helps me work them out. Very therapeutic."

My eyes narrow, suspicious. "Thoughts of what?"

"That's for me to know." He smiles, enjoying himself as usual, sending a shiver down my spine.

"You said my mom is here."

"Yes."

"And why should I believe you?"

This time, he does lift his gaze, a sincere-looking one. "Because I've never lied to you."

He has to be joking. "You lied about tracking my mom, you lied about the eye patch, you lied about nearly everything…" I trail off, his list of deception far too long to recount.

He sighs, leaning back against the headboard. "Okay, but when you live life in secret, it's hard to even know what the truth is anymore."

Our conversation is cut short when the lock clicks and a guard appears at the door. "It's time for dinner. Amelia is waiting."

I fold my arms over my chest. "I'm not going."

Wes looks at me, a curious glint in his eyes. "Don't you want to ask her where your mom is?"

I hate that he's right. At least if I get out of this room, I can start to figure out how this place works. I found Mom last time, I can do it again. But it's definitely not going to happen trapped in this stuffy room with Wes etching all his creepy thoughts into a leather-bound notebook.

Hesitant, I follow the guard out of the room, Wes trailing behind.

The hallway is much different than the decor in the room, lined with imposing steel doors, every few meters punctuated with a glowing blue light. I wonder who is inside of those rooms.

I notice the patterns in the floor tiles, counting the steps between each door. We take three rights and two lefts before we reach a large, metallic door at the end of the hallway. The guard enters a code on the keypad, and the door slides open with a hiss.

I try to memorize everything—the number of steps, the pattern of the lights, the sound of the doors opening. Anything that can help me figure out this labyrinth of doom. As I cross the threshold into the dining room, I steel myself for what's to come.

The dining room stands in stark contrast to the sterile hallway outside. It's warm, with a large, polished mahogany table set in the middle. An antique chandelier hangs from the ceiling, casting a soft, golden glow around the room. Fine china is set on the table, ornate and delicate, paired with silverware and crystal glasses. The aroma of food wafts through the space, making me even more queasy.

This place might be inviting if it were anywhere else.

Wes is the first to sit, his eyes lighting up at the sight of the food. I watch as he tucks into the spread—roasted duck, buttered vegetables, a basket of warm bread. He starts shoveling food into his mouth. "I'm not waiting. It's late and I haven't eaten all day," he says through a mouthful of food.

Barely a moment passes before the door opens and Amelia glides into the room. She's dressed immaculately in a form-fitting dress—midnight-blue fabric hugging her in all the right places. Her hair is swept into a neat bun, a few loose strands framing her perfect face.

"Welcome, Natalie, Wes." She smiles, taking the seat at the head of the table, acting like this is a fun family dinner. She takes a sip of her wine, her eyes trained on me.

I return her gaze, heart ricocheting against my ribs like a pinball. "Where is my mom?"

Amelia's smile doesn't waver, but she turns her gaze to Wes. There's an unspoken understanding between them that sets my nerves even more on edge.

"I want to know where my mom is, Amelia," I say, my voice booming through the dining room.

"We should eat." She casually reaches for her fork.

It takes every bit of restraint for me not to take my own fork and stab her.

"I'm not eating a thing here. For all I know, the food could be poisoned. Part of your sick game."

Amelia shakes her head. "I don't want to poison you, Natalie."

"Right, you want to use me in whatever sick game you're playing." My accusatory gaze never leaves hers. She doesn't deny it, and I press on. "Where's Henry?"

"He's at Lockwood, where he belongs," she replies coolly. "And you are here, where you belong. Your mother once followed the rules. You should too."

"My mother followed the rules and look where it got her—imprisoned, killed..." I trail off, my voice trembling.

Amelia frowns. "Is that how you see it? I hope you'll change your mind."

"What did my father *do* to you? Was it that bad to warrant all this torture?"

Something dangerous flits across her face, but she says nothing, slowly sipping her wine. She finally speaks. "Your father and I go way back."

Nothing she says or does makes sense.

Before I can press further, she interrupts. "There is something I'd like to share with you this evening. Wes came up with the idea." My stomach churns as she continues. "You two can live here, freely roam the halls, enjoy beautiful meals, enjoy each other… anything you dream of. My only condition is that you can't leave."

"That's not a dream, Amelia. That's my *nightmare*."

Wes shoots me a disgruntled look. As if I care what he thinks.

Amelia isn't fazed. "Well, how about this? I lifted the shield." She proclaims this as if it's the most natural thing in the world, as if I should know what the hell she's talking about.

I blink at her. "What shield?"

"The authority placed a shield on you when you were born. They wanted to ensure there would be no crossbreeding with other supernatural beings. This shield prevents you from procreating, and even from experiencing a simple kiss with someone who has supernatural powers." She pauses, a smirk playing on her lips as she glances towards Wes.

He's grinning, too, like a Cheshire cat.

A sickening feeling rises from my stomach, bubbling into my throat until I nearly choke.

"I've lifted that shield for you," she continues. "You're free now, Natalie. Free to be with Wes, as long as you stay within these walls. And if you should become pregnant, we will take care of the child."

The words crash into me like a freight train. I have zero interest in Wes, in being with him, sleeping with him, or having his child. The thought of it repulses me. And Wes is sitting there, loving this, grinning at her twisted offer.

"No," I say, standing. "I don't want this. I'm leaving."

But the moment I push up from the table, an invisible force pins my wrists down.

I stare down at them, straining against the hold. "What is this? What are you doing to me?"

"You need to learn how to live within these walls, Natalie," Amelia says, her voice slick with ice. "This is your life now."

Anger boils up inside me and I yank against the invisible restraints. I close my eyes, focusing all my energy. I can feel the familiar tingle in my hands, my power unlocking again, the sensation of stars pooling in my palms. And then, with a furious cry, I release them.

A burst of light, a shower of stars, pours from my palms, colliding with the table. The invisible bonds shatter and the tablecloth goes up in flames. The room fills with the scent of burning fabric.

Amelia watches it all, a curious look on her face. She gets up and walks over, waving a hand over the flames. They die down instantly, replaced by a thin wisp of smoke.

"These powers you've inherited are quite fascinating."

She keeps her gaze on me and I stare back at her, my heart rocketing into my throat. If she thinks she can keep me here again, to control me, she's got another thing coming.

CHAPTER SIXTEEN

HENRY

I trace my finger over the damp page of Adip's notebook, the sketched map still as mysterious as the man who drew it. An odd sense of anticipation churns in my gut.

"I'm going to follow this map. Find Natalie. Now."

Adip rubs his hands together in a mixture of nervous energy and determination. "I'll come with you."

I immediately shake my head. There's danger clinging to this map, to this entire situation, and I don't need Adip getting hurt.

"No, you should stay—"

"Her dad drew that map for *me*," Adip says, his voice wavering. He looks me straight in the eye. "What if I have to be there? What if it's something only I can do?"

I don't want to admit it, but he has a point. Her dad was only able to visit him for some reason. My reluctance finally recedes. "Fine. Let's go."

We set off through the campus, moving back to an area where everything seems distorted and unfamiliar.

A distant shuffle of footsteps punctures the silence, sending shockwaves up my spine. I yank Adip behind the gnarled trunk of a nearby tree.

Suddenly, our quest is breached by Ciel's voice, an unwelcome intrusion echoing through the stillness. "Hey, you guys? Are you back here?"

We come out from behind the tree, finding Ciel standing there in the moonlight. When she sees us, she hurries over, her frown turning into a grin.

"What are you doing out here?" Adip's voice is calm, but his eyes dart to me with a flicker of concern.

"I couldn't sleep and I saw you guys creeping around campus like you're playing hide and seek. What are you up to anyway?"

Adip shoots me a meaningful glance, then turns back to Ciel. "Nothing worth losing sleep over, babe. You should head back, get some rest."

But something in her eyes falters, a glimmer of unshed tears.

"Whoa, what's wrong?" Adip says.

"This may be weird, given our… situation, but I need to tell you something."

Adip nods, urging her on. "You know you can tell me anything."

She takes a deep breath, her voice dropping to a whisper. "I slept with someone else. But we're casual, right?" she quickly adds, looking into Adip's eyes for reassurance. "I just… I don't want it to be weird. I wanted to be honest with you."

Adip's silence hangs heavy in the air. Despite their supposed no-strings-attached agreement, something in the tension of his jaw-line tells a different story. He's right to be worried—anyone tangled up with Wes is in for a hellish ride.

He quickly gathers his composure. "Who was it?"

"Wes, that scholarship kid. Is it weird that I'm telling you this?"

"No, it's fine. It's cool," Adip deflects, but his withdrawal, the way he holds himself, betrays his words.

I attempt to steer us back on track. "Ciel, why don't you head back? Get some sleep, okay? It's late."

She offers a slow nod, her eyes still locked on Adip. It's better she remains oblivious to the danger we're stepping into.

As she turns and leaves, Adip and I head into the woods, the tree line casting long shadows as we venture deeper into the unknown. The tangle of branches and underbrush grows denser, the darkness thicker. He vents his frustration on the trees, yanking twigs off low-hanging branches.

"You okay?" I ask, breaking the silence.

"Yeah, sure," he says, unconvincing.

"Ciel mentioned the guy she was with… Wes," I say cautiously, watching Adip's face for a reaction.

He shrugs. "Doesn't matter. We're not exclusive."

"Yeah, but trust me, Wes isn't just some guy. He's trouble— big trouble."

Adip's gaze hardens, and I can tell he's taken my words to heart. He might not admit it, but the news about Ciel and Wes has affected him more than he lets on.

Ahead, a dilapidated part of the iron gate bars our path. Its rusted state suggests it's been forgotten for years. It's strange that I never noticed this part of the gate before, in the old timeline, before Amelia reset things. There's a gap just wide enough for a person to slip through. With a quick glance at Adip, I lead the way, squeezing through the narrow opening.

Once we're outside the gate, it feels as though we have stepped into another world. The path is unmarked and unclear, dense foliage pressing in from all sides. I take the lead, ripping down branches, clearing a path as we progress deeper.

Suddenly, the silence of the forest shatters as a resonating crack echoes through the air. We turn just in time to see a towering tree fall behind us, shaking the ground as it crashes. Then another, and another. The ground trembles under our feet, the noise deafening.

The only way to go is forward, and we take off running, Adip trailing behind. As I dart around a particularly gnarled old oak, I cast a quick glance over my shoulder, only to find that he's no longer behind me. Panic lodges in my gut, icy and sharp. I retrace my steps, the frenzied beat of my heart echoing in my ears.

I find him sprawled on the ground, his face coated with sweat. He's tangled in a bed of fallen branches, struggling to free himself. "Help me out of here!"

I extend my hand to help him up. He hauls himself up, stumbling a little before finding his balance, shooting me a nod of gratitude.

A high-pitched scream shreds through the chaos. My heart lurches as I turn to the noise, rushing towards the source. It's a woman's voice, stricken with sheer terror, and a chilling realization dawns on me—*it sounds like Ciel.*

I pivot, adrenaline pumping through my veins like liquid fire as I sprint towards the sound, finding her. A tree groans and creaks, teetering dangerously above her body. She's frozen in fear, trapped in a mess of branches as it sways above, about to crush her.

I throw myself towards her, lunging with every fiber of my being, aiming to knock her out of the deadly path. The air whips past us as we tumble to the side, sprawling on the ground, barely missing the monstrous tree as it crashes with a ground-shaking thud.

Shaken but unhurt, Ciel looks at me, her eyes wide with terror, breaths coming in shallow and rapid. There's no time for questions, no time for relief.

I pull her up as Adip approaches, my gaze swinging to him. "We need to keep moving."

Adip glares at Ciel. "Why did you follow us?" Adip snaps at her, fury simmering beneath his words.

Ciel flinches, her gaze darting between us. "Because you're mad at me, I know it. I know you."

"I'm not," Adip says, his tone icy. "Just drop it and move."

As the three of us move ahead, eventually, the chaos of fallen trees subsides. We slow down, catching our breath, only to find ourselves at the edge of a towering cliff—the same one on the map. The moonlight illuminates the stomach-churning drop into the rocky sea below.

Ciel manages a nervous laugh. "That would be some cliff dive, huh?"

My eyes are fixated on the dark water. "More like a death wish."

We made it to the final spot on the map, and the reality of our situation smacks into us as hard as the waves.

As we stare into the darkness, the blackened waters churn and roil, as if stirred by an invisible force.

Suddenly, a glow radiates from the depths of the sea, bathing the crashing waves in strange blue light. The water starts to stir more violently, waves rising higher and higher, their peaks gleaming. It's as though the sea is alive, its waves reaching out like giant arms, ready to pull us into its icy depths.

One wave crashes against the cliff, the force of it spraying us with cold seawater. Ciel shrieks as the water hits her skin.

Another wave rises, looming over us, a wall of water that threatens to swallow us whole.

"Run!" The word is barely out of my mouth when a monstrous wave crashes into us.

Adip, closest to the edge, is instantly swallowed by the water, his shocked yell cut short as he disappears with the receding wave. Ciel, teetering nearby, screams as she slips over the edge.

Ignoring the danger, I lunge for her, my fingers curling around her hand just in time. She dangles over the edge, her terrified eyes meeting mine as I struggle to hold on.

The water roars below us, ready to claim its next victim.

"Hold on!" I tighten my grip on her as another wave builds up, preparing to strike.

The wave comes like a speeding train, engulfing us with its cold, brutal force. I fight against the torrent, my grip on Ciel's hand slipping as the water attempts to wrench her from my hold. But I refuse to let go.

Another wave comes, its ferocity greater than the last.

Ciel's knuckles turn stark white as she clings on with the last of her strength. Her voice is barely audible above the crashing waves, but the fear in her eyes screams volumes. "Henry… I… I can't… hold on… much longer."

Another wave rears its head, a titanic mass of frothing sea rising against the backdrop of the moonlit sky. It's bigger, more merciless than the last, its thunderous roar drowning out our heavy, panic-stricken breaths.

"I need you to try!" But even as I speak, another monstrous wave descends upon us, a tsunami that swallows everything in its path.

There's no time to brace ourselves, no time to plan, to strategize. The water wraps around us with no mercy. Our world flips, turns into a chaotic whirl of foam and salt and roaring noise. We're helpless in its grasp, mere rag dolls against the relentless fury of the ocean.

I fight against the violent pull, but the sea is an unyielding enemy. My lungs scream for oxygen as the water crashes over us, fills my mouth, my nose, snuffing out the air.

The last of the moonlight illuminates Ciel's terrified face just before the water yanks her away, her fingers slipping from my grasp. Her scream is swallowed by the water, her figure distorted by the whirl of bubbles and churned-up sand. I reach out for her, but the current is too strong, and she's swept away into the darkness.

A strangled scream rips from my chest, bubbles of air escaping my lips and rushing upwards, towards the rapidly receding surface. The sea couldn't give a fuck about my voice as it yanks my body down, claiming me whole.

CHAPTER SEVENTEEN

NATALIE

Silence descends over the dining room, a strange calm following my outburst. The charred tablecloth, the smell of burned fabric lingering in the air, is the only memory of the power I've just unleashed.

Amelia stands at the head of the table. "Such a fascinating power." Her curious gaze trails over me. "I presume it's from your mother's side. Celestial, isn't it?"

A bitter laugh escapes me. "Why don't you ask her yourself?" The words hang heavy in the room, a thinly veiled challenge, a plea for information about my mom.

Amelia's expression doesn't waver. "Your mother never used her powers while living under authority rule. She behaved. We never got the chance to witness such a spectacle."

"How did you meet her anyway? Was it through my father?"

My question grinds the conversation to a halt, the air between us fraught with tension, each word hanging like a sword ready to drop. An uneasy silence settles in as I wait for Amelia to answer.

She turns away, her elegant fingers trailing over the burned tablecloth. "Let's save that story for another time. You should really eat something, Natalie."

The sight of the lavish spread in front of me stirs a pang of hunger, but I push it away, setting my jaw in defiance. "I'd rather starve."

Amelia doesn't miss a beat. "And waste away? I certainly hope not." She pours herself another glass of wine, her every movement calculated, controlled. "It would be a shame if you became too weak."

A spark of anger ignites within me. "At least you can't experiment on me then."

The rest of the dinner is a silent affair. Amelia and Wes finish their meals, exchanging occasional glances and muffled words, while I sit with my arms crossed, my stomach growling in protest.

As the tortuous dinner comes to an end, we're ushered back to our room by one of the guards. I walk in silence, Wes trailing behind. Each step feels heavier than the last.

Back in the bedroom, the weight of everything sets in. My thoughts spin in a chaotic whirl, Amelia's words playing over and over in my mind. She's lifted some bizarre shield and now I'm supposed to play out this arranged marriage bullshit with Wes? No fucking way.

Tears well up in my eyes as I sink into an oversized chair across from the bed, but I blink them back. Wes takes the bed. His journal lies open on the side table.

As the quiet settles in, a question burns in my mind, the unfairness of it all pushing me to break the silence. I turn to Wes, my gaze hardened, my words laced with a bitter edge. "Aren't you mad that she's manipulating you?"

Wes looks at me in confusion. "Not at all. It led me to what I want...you."

His words land like a punch, stirring my nausea. I pull my knees to my chest, looking anywhere but at him.

"Come on, Covington." His voice breaks through my anger.

"You should just join me in bed. I promise, I won't even touch you. I'm Switzerland, I swear."

"No." My reply is firm, resolute. I will never share a bed with him. He's anything but neutral. Switzerland, my ass.

Resigning to my decision, he starts journaling again. The scratching sound of his pen against the paper grates on my nerves, each stroke a bitter reminder of our circumstances.

The night stretches on, every tick of the clock marking the passing time, the relentless echo filling the room. Despite my best efforts, my eyelids grow heavy, my body betraying me.

I don't recall at what point I surrender to the exhaustion, but the last thing I remember is the soft scratch of Wes's pen.

The sound of a door creaking open stirs me from my sleep. My eyes flutter open to the darkness. I'm startled to find a blanket draped over me, its warmth a sharp contrast to the cold reality standing above me.

It's Wes, his figure silhouetted in the darkness. His eyes meet mine, a silence stretching between us, his gaze holding an unspoken question.

I pull the blanket closer, wrapping it around myself like a protective shield. "Did you…?" My voice is raspy from sleep, my question trailing off as I gesture towards the blanket.

He shrugs, an unreadable expression on his face. "I didn't want you to be cold."

His simple reply causes a strange sensation to bubble up within me. It's not gratitude or anger, but a more complex emotion I can't quite place. I push it aside, reminding myself of where we are, of who he is. I can't afford to forget, not even for a moment, not even if he shows a shred of kindness.

The world shifts around me, the edges blurring and blending in an unfamiliar pattern, the room spinning slightly. This is not the cold, harsh reality I'm living in. This is different, hazy.

Wes sinks to his knees in front of me, his face softened, his eyes swimming with regret. "I'm sorry, Natalie," he says. He seems… earnest. Strange. "I'm sorry for everything you've been through. All I've ever wanted is for you to be happy. I thought… I *think* we could be happy here, together."

I attempt to reply, to counter his delusion, but my words are trapped in my throat, as if the air in this room is turning against me.

Slowly, with a softness that startles me, he reaches out, his hand coming to rest on the edge of my blanket. I shift away instinctively, but he persists, gently tucking the blanket around my legs, his hand brushing against my now-bare thigh. What happened to my clothes?

An unexpected rush courses through me, but I quickly bat it away. I don't want to feel anything from his touch.

He leans closer to me. "You say you don't want me, but I see it, Natalie. Your body shows it. It always did."

I swallow hard as my body starts to shiver—from the cold, his touch, I'm not sure. I know I hate him. I hate what he's done. And yet, in this strange moment, a feeling I don't understand, a feeling I can't name, flickers within me.

"We don't need to pretend anymore," he says, his eyes never leaving mine. "It can just be you and me. I can make you feel good. Anything you want."

His hand disappears under the blanket, his fingers tracing a path up my thigh, eliciting a gasp from my throat. It's then I realize that my sweats have vanished, replaced by a nude-colored, silk night-gown—short, with spaghetti straps. I glance down at the thin fabric that's barely covering my body, heart thudding against my chest.

Wes seems to sense my confusion. "I helped you get changed."

Panic sets in, the world shifting and spinning even faster. This is a dream, it has to be. But it feels so real, so vivid, I can't seem to pull myself out of it.

Grasping his hand, I attempt to drive it away, but he tightens his grip on my thigh. His voice, husky with command, cuts through. "Don't push me away." His breath is hot against my skin as he disappears under the blanket, moving between my thighs, running his hands up the silky fabric. "Let me change your mind."

Instinctively, I squeeze my legs together, a futile attempt to ward him off. Yet a part of me betrays my revulsion, a part that craves his touch. This can't be. I don't feel this way. *This can't be real.*

"Stop… stop… stop."

I'm jolted awake, breath lodging in my throat. The room around me is still, dark, my body curled on the chair. I glance down to see myself dressed in Henry's sweats still, the fabric cozy against my skin.

Across the room, Wes is awake, watching me, his green eyes glittering in the darkness. A laugh, low and mocking, escapes his lips.

"What?" I push myself up, my muscles protesting against the sudden movement. There's a blanket over me and I realize he must have placed it there. With a repulsed gasp, I fling it off like it's made of fire.

"Nothing," he says, a smirk tugging at the corners of his lips. "That was… fun."

My heart lurches. "What was?"

"I just walked into your dream," Wes says, his smirk broadening. "Didn't quite go as planned, but I think with some practice…"

"What the hell do you mean you *walked* into my dream? You're invading my sleep now?" Disgust coils over my skin.

"Covington, you won't let me anywhere near you while you're awake. We're alone in a bedroom together. What am I supposed to do?"

Bile rises in my throat as I press him for information. "What is this? More of your sick little magic tricks?"

"No, it's one of my powers. Another string to my bow, if you will. A power I happened upon…accidentally, I guess you could say."

I choke back my contempt. His fingers toy with the pen lying next to his journal.

"Get the fuck out of my head." I push to my feet. My body feels heavy, drained, but the anger pulsing through my veins gives me strength.

All I know is I can't be here with him another second longer.

CHAPTER EIGHTEEN

HENRY

COLD, RELENTLESS WAVES slap against my face, each one a cruel reminder of my brutal reality.

I sputter, my throat raw from the saltwater as I struggle to breathe. The grainy sand beneath me digs into my back, every pebble imprinted into my flesh as I struggle to sit up.

A searing pain radiates through my body. My hand shakes as it finds the handle of a dagger plunged mercilessly into my chest. Blood pools out, soaking the sandy grit under my back, the metallic scent stealing away bits of my consciousness. The world spins around me, a blurry, nightmarish kaleidoscope of shadow and dim moonlight.

Natalie is ahead—I notice her silhouette. Her voice comes to me in distant echoes, floating over the wind. She's talking to Cy—their conversation a whispered secret that my dying mind can't decipher. I strain to understand, to grasp the last lifelines of connection before they vanish.

Cy's words pierce through the howling wind. "Natalie, listen to me. I've… I've done terrible things, things I'm not proud of."

His voice, tinged with a regret so raw it feels as though I'm intruding on a private moment, leaves a bitter taste in my mouth. This isn't what Natalie deserves… her absentee father trying to gain her sympathy.

Her shaky breaths falter at his confession. Strands of waterlogged hair cling to her face as if trying to shield her from the ugly truth. "What are you saying?"

A look of profound sadness settles on Cy's face, a stark contrast to the cool, detached man I've seen. "I hurt the people I loved… including your mother."

Something shifts within me. A cold dread snakes its way down my spine, tightening its hold with every word Cy speaks. Natalie's mother…she doesn't deserve to have her memory tarnished by the confession of a man who abandoned her and his daughter.

"I've failed everyone," Cy says. "But I don't… I can't fail you anymore."

Before Natalie can comprehend his words, before she can brace herself against whatever emotional tidal wave he's about to unleash, Cy's hand latches on to hers. It's sudden, unexpected, and the scream that rips through Natalie's throat is terrifying.

Her body seizes up, her scream sliced into eerie fragments as she convulses, her body jerking violently under his hold. Rage grips me as I watch, paralyzed by the sudden onslaught. The scene unfolding before me paints a picture I don't want to see—a father causing his daughter—*the girl I love*—unimaginable pain.

Natalie's suffering under her father's grip cuts through the numbing shock, igniting even more fury in my bones. I need to stop this, to save her.

I surge forward, intent on pulling them apart, but I'm too weak, too slow. The world around me blurs, my vision fading as my life trickles away.

I scream, or at least I think I do. No sound escapes my lips, my voice a pathetic wheeze lost in the pounding surf. I try to move, to crawl, to get to her, but my body refuses to cooperate. I'm trapped in my own dying shell, a spectator to my own gruesome end… and Natalie's.

Natalie fights, writhing against the brutal hold her father has on her. Desperation claws at me, my heart pounding against the blade embedded in my chest. I can't save her, can't reach her. The sickening reality settles heavy in my stomach, a poisonous reminder of my helplessness.

My sight begins to dim, the world around me shrinking, consumed by the overwhelming darkness.

I'm dying, and there's nothing I can do about it.

The last thing I see is Natalie, her figure outlined against the moonlit waves, convulsing in the grip of the man who claims to be her father. And then, everything goes black.

I jolt awake, my body racked with violent coughs as I spit the water from my lungs. My skin feels raw under the weak daylight, the sky a sheet of gray above. I press a hand to my chest, but the cruel sting of the dagger is gone.

Was it all a dream? Or a vision?

Pressing up onto my hands, I scan the surrounding area, searching for Natalie. My stomach twists violently when I discover there's no sign of her.

Instead, Adip catches my eye, hunched over nearby and gasping for breath. Without a second thought, I race over to him.

His shivering body straightens up, spitting out sand. "What the hell happened? Where are we?"

His question hangs in the air, unanswered, as we take in our surroundings. The beach is deserted except for us, the waves crashing against the shoreline, softer than before. But it's not the sea that draws my attention, it's the imposing structure looming ahead, partially hidden by the thicket of trees—a building with Gothic architecture, like a fortress in nature, a dark silhouette against the cloudy sky. Violet flowers creep up its black stone walls.

I tear my gaze away from the building, focusing on the skyline in the opposite direction, hovering over the shore.

A shiver chases down my spine as I recognize the distinctive silhouettes—the Hagia Sophia, the Blue Mosque, the Bosphorus Bridge. *Istanbul.* I saw this view countless times during my ocean cleanup mission. But that was in Turkey.

Are we... in Turkey?

I squint at the landmarks, their familiar shapes stirring up a whirlwind of questions. How the fuck did we end up here, thousands of miles away from where we should be? Did Natalie's father somehow lead us here... or transport us?

"Ciel." Adip's gaze darts around the deserted beach. "Where's Ciel?"

The urgency in his voice ignites a spark of panic in my chest. We call out for her, our voices bouncing off the towering rocks, swallowed by the crashing waves, but all we're met with is silence.

We scour the shoreline, our eyes tracing the waves as they retreat back into the sea, searching the scattered rocks protruding from the sand like weathered tombstones. But Ciel is nowhere in sight.

Adip's steps falter, his eyes glossy, his voice choked with emotion. "No, I... can't lose her, man. I... I'm in love her. Ever since I first met her. Long before Lockwood. She just doesn't know." His confession hangs heavy in the salty air, raw and vulnerable.

I'm not sure what to say in this fucked-up situation, especially when we've both lost people we love.

Suddenly, a flicker of movement in the distance pulls my gaze. Lying motionless at the edge of the shore, the waves lapping gently over her, is Ciel.

Adrenaline floods my veins as we bolt towards her. Adip reaches her first, dropping to his knees in the wet sand. His hands tremble as he begins the rhythmic push of chest compressions, his panicked whispers to Ciel morphing into desperate pleas.

We fight against time and odds, and I can't help but feel a surge of despair. Here we are, stranded on some coastal island in Turkey, in search of the ones we love, not knowing if they're safe or even alive. The situation is a relentless undercurrent, threatening to pull us under.

Ciel remains still as Adip continues his efforts to revive her, his efforts met with chilling silence until suddenly, she coughs up seawater.

Alive.

Relief washes over us as Adip cradles her in his arms.

As he comforts Ciel, my eyes drift back to the Gothic structure looming in the distance. "Maybe Natalie's father brought us here," I say. "Maybe Natalie's in that place."

Ciel's voice is weak but laced with confusion. "Natalie's father? What?"

"I'll fill you in," Adip says as he pulls Ciel to her feet.

My thoughts wander back to Natalie, the way she was convulsing—the raw fear in her eyes. That nightmare—or vision—is a splinter lodged deep within my mind, a painful reminder of what might happen to her.

A mixture of fear, anger, and determination courses through my veins—a volatile cocktail, fueling me, driving me forward.

Behind me, Adip is still comforting Ciel, his words just audible above the incessant sound of the waves. Their murmured conversation seems distant, like an echo bouncing off the walls of my focus. All I can think about is Natalie.

I force my gaze back to the building that stands between us and hopefully her.

As we walk towards the building, the structure grows larger and more intimidating. But my resolve is steel. She's in there—the closer we get, I can feel it—and nothing on this damned island or in that cursed building is going to stop me from getting her back.

I clench my jaw, steeling myself for the storm that's surely waiting for us within those walls. Sand crunches beneath my feet as I stride ahead, pulse thundering in my ears, drowning out everything but a single, driving thought: *Find Natalie. Find her, no matter what it takes.*

CHAPTER NINETEEN

NATALIE

THE SKY'S A sickly gray, like someone sucked all the joy out of the universe. Which, come to think of it, is a pretty good metaphor for my life right now. I'm running on fumes after a nightmare-ridden evening courtesy of Wes, trying to ignore the gnawing pain in my stomach from lack of food.

Across the table, Wes devours the extravagant breakfast spread like he doesn't have a care in the world. He's content, so fucking pleased with himself, while I'm here, starving, on edge, *trapped*.

But that's Wes for you—always living in his own world, by his rules.

Amelia looks between us. "I trust your night was… enjoyable?" She points a look in my direction.

"You can't expect me to play house and sleep with whoever you choose. This isn't a twisted reality show. I'm not some prisoner you can breed."

Amelia maintains her calm, a smile fixed on her face. "Oh, on the contrary. You wouldn't be keeping the child if you did conceive."

Before I can vomit into my untouched breakfast, one of her

servants enters, setting a cup of cinnamon tea in front of me. The fragrant steam wafts up, but the inviting aroma does nothing to ease my disgust.

Breaking the silence, Wes turns his attention to Amelia. "Maybe Natalie's mom could join us for dinner tonight."

My heart drops. The room spins. He knows my mother is here… but he said he didn't. Is he trying to bait Amelia? Or lying, once again?

Amelia falters. "We… we've already discussed this."

Wes tilts his head, feigning innocence. "Actually, we haven't. If you want Natalie to feel welcome in this place, she should be reunited with her mom."

I can see Amelia's discomfort grow. The tension in the room is a live wire. "It's a sensitive subject, best left untouched for the time being."

In a burst of rage, I seize the cup of tea and smash it onto the marble floor. The porcelain shatters, splattering hot tea and shards of glass everywhere. "That's enough!" I push away from the table, standing up, the chair grinding against the stone floor.

Amelia and Wes can keep their breakfast, their schemes, and their twisted agendas. All I want is my freedom, my mother, and Henry. And I won't stop until I get them back.

Fury coursing through my veins, I stride towards the door, attempting to twist it open. Of course it won't open—I certainly didn't expect Amelia to keep her word.

"You said I was free to roam the halls here. So why the hell is this door locked?"

Amelia and I engage in a tense standoff, her eyes locked with mine. Then, I hear the faint click of the door unlocking. A smug smile flits across Amelia's face, but I don't stick around to confront her.

Storming out, I find myself navigating the labyrinth-like corridors of this hellscape. The hallways stretch endlessly, a maze of oak-paneled walls covered in ornate paintings. The dark hardwood floors, the heavy, embroidered drapes hanging off windows, the cold marble statues tucked into shadowy corners—everything reeks of old wealth and secrets.

Room after room, I try the handles, the doors opening with surprising ease. Each room appears grander than the last, a showcase of opulence, yet still cold and impersonal.

Most importantly, my mother isn't inside any one of them.

I move to the next door, its handle refusing to budge under my grasp. If this one is locked, that means I need to get inside.

I take a deep breath, focusing my thoughts on my powers, sending energy from my hand to the knob. I'm not quite sure how to wield or control my powers yet, but this seems to be working as the familiar glow of my ability sparks to life, stars twinkling in my palms like a celestial tapestry.

The handle shifts under the glow, a soft click reverberating through the silence. Pushing the door open, I step inside and my breath catches in my throat.

The room is filled with that strange, glass contraption, its polished surface reflecting the dim light filtering in from the narrow windows—the same contraption Amelia used to reset time. Around it, walls are lined with clocks of every shape and size, their rhythmic ticking filling the room in an eerie lullaby. The air in the room seems to ripple and shudder, as if trapped in a continuous loop of time. I step carefully, the steady rhythm of the ticking clocks echoing in my ears. This is Amelia's time machine, a monstrous construct of glass, gears, and unbearable loneliness. A place where time stands still, and yet runs away.

Caught in the eerie glow of the contraption, I wrestle with my instincts. Should I destroy this thing?

The consequences dawn on me, the horrifying thought of being severed from my mother and Henry indefinitely. I can't risk it. I have to find them first. Then destroy it.

My gaze flits across the room, eventually landing on a wall lined with monitors. I approach them, expecting to see rooms within this building—but the monitors show Lockwood instead.

I watch in disbelief as the footage flickers to Henry in Adip's room. In the dim glow of the monitors, I watch things unfold.

The window in Adip's room unlatches seemingly on its own, and water begins to seep in, forming a puddle on the floor. Each droplet glimmers in the faint light, casting eerie shadows that creep along the walls. The sensation ripples up my spine, as if I, too, am there, watching this in person.

A figure materializes from the pool, water droplets shimmering down his tall frame. His light-brown hair is wet, clinging to his forehead and his eyes, so blue and intense, they seem to pierce through the screen. They're so mesmerizing, I nearly miss the faint scar that lingers on his cheek. Is this man supposed to be… *my real father?*

He's not solid, not quite there, an illusion of water and mystery. He doesn't even notice Henry's attempts to grab his attention.

"Are you Natalie's father?" Henry calls out, his voice swallowed by the room.

The specter that is supposed to be my father glides towards Adip, as if he didn't hear the question.

"I see you found a way in here." Amelia's voice slithers in from behind, cutting through my focus.

I don't remove my gaze from the screen. "That's my father?"

She breathes a heavy sigh. "Yes."

Suddenly, my father lunges ahead, attacking a sleeping Adip. A three-pronged spear materializes and he plunges it into Adip's stomach. Adip wakes with a start, his scream echoing through the video. I clench my hands on the table in front of me, a silent cry escaping my lips.

Henry tries to intervene, but the water on the floor betrays him. He slips, falls, and my father capitalizes on the moment. The trident plunges down, and I can almost hear the sickening thud as it pierces Henry's chest. The room spins around me as I struggle to breathe, the glow of the monitors blinding, the taste of horror bitter on my tongue.

I yell out, the sound piercing the stillness. And then Amelia laughs, her harsh response ricocheting off the walls, chilling me to the bone.

I whirl around, my anger flaring. "Why the hell are you laughing?"

"That's exactly how I remember your father. That's exactly how he treated me."

Fear and horror wash over me. If the monitors are showing the truth, that means… Adip… *Henry…*

No, only a dagger can kill Henry. I hold out hope, trying to make sense of the scene unfolding before me, hoping it's just another one of Amelia's twisted games playing out as a movie and not reality.

"This isn't real, is it? Just another one of your illusions."

There's a long silence, which I take to mean she's fucking with me again.

Then finally, Amelia speaks. "I know it doesn't seem like it, but I'm only trying to protect you, Natalie." Her voice is casual, as if we're discussing the weather and not my father's malevolence.

"No. I don't believe a word you say."

"Your father is more powerful than you realize. He's a very dangerous man."

A lump forms in my throat as I swallow back my rising panic. "You already admitted before that you're testing me…to figure out my powers… to use me."

"Information is power. Yes, I need to understand you, the extent of your abilities. But only to keep you safe."

"Safe?" I scoff, my rage flaring up. "How does any of this make me safe? You've locked me up, kept my mother from me, tortured me and people I love, and now… now you're telling me that it's all because of my father, a man I've never even met."

Amelia leans in closer, her eyes narrowing. "I've known your father, Cy, for a long time. I'm the only person who knows who he *truly* is."

I snort in disbelief. "So you expect me to trust you? To believe that you're suddenly on my side?"

"I don't expect you to trust me, Natalie," Amelia says, her voice eerily calm. "But I do want the best for you. Unlike your father."

She turns to leave, but I stop her. "I don't believe you. Everything that comes out of your mouth is bullshit."

"Then you're more like him than you realize."

CHAPTER TWENTY

HENRY

THE GOTHIC BUILDING casts a long, dark shadow, standing tall like a warning.

As I lead Ciel and Adip through the property, I can't shake the feeling of something unnatural clinging to this place. Like the building is not just a structure, but something with a consciousness of its own.

As we get closer, I notice that the building's exterior is impenetrable—no doors, no windows, no signs of an entry point. It's as if it wasn't meant for people to go in or come out. It doesn't make sense.

"It's like a fortress," Adip says, scanning the stone walls.

"Fortresses have gates. Entrances. This…" My voice trails off. This isn't a fortress. It's a fucking tomb. A sudden pang slices through my temple, forcing me to clutch my head. I blink against the pain, a new vision swimming.

And then I see…

A cave, sprawling and intricate, beneath the building. An underground maze accessible only by a singular secret point—a hidden entrance marked by an ancient symbol—a blooming violet flower, identical to the ones creeping up the building's exterior.

My vision fades, replaced by the reality of the stone structure standing before us. I glance at the ground, the tangle of violet flowers suddenly taking on a whole new meaning.

The ease of my vision is unsettling, almost too convenient, which probably means Amelia is aware of our presence and is intentionally luring us inside. Which is fine by me, because I'll do whatever it takes to get to Natalie, even if it means playing more of Amelia's twisted fucking games.

"This way," I say, more to myself than Adip and Ciel.

We trail the growth of flowers to a less conspicuous section of the stone wall. With closer inspection, I spot a pattern in the placement of these flowers, encircling a particular section of the wall, almost like they're marking a point.

Sucking in a deep breath, I press my hand against it. There's a shudder, and then, slowly, the stone surface grinds aside, revealing a hidden passage. The wall moves just enough to allow one person to slip through. A perfectly camouflaged entrance.

I look back at Adip and Ciel, their faces mirroring my shock. I'm not sure whether they trust my intuition or are just too shell-shocked to question it. But either way, we're on the same page.

"The entrance," I say, pulling the hidden door open, revealing a steep staircase disappearing into darkness.

As we each step through, a gust of cold, stale air hits us. An icy draft curls up, littering goosebumps across my skin. As we move further down, the light from the entrance grows fainter, leaving us shrouded in near-complete darkness. Each step down brings another pang of anxiety and a surge of determination. I can feel her... *Natalie...*

I know she's close.

Suddenly, Adip's foot slips on a loose stone, sending him stumbling against the cold wall. He catches himself just in time. "Fuck." His voice cuts through the silence.

Ciel clings to his arm, her wide eyes reflecting off what little light we have left.

Once he regains his footing, we resume our descent. The temperature drops with every step, the cold seeping into my bones.

With a shiver, I pull my coat tighter around me, my thoughts flickering back to Natalie. Her face swims into my mind, an island of warmth in this cold, unfeeling place.

When we reach the bottom of the staircase, tunnels snake out in every direction, a complex network of uncertainty. I can't shake the fact that we're being led, being watched.

Then, another vision slams into my brain.

Natalie. *Her fear-streaked face appears in front of one of the tunnels, bathed in crimson light, her skin clammy and pale, eyes wide with terror.*

The vision is like a magnetic pull, a tether anchoring us together.

"This way," I say, turning left where my vision led.

Adip and Ciel exchange uncertain looks but follow me anyway.

"We should mark our path," Adip says, breaking off a chunk of chalky stone from the wall.

The path twists and turns, and with each step, the feeling that Natalie is near intensifies. It's a feeling that's hard to describe, like hot lava coursing through my veins, seeping into my bones—an internal inferno that would be unbearable if it weren't for its purpose: her.

Every step, every breath is laced with her—Natalie. It keeps me going, the insatiable need to see her alive, to hold her, to make sure this is the last time we're separated. Being apart from her is as tormenting as it is motivating.

Every so often, Adip cracks off another piece from the wall, a breadcrumb trail for us to find our way back. But I can't afford to think about the way back. Not when everything I want lies ahead.

We stumble upon a massive, ornate door, etched with ancient symbols. This is it. I can feel her behind this door. I don't know how I know, but I do.

"Wait, Henry." Ciel grabs my arm, her grip firm. "We don't know what's behind—"

Another vision slams into my brain.

Natalie again, but this time, she's not alone. She's with Wes. He has her cornered against a wall, his head lowering towards her neck in a grotesque display of control. Her face contorts in revulsion, but there's a certain resignation in her eyes, as if she's accepted this grim scenario as her reality... her future.

My vision ends, igniting a rage so fierce it threatens to consume me. *No. No fucking way.* My hands ball into fists, knuckles bleaching to a stark white as my anger whips into a frenzy. Over my dead body will this be her reality.

"I'm going in." I wrench my arm free from Ciel, stepping up to the door. "Natalie's in there."

I press against the door, but the stone won't budge. I try again, my muscles straining under the effort, but the stone remains immovable. Adip joins me, but our collective effort does nothing.

This is an obstacle strategically placed by Amelia, no doubt. She wants us here, yet she's thrown this barrier in our path. Why?

My gaze roams over the door, the coarse texture of the stone cool beneath my palm. And that's when I notice it—an inscription of some sort, ancient symbols intermingling with an unknown script.

I reach out, tracing the cold carvings with my fingers. They wind together to form a circular pattern, like an intricate maze within the stone itself.

Adip moves closer, brow furrowing as he studies the inscription. "Hang on, this... this looks familiar," he says, his voice trailing off as he searches his memory.

Suddenly, he reaches into his pocket and pulls out the map Natalie's father drew for us. He unfolds the delicate paper, still damp. His finger stops at one point, a small drawing that's remarkably similar to the one inscribed on the door.

"There." Adip points to the symbol. It's accompanied by a set of words written in the same cryptic script as the inscription. "This is the same symbol that's on the door. It's a phrase… a key, maybe?"

I step closer, looking down at the map, then back up at the door. The similarities are uncanny. But how do we use this phrase, this key, to unlock the damn door?

On the map, right next to the inscription, Cy sketched a hand, with the index and middle fingers pressed together and pointing at the center of the maze symbol. An instruction?

Lifting my hand, I mimic the gesture indicated on the map, pressing my fingers into the heart of the engraved maze. But the door remains shut.

"It's not working."

Adip steps forward. "Let me try."

He mimics the same pattern I tried, his index and middle fingers meeting at the center. There's a long pause, a heavy silence that hangs between us, before the stillness is shattered by a loud, grating noise. The enormous stone door shudders, then groans open, revealing a pathway into the darkness beyond.

Relief surges within me, washing away the initial frustration. I clasp Adip's shoulder. "Thanks, man."

Adip gives a small nod, his gaze locked onto the dark passage before us.

We're coming, Natalie. Hang on.

CHAPTER TWENTY-ONE

NATALIE

THE MOMENT AMELIA leaves the room, a wave of familiarity floods over me. The sensation, as clear as if Henry were standing right beside me, stirs a sliver of hope in my heart. I don't see him on the monitors, but he's close. I know it. I feel it.

Closing my eyes, I focus on him, desperate for that thread of connection. I know what I saw on this monitor had to be a lie. Just more of Amelia's games.

When I blink my eyes open, they're there—Henry, Adip, and Ciel appear on one of the monitors. They're trudging through what seems to be a dark cave. My heart lurches at the sight of them. I squint at the screen, trying to figure out where exactly they are in this place.

I need to create some sort of distraction—something that can lead them to me. I'm standing in front of the building's security system, but I don't know the first thing about this technology. I feel a stab of frustration, wishing my gifts had more to do with hacking computers than shooting stars from my palms.

My gaze moves on, landing on an electrical box wedged into

a corner of the room. Overloading the building's electrical system to create a blackout seems like a great idea for a split second. The resulting confusion might provide an opening for Henry, Adip, and Ciel to navigate this place unnoticed.

But total darkness might not necessarily lead them to me. Instead, it could be like tossing them into a labyrinth without a flashlight, drawing them further into the unknown. In the worst-case scenario, they could even get separated in the chaos. I shake my head. I can't risk it. I can't risk them.

As I grapple with my dwindling options, my attention lands on an object hanging on the wall—an alarm. A sense of hope surges through me. If I could set that off, it would definitely create a commotion—a loud, ringing commotion that might guide them straight to me.

I gnaw on my lower lip as I consider this. It's still a risk, but one I'm willing to take. I edge towards the alarm, my heart rocketing into my throat. This could be it. The lifeline that reunites me with Henry.

I yank the red lever down. The shrill sound that follows is deafening, reverberating through the room. I wince at the sudden noise as I cut my gaze back to the monitor, watching as Henry, Adip, and Ciel freeze in shock. The piercing sound makes them look up, their eyes wide, their bodies tensed.

Got their attention.

They start to move toward the sound. It's working.

The alarm still blaring, I turn and slip through the door, anxiety coiling through my chest. The urgency of the alarm has the guards running in the opposite direction, their hurried steps echoing against the stone walls. As I slink down the hall, it's almost like I'm invisible.

I venture further, each step hopefully drawing me closer to Henry. But just as I'm about to turn a corner, my body slams into a solid figure.

I stagger back, momentarily disoriented. When I look up, my blood freezes.

Wes.

His green eyes widen with surprise, then narrow with suspicion. "What are you doing?" he demands with a sly grin, his gaze sliding over me. "Did you set off that alarm?"

"No." I think fast, pasting a terrified look on my face. Then I reach out and clasp his hand, eyeing his shocked expression. He eyes our interlocked hands but doesn't pull away, a flicker of confusion passing over his face.

Good. *Keep him off balance.*

The question tumbles from my lips, the start of a new lie—one I'm hoping he buys. "Do you know where the caves are?"

Wes doesn't respond, but his silence tells me everything I need to know.

I bite back a victorious smile. "I was in that room with the security cameras." My voice quakes with feigned fear. "The monitors… they showed this cave. My mom was there." The lie tastes bitter on my tongue, but if it gets me one step closer to Henry, it's a price I'm willing to pay. Besides, we're much stronger together. I know we can defeat Amelia and Wes, get Adip and Ciel to safety, and most importantly, find Mom.

"Really? Your mom's down there?" Wes's voice is laced with uncertainty, a clear sign that my act is working.

"Can you help me get there?"

He pauses for a moment, scrutinizing me.

My blood runs cold, but I hold his gaze, hoping my lie hasn't crumbled. "Please, Wes." I layer my words with urgency. "I know things haven't been great between us. I just want to find my mom more than anything."

Wes continues to eye me, his brow furrowed. "And if I help you, what do I get in return?"

Of course he wants something for the favor, and I know what that is, but I manage to keep my composure.

"I'll sleep next to you tonight," I find myself saying, and the words send a sharp, vile stab to my gut. It's a promise I have no intention of keeping, not when I hope to be reunited with Henry by the time night falls. But it's the bait Wes needs, the incentive that will hopefully push him to help me.

Wes studies me for another beat, as if attempting to read my thoughts.

I hold my breath, hoping that he buys my desperate act. I need him to believe me, to trust me, if only for a moment. I need him to lead me to Henry.

And then, finally, he nods. "Alright."

I force myself to maintain a façade of nervous anticipation, squeezing his hand for good measure. "Thank you."

As Wes nods again, relief floods my system, only to drain away the instant he grips my arm and slams me into the wall. The alarm's blaring seems to grow louder, its insistent wail a jarring counterpoint to the sudden tension between Wes and me.

"You're not lying to me, are you?" His words come out in a hiss, his face so close to mine I can feel the heat of his breath ghosting over my lips.

"No." I force out the words, keeping my voice steady.

His eyes, filled with doubt and suspicion, bore into mine. "I don't believe you." He leans into my neck, his voice a threatening purr against my skin.

Fear skitters down my spine, but I refuse to let it conquer me. I've come too far, risked too much to let Wes ruin everything now.

"I'm not lying to you. I'm accepting what's happening here, our situation. I know you want to help me...that you love me. So do it. Help me find my mom."

Something flickers in his eyes, but he doesn't challenge me. Instead, he takes my hand and begins leading me down the dimly lit corridor.

With each step, my heart pounds against my ribcage, matching the urgency of my thoughts. I need to keep Wes convinced. I need to find Henry.

I need to escape this fucking place.

As we move deeper into the corridors, I fight to keep my breath steady, my steps sure. The walls close in, suffocating, oppressive, but I can't afford to panic. Not when I'm so close.

Every noise, every shadow, every alarm ring fills me with dread. But fear is not an option. It never has been. Not when my freedom, my survival, hangs in the balance. I need to be strong. For me. For Adip and Ciel. For Mom. For Henry.

And I will be. Because if there's one thing I've learned about myself, it's that I am a survivor. I've made it this far, and I refuse to back down now.

Even if it means playing nice with Wes. Even if it means burying the fear, the disgust, the uncertainty.

This is a game of survival. And I intend to win.

The moment the blaring alarm ceases, my heart thumps harder. I was counting on the chaos to cover our movements, to buy us time. Now, every footstep seems to echo, the silence of the corridor suffocating.

"Almost there," Wes says, his grip on my hand unyielding as he steers me through the winding halls.

Left. Right. Left again. The pattern quickly blurs, the ever-changing path making it impossible to memorize the route. A thought nags at the back of my mind—Amelia is probably watching us. She doesn't strike me as the kind of person who would race outside for a fire drill. Panic flares in my chest at the thought, but I squash it down, trying to focus on my mission.

Suddenly, Wes pulls me into a room. I take in the scene before me, my heart plummeting. This isn't the cave entrance. It's not a stairwell leading downwards.

It's an office.

And Amelia is behind the desk.

Betrayal scores through my bones. I glare at Wes, the depth of his treachery a gut punch. Not that I should be surprised.

His gaze avoids mine, landing on Amelia. "Natalie saw her mom in the caves on the security monitor. Is that true? Do you have her there?"

Amelia's lips curl into a chilling smile. "No. Why would you think that?"

"Because she said…" Wes begins, turning to look at me, but I'm already nodding in agreement. Stick to the story, even when it feels pointless.

Amelia chuckles, a disturbing sound that makes my skin crawl. "You thought pulling the alarm would lead Henry to you? I have eyes and ears everywhere."

Wes's head whips around to me, betrayal burning in his eyes now, as if he hadn't just walked me straight into a trap.

Amelia continues, her voice sickeningly sweet. "Oh, don't worry, Natalie. I know your friends have arrived."

Ice-cold panic freezes my veins as she summons the guards. I barely have time to process her words before strong arms grip me, yanking me away. Fear seizes me, but I fight, lashing out and trying to break free, trying to summon my powers.

But their hold is relentless. As they drag me away, all I can do is let my desperation fuel me.

I won't give up. Not yet. Not ever.

I am stronger than they think, and I will find a way out.

CHAPTER TWENTY-TWO

HENRY

THE BLARING ALARM abruptly ceases and we're left standing, alone, trapped. The doorway seems to have led to even more confusion, an even deeper maze with no end in sight. My mind races for our next move.

A figure steps out from the looming shadows of the cave's mouth. Dressed entirely in black with a stark-white mask obscuring their face, there's no mistaking who it is—a member of the Armory.

Instantly, my body reacts, every muscle tensing. I slide in front of Ciel and Adip, becoming a human shield, my eyes locked on to the approaching figure.

Then, with a swift motion, the person pulls off their mask. A chill spiders down my body. It's a face I know.

His name is Oscar.

Oscar—the one who gave me my first entrance into the Armory in the original timeline. Before Amelia hit the reset button.

But in this timeline, we haven't officially met yet.

His steely gaze meets mine, but there's an unreadable expression in his eyes. In my mind, I replay our previous encounters, the first time we met, trying to glean any insights that might help me now.

With a calculated calmness, I raise my hands in a universal sign of surrender. "I'm not looking for a fight."

Oscar regards me with skepticism, his eyes narrowing as he gives a nonchalant crack to his neck. His smug demeanor grates on my nerves, but I know I need to tread carefully here.

Taking a deep breath, I drop a bombshell—the same bombshell I dropped when I first approached the Armory in the last timeline.

"I'm considering…joining you."

Ciel gasps audibly behind me, her disbelief ringing loud in the silent cave. Before she can say anything more, Adip muffles her outcry with his hand.

Oscar snorts in derisive laughter, his gaze chilling and cold. "So you're playing *that* card again, Henry? Just like you did before. Coming to us, claiming that Natalie Covington betrayed you, that you wanted to sever all ties with her. Why can't you quit that girl?"

A jolt of surprise shoots through me. *He remembers.* He knows my name. Amelia either shared the truth with him, or his memories somehow remained intact. Or she brainwashed him. Likely all three.

"Because I love her," I say.

A twisted laugh bursts from Oscar's lips. "Love." He sneers, as if it's the most ridiculous thing he's ever heard. "Such a futile emotion. It blinds you, distorts reality."

His words are meant to provoke me, but I remain unfazed. I know the truth of my feelings, what I have with Natalie, and nothing he says can change that.

"I know what's going on," I say.

Oscar studies me, a cruel glint in his eyes. "No, Henry, you don't."

Abruptly, a vision crashes into my consciousness, flooding my senses.

I'm standing on a beach, right at the brink of a cliff. The skyline of Istanbul stretches out before me. Natalie and Amelia are there.

Then, everything spirals out of control. A dagger flies from Amelia's hand, burying itself deep into my chest. Pain explodes within me, ricocheting through my body in sharp, unbearable waves. I stumble backward, the shock almost numbing the physical torment. Natalie lets out a terrified scream, rushing towards me.

"I can fix this! I can reset everything!" her voice cries out in panic.

Amelia's cold voice cuts through the chaos, her words laced with ruthless finality. "No, Natalie, you can't. The single thread that could have undone this knot—you severed it."

Life ebbs away, blood seeping out, staining the sand below. As my eyelids flutter shut, the last thing I see is Natalie's horrified face, her tear-filled eyes mirroring my pain.

A chill slices down my spine as I snap out of the vision. I push the horrifying thoughts away, focusing back on Oscar.

"This won't end well for you, Henry," Oscar warns.

I swallow hard, wondering if he's somehow clued in to my grim vision.

"Why the hell are you even working for Amelia?"

"Because we have no other options. She's our leader. There's no alternative unless I want to end up like you."

Rage scorches through my veins. "Move out of my way."

He gives me a firm shake of his head. "Can't."

Suddenly, from the shadows, at least a dozen Armory members fan out behind him, ready to take us down.

Adrenaline surges through me, pulling my focus into sharp clarity. There's no time for fear, no time for doubt.

It's either fight or fucking die.

The first one lunges, and I dodge easily, disarming him. My fist collides with his jaw, a satisfying crunch echoing in the cave as he crumples. One down.

The second one is faster, but not fast enough. I use his own momentum against him, spinning to the side and driving my elbow into his ribs. He gasps, winded, and I deliver a swift knee to his face. He, too, goes down.

A third and fourth attack simultaneously, but I've been trained for this—trained by them. I block a punch, spin, and land a roundhouse kick on the fourth one. He staggers back, but the third one isn't deterred. He comes at me with a dagger.

I barely have time to move, the blade grazing my arm. Pain flares, but I grit my teeth, reaching up to catch his wrist. I twist sharply, and with a cry of pain, he drops the knife. I kick it away, then take him down with a swift jab to his throat.

One by one, I fight them, my body moving on autopilot as I dodge, weave, strike. It's brutal, it's bloody, but it's the only way out. The vision of my impending death lingers in the back of my mind, driving me forward with a desperation I've never felt before.

Oscar approaches me with a deadly calmness, his stride predatory, his eyes burning with a fierce determination. He's lunges at me, fast, his movements honed by training and time. I can tell that he's been waiting for this confrontation.

I take a hard hit to my ribs that nearly crumbles my stance, but I grit my teeth, refusing to show weakness. I pivot, landing a blow to his midsection that has him doubling over. I use the momentum to deliver an uppercut that sends him sprawling backwards, knocking himself out against the stone wall.

Out of the corner of my eye, I see Adip battling his own opponent. His punches are solid, precise. His strength is… shocking.

A distressed cry echoes through the cave, snapping my attention towards the source. Ciel is being dragged down by another member of the Armory. I move to intervene, but it's a trap. I'm blindsided, my defense thrown off balance as his fist crashes into my face over and over, and I'm unable to duck the blows.

Suddenly, Adip is there, moving with an agility and speed that's not even human. With a powerful thrust, he sends the Armory member flying away from me, crashing into the cave wall. How the hell did he just do that?

He checks on Ciel, helping her to her feet, as I study him.

As the dust settles, we scan the cave. The remaining Armory members are defeated, their bodies scattered across the cave floor. For now, it seems, we've won. At least long enough to get past them and inside this place.

I turn to Adip, watching him help Ciel steady her breathing. "How did you get so strong?"

He shakes his head, his eyes reflecting the same surprise I feel. "I don't know." He flexes his hand as if it belongs to someone else. "It's like something took over my body. Like I wasn't entirely…me."

I study Adip's flustered face as he contemplates his own strength. Dread gnaws at my gut. Was that Adip? Or had something else taken him over? The intensity of his actions, the raw, untamed power—it doesn't align with the Adip I know. It was as if some invisible force had commandeered his body, commanding his muscles and senses with frightening ease, like a puppet master pulling at unseen strings.

My mind whirs, flicking back through memories like a detective sifting through a case file. And then it hits me—Natalie's father, and the intricate puzzle pieces he seemed to have masterfully arranged to guide us to this very moment.

Could he be responsible for this sudden surge in Adip's strength? Is he capable of taking over Adip's body, lending his own powers, fighting in his place? The idea sends my thoughts into a spiral. What else can this man do?

Uncertainty and dread hang in the air as I force myself to focus on the here and now. I glance at Adip once more, a sense of grim resolve hardening within me. Regardless of who—or what—fueled his strength, we're still a team right now.

As these thoughts swirl through my mind, something else tugs at my attention—a flicker in the darkness that hadn't been there before. Light. Dim at first, but steadily growing brighter, spilling into the cave. It's coming from a source ahead of us, too deliberate to be natural.

"Down there." I point as Adip and Ciel follow my gaze.

An open door stands ajar ahead, revealing a sliver of a hallway. An invitation?

More likely a trap.

We exchange glances, our decision unspoken but unanimously understood. We need to find Natalie.

The three of us move as one, cautious yet determined, towards the light, ready to face whatever lies beyond the door.

As we approach, the cave's chill gives way to a rush of warmer air, carrying with it the faint but unmistakable hum of machinery. Electricity. Technology.

We're closer to Natalie, I'm sure of it. As we reach the door, I tighten my grip on the handle, and with a deep breath, push the door open.

Light floods into the cave as I step through, into the unknown.

CHAPTER TWENTY-THREE

NATALIE

IN AN ADRENALINE-LACED blur, I'm yanked through the stark-white halls by two hulking guards, their grips unyielding. My legs kick at the air, my screams swallowed by the hollow echoes of the sterile corridor. The betrayal, the shock, the fear—it all whips around inside me.

The guards stop in front of the familiar door of my room, my supposed sanctuary in this awful place. They fling me inside with an impersonal force that sends me sprawling onto the bed. The door slams shut with a thud that reverberates through the silence of the room, the click of the lock feeling like a death sentence.

I scramble up, throwing myself against the door, my palms slamming into the hard wood. It's locked, of course. My chest heaves, the bitter sting of helplessness crawling up my throat.

Exhaling in frustrated defeat, I step away from the door, raking a hand through my hair. I need to get out. I need to find Henry. My heart swells with a desperate resolve. I can do this—I can summon my powers. I've done it before.

I hold my hand out, focusing all my energy into my palm. I

visualize it, the stars igniting in a radiant celestial outpour, the power washing over me like a warm wave. But nothing happens. No stars. No light. Just the chilling reality of my situation, stark and cold.

Anguish gnaws at my insides, tearing at my resolve. My hand falls back to my side, a useless appendage. Why aren't my powers working? What has Amelia done to me now?

And then I hear it—the soft exhale of breath, the shuffle of a foot. I whirl around and the sight that greets me sends a jolt of horror through my veins.

Wes. Standing in the middle of the room. My heart lurches in my chest. How the hell did he get in here? He seems just as confused as I am.

"Amelia…" His eyes flame with an anger that mirrors my own. "She must have transported me here, with you." The words are bitter and raw. "You lied to me, again," he says, cold as the silence that settles between us.

I take a step back, feeling the sting of his words. "I'm trying to find my mom, Wes. Can you blame me for that?"

"No." His words shoot back, eyes hard and unyielding. "You want to find Henry. You couldn't care less about your mom."

His words hit like a physical blow and I recoil, anger surging within me. "That's not true. Don't you dare say that again."

"Covington, I'm trying to help you. That's all I've ever tried to do. Want you. Love you. Help you."

"I don't want your love or your help. How many times do I need to tell you that?"

"If only you'd come around to my side of things." He sighs, rubbing his forehead in frustration. "To just let things be. We could be happy together. You'll have your mom back. Amelia has already struck a bargain with us."

"Yeah, a bargain to keep me imprisoned here for life."

His eyes fill with a desperate plea. "Yes, with me. A guy who fucking loves you, who kills for you, who would do anything you wanted."

My words fly out like daggers. "If that's the case, you'd let me go. If you loved me, cared for me at all, you wouldn't force me to be with you."

He's silent for a moment, his gaze never leaving mine. "I'll leave you alone, for now," he finally says. "But you *will* join me in that bed later."

My anger spikes at his disgusting order. "That was the bargain if you led me to the cave to find my mom. And you didn't."

He crosses the room in quick strides, stopping just short of the bedside table where his journal rests. "You're not really in a position to bargain," he says, knocking his journal onto the floor with a swift movement, twisting his gaze as if he wants me to notice what he's doing.

He turns abruptly on his heel, heading to the door. I watch, my heart leaping into my throat, as he reaches out, his hand easily turning the handle that refused to budge for me.

In a moment of panic, I rush after him, hoping to escape. The door slams shut before I can get out. I smack my palm against it in frustration, turning the handle in vain. It's locked again, trapping me in this gilded cage, the last echo of Wes's departure a chilling reminder of my captivity.

My gaze, drawn to the fallen journal like a moth to a flame, doesn't waver for a second. The faded leather peels off at the corners, pages sticking out—dog-eared reminders of past thoughts.

I approach it with hesitation, half expecting Wes to emerge at any moment and snatch it away. But he doesn't. Does he want me to pick it up? To read it?

With a deep breath, I bend down and grab his tome of tortured thoughts. The journal feels heavy in my hands, the pages thick and rough under my fingertips.

I open it and start flipping through. Sketches of what appear to be hand-scrawled blueprints of this very building sprawl across the pages, detailed and labeled. There are other pages filled with notes on magic, cryptic comments, and arcane symbols.

Intrigued and apprehensive, I turn back to the first page. The inscription there makes my heart skip a beat.

With Amelia able to read my mind, it's hard to repair things with Natalie.

I recoil as if the journal has bitten me. Amelia can read Wes's mind? She's been doing that the whole time?

A chill creeps down my spine at the thought. That would mean… if Wes even entertained the thought of helping me, Amelia would know.

The realization hits me like a punch in the gut. Wes's behavior here—it could be because he's playing a part for Amelia. He wanted me to read this journal, didn't he? It's a way of relaying information without uttering a word, without risking Amelia's telepathic scrutiny.

Could Wes be… somewhat on my side?

The disgust I've been harboring for him shrinks ever so slightly. But I can't shake the feeling that I'm still a pawn in a larger game. A twisted chess match where I can't trust the knights supposedly protecting me.

And Wes… he's always playing a game I can't quite figure out.

The sickening swoop of my stomach intensifies as I return to the pages of his journal. There's an entry written with an air of frustrated fascination that catches my attention, detailing his inability to penetrate my thoughts.

Amelia can't read Natalie's mind, which infuriates her. How I wish I could have a glimpse into Natalie's thoughts, to know what she truly thinks of me. I feel it in my bones that she wants me, loves me even. We are meant to burn slow.

A wave of nausea washes over me, turning my insides sour.

I swallow the bile that threatens to rise, forcing myself to read on. The next entry delves into magic—Wes's recollection of a book once belonging to his uncle, filled with complex spells. His memories are vague and hazy, yet peppered with sporadic moments of clarity. He mentions channeling energy, and the importance of visualization. I make a mental note to come back to this.

Then, I stumble upon something that chills me to the bone.

On the next page is a family tree—*my family tree*. My name sits at the center. My mother's name branches out to the right.

The space for my father's name is left hauntingly empty, bearing only two enigmatic words: *Black Sea.*

My brow furrows in confusion. What could that possibly mean? Next to my father's designation, where one might chart extended family, there's an intricate sketch of flowers entwined with flames. It's a beautiful rendering, filled with an odd sort of melancholy that tugs at my heart.

Knowing Wes, I doubt this is just a random doodle.

A series of meticulously detailed maps of the building sprawl across the following pages. Wes must have devoted hours to combing this place—returning to his journal to capture all the crevices.

His alarming commitment might prove beneficial in this case. One spot, in particular, stands out.

It appears to depict a descent into the lower levels of the building, an almost underworld-like place. I can't help but wonder if that's where Henry could be.

Dread knots in my stomach at the thought, mingled with a spark of hope.

CHAPTER TWENTY-FOUR

HENRY

THE ROOM CLOSES in as the door slams shut behind me, separating me from Adip and Ciel. I whip around, reaching out for the doorknob, but my hands close around thin air. The door has disappeared, swallowed up by the wall. The realization hits me hard and fast, making my chest tighten in panic.

"No," I mutter, feeling along the wall, desperate for a latch, a handle, anything that would lead to an exit. But the wall is smooth and unyielding.

Just more of Amelia's bullshit.

I draw in a deep breath, willing myself to stay calm. Losing it now won't help. But the anger is still there, a relentless tide battering against my self-control.

The room is shrouded in near-complete darkness, the dim light from the high window barely enough to see by. Squinting into the black, I stumble forward, reaching out to the shapes materializing out of the shadows.

Antique furniture clutters the space, bearing the unmistakable marks of age. Stacked boxes form a labyrinth of towering obstacles.

I push through, my fingers skimming over dusty surfaces and ridged edges. Then something else emerges from the darkness—a hulking shape, mechanical and menacing.

Steadying myself, I step closer, reaching out to touch the cold metal. At that instant, a sharp click sounds, and a harsh, fluorescent light flickers on overhead, nearly blinding me.

Blinking away the spots in my eyes, I squint at the object now bathed in an unforgiving white light. It's a vile contraption of chains and metal clasps, a sickening mix of torture and science. The metallic surface is stained with a hue too dark and sinister to be anything but dried blood.

My stomach lurches, the stark-white light too bright, too revealing. I close my eyes against the gruesome sight, against the undeniable evidence of Amelia's continued monstrosity.

I'm trapped in here. Alone. In a twisted laboratory of horrors.

I open my eyes, forcing myself to look again at the monstrous contraption. But it's not the torture device that scares me. It's the cold, hard realization that Amelia will never stop unless we make her.

A surge of determination washes over me, driving back the panic. If I'm going to get out of here, to save Natalie, to reunite with Adip and Ciel, I can't let this room break me.

I search the room again, ignoring the grisly centerpiece. There has to be a way out of here. There has to be. The harsh fluorescent light continues to carve sharp shadows into the room, turning harmless objects into twisted, monstrous silhouettes. A part of me is screaming to find an off switch for the blinding light, but a more primal part of me—the part that's reeling in disgust from the dark stains of dried blood—prefers this cruel brightness over being left alone in the dark with the silent screams of those who've been chained here.

I force myself away from the mechanical horror, venturing deeper into the room. My hands reach out for a stack of clutter on a rickety table. Wiping away layers of dust, I'm confronted with a collection of neatly bound documents—patient charts, marked with dates, coded entries, and a signature that strikes me like a punch to the gut: Amelia Collins.

My mouth dries, anxiety coating my throat as I leaf through the papers. Each document is filled with incomprehensible medical jargon, strange symbols, and cryptic notes. But one word keeps popping up on each form: *RELEASE*.

I frown, the creased paper crinkling under my tight grip. Release? Does that mean these people…were set free by Amelia? Not held captive against their will?

Sifting through more of the documents, I look for a name, a clue, anything that might shed light on what's going on. But the names are as foreign to me as the jargon. The realization that I don't recognize any of these names sets me on edge. How long has this been going on? How many lives have been touched by this horror?

My blood chills, noticing the dates on the papers range over years, some even decades old. How long has Amelia been doing this? How deep does this rabbit hole go?

I drop the document in my hand, my mind whirling with unanswered questions. Something is hidden beneath layers of lies and secrecy, and for the first time, I'm not sure if I want to uncover it.

But as images of Natalie, of her wide-eyed fear and unwavering determination, flood my mind, my resolve hardens. I need to know. I need to understand what Amelia is doing. For Natalie. For all of us to get the fuck out of here.

I continue digging through the pile of patient charts, my brain working overtime to piece together the cryptic puzzle laid out in front of me.

The room, once a symbol of untold horrors, now feels like a confounding maze, its secrets guarded behind Amelia's cryptic codes and unsettling release forms. The mystery deepens with every passing minute, the tension winding up inside me like a coiled spring.

Fear claws at my insides as I reach out to where the door used to be, the void colder than the surrounding air. I trace the edges, feeling for the slightest catch or indication of a magical barrier. Amelia's magic—it's subtle and often defies comprehension. Energy ripples under my fingertips.

For a moment, frustration clouds my mind, a flurry of fear and anger. But I've been in worse situations. I've fought back against stronger tides. I can't allow myself to be defeated now.

Channeling my focus, I gather what little control I can muster over the elements around me, imagining my energy as a tactile force extending from my fingertips and reaching out into the room. The chains and clasps of the torture device rattle slightly, the rusted metal emitting an eerie resonance. It's not much, but it's a start. My power, however, seems to be waning, diminishing under the weight of this place. It's as if this room is draining me, weakening my control over the elements.

I shift my focus, scanning the room for an alternative exit. Maybe there's a hidden passage, concealed door, a trap. You never know what a place like this could hold. The floor is solid beneath my feet, but the walls are rough, irregular, as if hastily constructed.

Dust chokes the air as I move piles of abandoned boxes and examine each wall meticulously. The texture changes under my fingertips, the irregularities of stone giving way to a smoother surface.

Pushing past the scattered papers and grime-covered objects, I focus on the smoother section of the wall. Hidden compartments—this building is full of fucking surprises.

The discrepancies are minor but significant. I retrieve a metal piece from the torturous contraption, its jagged edges gnarled but sturdy, and pry at the suspicious panel. The metallic sound reverberates in the tight space. The final click that signals success sends a rush of adrenaline through my core.

The panel swings open with a low creak, revealing a dark, narrow passage behind it. Cold air seeps out, carrying with it a dank, musty scent—the smell of abandonment and decay. The smell sticks in my throat, sour and persistent, like stale fear. But fear isn't a luxury I can afford right now.

Hesitant, I step into the passage, the unknown darkness swallowing me as the hidden door closes behind. The only sound is the steady thump of my heart echoing ominously in my ears. After a few paces, I hit a dead end that leads to another door. With a forceful push, it swings open into a small cell.

The cell is dark, but I notice the outline of a figure slumped in the far corner, so still that for a chilling moment, I'm afraid I've come too late. But as I move closer, a weak gasp confirms life, however fragile.

Cautiously, I kneel down beside the crumpled figure, turning her over. The frail woman gasps in surprise, fear pooling in her eyes. As my eyes adjust, the reality of the situation hits me like a tidal wave, both horrifying and surreal.

It's Natalie's mother.

CHAPTER TWENTY-FIVE
NATALIE

THERE'S A STRANGE mix of revulsion and gratitude as I page through Wes's journal. My instincts tell me not to trust him, not completely, but his musings could be my only chance of escape. Every moment not with me, he must have been wandering these halls, mapping out this prison.

Panic claws up my throat and the room seems to close in around me as I pour over his words and drawings, desperately searching for a clue, a spell, anything to get me out of here.

My fingers tremble as I turn the pages, taking in the detailed maps, coded sequences, and sketches. There must be something here that can help me.

There are no overt headings like "undoing a magical lock." Wes is smarter than that—he wouldn't leave such obvious clues. Especially not if Amelia is reading his mind. He's hidden the information in layers, wrapped it in riddles. His handwriting is a maze in itself, a combination of ancient scripts, alchemical symbols, and mathematical equations. Some words stand out, veiled references to doors, pathways, openings. Others are lost to me, probably purposely obscured by Wes, considering Amelia is always watching.

One particular sketch draws my attention. It's beautifully rendered, half concealed by the adjoining text. I didn't know Wes could draw so well, but what really catches my eye is the striking resemblance between the drawing and a painting in front of me, on the wall next to the lock.

Could it be a clue? My heart tumbles into my throat as I study the drawing more closely, comparing it to the actual painting. They are identical, down to the last detail. The words partially scrawled over it seem to call to me, riddled with meaning: *Embrace the tear that falls at dawn, hold the ache where warmth is gone.*

A pang of sorrow strikes my heart. Mom. Her laughter, her gentle touch, all gone. It's hard not to let the memory envelop me, feeling the cold embrace of her loss—twice. I can only hope that she's here, that I haven't lost her forever.

I continue reading his words: *Touch the fear that froze your soul, grasp the night that took control.*

My breath catches as a vivid memory from that night at Lockwood returns. The terror, the pain, the cold knife at my throat. My hands tremble, recreating the fear that once paralyzed me.

Reach the heart that beats as two, feel the love that's pure and true.

A soft smile plays on my lips as I think of Henry. The way he looks at me, how everything about him pierces my soul.

Caress the water in a serpent's path. Dance the waves, embrace the wrath.

I frown, stumbling on this one. Water? Serpents? What does that mean? Fragments of conversations whirl in my mind—Adip's mysterious dreams, mentions of my father. Water has been a recurring theme, but what does it signify?

My eyes drift to more words beneath the riddle. *The rhythm of tides flow through your fingers.*

I stand up, approaching the door, my mind still wrestling with the statement. I raise my hand, moving my fingers in a fluid, wavy motion.

The door responds with a sudden pop, and I freeze. It's cracked open just an inch, a sliver of light piercing the dim room. My heart hammers against my ribcage, a mixture of triumph and terror.

Wes's words, his riddles, his magic? They were the key. I clutch his journal tightly to my chest, stepping out into the hallway. It's empty, the silence almost suffocating as I move slowly, eyes darting from one shadow to the next. The map that Wes drew out guides my trembling steps, a path winding through the labyrinth of this place.

A single door at the end of the hallway beckons, and with cautious hope, I inch my way down a long staircase. It leads into a vast basement, a place where time seems to have stood still.

Gothic arches loom overhead, casting shadows along the walls. The air is musty, filled with the scent of decaying wood. Rows of ancient trunks and boxes stretch into the darkness, their contents hidden beneath layers of dust and cobwebs.

Curiosity tugs at me, and I find myself drawn to an old trunk. Lifting the lid, I'm met with the sight of a varsity letterman jacket— hunter green with white letters, *Lockwood* spelled out across the front. It's old, men's sized, XL. These are not the current Lockwood school colors.

My hands tremble as I continue to dig, unearthing a pile of old Polaroid photos. A group of girls, all smiles and laughter, wearing hunter-green skirts, thigh-highs, white blouses, blazers bearing the Lockwood "L." Boys in matching green uniforms, a young Amelia standing among them.

My stomach churns as I notice one photo in particular. Amelia standing next to a guy—much taller, sandy-brown hair, and the brightest blue eyes. I swallow hard. There's something familiar about this man, but I've never seen him before. Amelia is nuzzling into him, her affection clear in every pose. More photos of them together, their love captured in each embrace, every stolen kiss.

One close-up catches my eye—a pair of blue eyes so intense they seem to pierce my soul. Eyes just like Henry and Adip described. A sense of dread overwhelms me. This… this can't be my father. It can't be.

"Find something interesting?"

My hands freeze, the photos slipping from my grasp as Amelia's voice rings out behind me, cold and taunting.

I whirl around, my body going rigid as I meet her eyes. A cruel smile plays on her lips as she steps closer, her gaze never leaving mine.

The room seems to close in around me, the walls echoing with secrets and lies. My mouth opens, questions about the photos ready to spill out, when the doors burst open. Two of Amelia's guards drag Wes into the room, throwing him to the ground with brutal force. He lands with a heavy thud, spitting blood from his mouth. His face is contorted in pain, but his eyes find mine, filled with something I can't quite decipher.

"You betrayed me, didn't you?" Amelia's voice is cold, dripping with venom. "You taught her how to escape that room."

Wes struggles to breathe, his voice ragged. "I didn't."

Amelia's eyes narrow, and she snaps her fingers. The guards stomp down on Wes's back, eliciting a cry of agony.

I hide Wes's book behind me, slipping it into a nearby box unnoticed. "He didn't help me," I say, my voice shaking. "I figured it out myself. I have powers, remember?"

"Your powers wouldn't break you out of that room. You used magic—magic that *he* taught you," Amelia says, her gaze fixed on me.

"How would you know? You yourself said you don't know my full capabilities."

Amelia's lips twist into a sneer, and she calls my bluff. "Bullshit."

Her attention turns back to Wes, her voice softening. "You know what you have to do to prove your loyalty to me."

Wes hesitates, his face pale and his body trembling. He rises to his feet, staggering over to me. He stares into my eyes, and I'm struck by the desperation in his gaze, as if he's pleading with me to trust him. Fear coils in my stomach, and I take a step back.

Then, with a speed I never saw coming, he yanks his dagger from his pocket and plunges it into my stomach.

Pain explodes through my body, a white-hot agony that rips through my flesh and tears into my soul. My breath catches in my throat, a strangled cry escaping my lips as I stagger back, clutching at the wound. The world spins, and I stumble, Wes's face a blur, his eyes filled with an anguish that mirrors my own.

Blood pours from the wound, warm and wet as it soaks through my clothes. The pain is unbearable, a relentless torment that threatens to consume me. I collapse to the ground, gasping for breath, every nerve on fire.

Wes's face looms above me, his eyes filled with tears, his hands trembling as he reaches out to me. But I can't feel him, can't hear his words of apology. All I can feel is the agony of betrayal, the sharp sting of the blade still buried in my flesh.

Amelia's laughter rings in my ears, cold and cruel as she watches me writhe in pain. Her victory is complete, her power over Wes proven. She's won, and I'm left broken and bleeding on the floor, my trust shattered, my hope destroyed.

The room fades to darkness, and I'm left with nothing but the pain and the haunting realization that everything I thought I knew was a lie. Wes's latest betrayal cuts deeper than any blade, and if I am immortal, if I make it out alive, I know that I'll never be the same again.

CHAPTER TWENTY-SIX

HENRY

THE DIM LIGHT of the cell flickers over Madeline's frail form. Her skin is pale, her green eyes hollow, and her body weakened, yet there's a spark of determination in her gaze. I see Natalie in her, fierce and unbreakable.

"Natalie, my baby, where is she? Why am I here? Where have they taken her?" Madeline's voice is frantic, her confusion tangible.

I take her hand because it's all I can think to do in this fucked-up situation. She's cold, trembling, and I want to offer her comfort. "I think Natalie is here. I came for her, to try and get both of you out."

Madeline tenses, releasing my hand. "Who are you?" Her eyes search mine, full of fear and suspicion.

The realization hits me like a ton of bricks— Amelia erased her memory when she turned back time. In this timeline, Madeline never met me.

"I'm her… Natalie's… boyfriend." The words feel strange in my mouth. We haven't labeled anything, but I assume that's what we are. Soulmates might be more like it.

"Boyfriend? She's a baby." Madeline pushes up, slinking away from me, pressing against the wall, like she's terrified *of me*. "Who the hell are you? What have you done with her?"

She thinks Natalie is a baby? My heart drops into my stomach. When Amelia reset time, something must have distorted Madeline's memory, erasing some, but not all.

"No, Madeline, Mrs. Covington… listen…" I stumble over my words, desperation splicing through my core.

"Don't call me that. It's not my last name. I didn't want to marry that man. I don't want his name. Get away from me. Stay away." She begins screaming, her voice echoing through the cell, and I feel a surge of sympathy mixed with growing dread. Her body begins to tremble, panic clearly setting in. "You took her, didn't you? You took my baby girl!" She's nearly hysterical, her eyes wide with terror.

"Please listen to me. Natalie's not a baby anymore. Your daughter is eighteen years old." I force the words out, hoping she'll understand.

"Eighteen?" The word seems to catch her attention, and she looks at me, bewildered. "No, no, she's just a baby. Where is she? Is this all because of Cy? Are you working for him?" Madeline's face crumples, tears spilling from her eyes. "Amelia said she would keep me and the baby safe." Her voice falters, giving way to tears, her body trembling under the weight of her sorrow.

My mind reels, confusion and horror warring within me. Amelia? Safe? The words don't make sense, not with what I've seen, not with what I know of that woman.

"Please, Mrs. Cov—Madeline, I'm trying to help you and your daughter. And I need you to help me understand. What happened? How did you end up here?" My voice is urgent, my fear for her, for Natalie, growing by the second.

Her eyes, clouded with confusion and pain, suddenly lock on to mine. The pieces of the puzzle are there, but they're scattered, hidden in shadows and secrets. Desperation mixes with determination as I grapple for a way to reach her, to jog her memory, to rebuild the bridges Amelia has burned.

"I think something happened to your memory when Amelia reset things. Natalie found you before. I was with her. And Amelia, she's experimenting on Natalie, to see how powerful she is," I say, each word aching in my throat.

Madeline's face twists in horror and she shakes her head, becoming more panicked. "No, Amelia would never do that. She's my friend."

The admission stabs at me, and I can hardly bear to tell her the truth. "Amelia is the reason you're locked up in this room. Whatever she told you, it's a lie."

Her face contorts, and she seems to be struggling to process.

"How old do you think you are?" I say.

"I'm nineteen," she says, her voice faint.

"No, you're not. Your *daughter* is eighteen." The words hang heavy in the air, a cruel reminder of the twisted reality we're trapped in. I wish I had a mirror to show her. "Please, can you tell me any-thing you remember? What happened right before you got here?" I say.

"That's a long story. A long, complicated, unbelievable story." Her voice is hollow, lost.

"Please." My hand reaches out for hers, desperate to offer comfort.

Her eyes flick to mine, and I can see the skepticism, the uncertainty.

I turn over my arm, revealing my precog marking, hoping it might open some element of trust—a connection between us. "I love your daughter, Madeline. Please. I only want to help."

She stares at me, embittered. "You remind me of him."

"Who?"

"Cy. Her…father."

I plead, my voice cracking with desperation. "You have to believe me, Mrs. Covington. Amelia is *not* your friend. She's manipulated you. She's twisted everything to fit her agenda. *She* is the one who put you here. I think Cy... maybe he was trying to reach you, to help you."

"No. He lied to me. It's his fault...and mine for falling for it. For him."

A cold dread settles over me, and I shake my head, disbelief warring with horror. "No, no, Amelia has warped everything. *She's* the one who lied to you, tricked you. *She's* the evil one here."

Madeline swipes away her tears and steels herself. "No. You've got it wrong. It was Cy who deceived me. Cy who lied to me, tricked me. He said we were the same, that he was like me, but we're nothing alike. He made me believe in something that wasn't true. I got pregnant. Amelia helped me see. She helped me out of a dangerous situation. She's the only one I could trust." Her voice is raw, filled with betrayal.

A sharp pain crushes my chest. How could everything have gone so wrong? How could Amelia have twisted the truth so completely that Madeline can't see what's right in front of her?

"No, Madeline, please listen to me," I beg. "Amelia is manipulating you. She's using you for her own purposes. She doesn't care about you or your daughter. I've seen what she's capable of. She's twisted and cruel."

Madeline looks at me, her eyes filled with torment, doubt, and fractured memories. The woman before me is broken, torn between two worlds, two truths. I can see her struggling to reconcile what she believes with what I'm telling her.

"Your daughter is grown up now and she's terrified for you. She knows Amelia's true nature. We are here to find you, to help you."

Madeline's face goes pale. "What does Natalie know?" Her whisper is filled with hope and fear.

"That she loves you. She's fighting for you. And so am I. Please, trust me. Help me understand what happened so we can get out of here and make everything right."

The room is filled with a heavy silence as Madeline considers my words. I can see her mind working, weighing the evidence, trying to untangle the web of lies and deceit that Amelia has woven around her.

The connection to her past, the pieces fitting together, it's all there. I can almost taste the urgency as I prompt her again. "Start with how you met Natalie's father, Cy."

Her eyes glaze over, lost in memories. "I'm a Cambion and Astral. The authority never understood me, my powers, or what I was capable of. I lived with them until eventually, they allowed me to leave and live in the world. Once I was out, I was a bit reckless, I suppose. I got myself into trouble one night, I was nearly attacked, and then…" Her voice trails off.

I nod, encouraging her to keep going. "And then…?"

"This guy with wings swooped in. I didn't know who he was—*what he was*—at first, but he saved me. Later, I found out he was a guardian angel…Oman. We became fast friends, even though he said he was new to discovering his powers. He was struggling and needed a friend. He invited me to hang with him in Istanbul for the summer at one of his father's hotels. I was shaken up from the attack and didn't have a plan, so I went."

I hang on her every word, the story both fascinating and troubling.

"We went to Istanbul, and that's where I found out he had a friend in town. Cy. The first time I saw him, there was something about him, something…irresistible. I stupidly began digging into him, trying to understand who he was. I suppose being locked away with the authority all those years made me overly reckless, somewhat obsessed. I knew deep down it was a mistake, but I couldn't help myself."

She pauses, her eyes narrowing, the pain of the memories etched on her face. "Cy caught me once, at his father's party, going through their things. That's when he became a bit obsessed with me. We were drawn to each other, two lost souls trying to find our place in the world. Or so I thought." Her voice cracks, and I can see her fighting back tears. "That's also when I met Amelia. She warned me about Cy, told me to stay away from him. She grew up with him, knew him well. But I didn't listen. I was infatuated, and it was like something out of a fairy tale. He told me he was a Cambion and Astral, just like me. It felt like destiny."

"And then what happened?"

Her face contorts with pain, the memories clearly tormenting her, and lowers her gaze. "His father found out about us. He was furious, couldn't accept that Cy was in love with me. He saw me as a threat."

She looks at me, her eyes wide with terror. "And then his father tried to kill me."

CHAPTER TWENTY-SEVEN

NATALIE

I WAKE UP with a start, my heart pounding in my chest, a scream trapped in my throat. Sweat trickles down my forehead, and I'm paralyzed by panic. The dark room spins around me, and all I can remember is the cold, sharp blade of Wes's dagger as it pierced my flesh.

Frantically, I place my hand on my abdomen, expecting to feel the wound, the searing pain. But there's nothing there.

The comfort of Henry's sweats is gone, replaced by a delicate tank top and silky pants that might pass as pajamas. They sit unfamiliar and intrusive against my skin. I lift the tank, confused and terrified, but my skin is unbroken. Was it all a dream? Was the horror I felt nothing more than a twisted figment of my imagination?

As I try to sit up, something stops me. I can't move. Panic rises again, choking me, and my eyes struggle to adjust to the darkness. Slowly, I realize that I'm restrained, strapped down to a bed. There's an IV in my arm, and fear grips me like a vice.

What is happening? Where am I now? Desperation and anger build within me, a fiery rage that threatens to consume me. I have to get out. I have to escape.

I pull against the restraints, but nothing is happening. My body is weak, my mind a whirlpool of confusion and terror. But I won't give up. I can't give up.

Using my teeth, I manage to grasp the tube of the IV, the metallic taste of blood filling my mouth as I rip it out of my arm. Blood splatters, but I don't care. I have to get to Henry, get us all the hell out of this place.

The thought of Henry brings a fresh wave of determination. I remember how I was able to get out of the bedroom, the spell that saved me. Thinking of my mom, of the attack at Lockwood, of Henry, I make the wave motion with my hand, praying, hoping, begging for it to work like it did before.

"Come on…" I whisper, tears of frustration stinging my eyes. I continue the pattern again, my hand trembling, my heart pounding.

And then, miraculously, the restraint on my right wrist breaks. I gasp, a triumphant sob escaping my lips. I'm one step closer to freedom, one step closer to safety.

But I'm not out yet. The dark room is still a prison, the shadows hiding unknown dangers. I have to be careful, have to be strong.

As I continue to work on the remaining restraints, my mind races, the memories of Wes's latest betrayal, the horror of the attack, the uncertainty of what lies ahead, all swirling together in a chaotic storm.

My hands tremble as I free myself from the last restraint, my body still weak but driven by an adrenaline-fueled determination. I look around the room, taking in the sterile surroundings. It's some kind of patient room, reminiscent of a hospital, but with an unsettling air that chills me to the bone.

Digging through the drawers, I search for a weapon. I know that nothing but a dagger will truly kill these beings, but something—anything—might fend them off, give me a chance to escape. My fingers close around a pair of sharp scissors, and I pull them out, looking down at them, my anger growing for this entire situation.

As my rage swells, something inside me begins to change. A warmth spreads through my body, starting in my chest and radiating outwards. My hand starts to glow, and tiny stars reflect on the scissors, casting a glimmering light that dances across the room.

I can feel it, a power building within me, something more potent and intense than anything I've ever felt before. I'm not helpless. I'm not weak. I'm strong, and I can fight back.

Clutching the scissors, I storm over to the door. It's locked, of course, but that won't stop me. Not now. Not ever.

With a swift movement, I channel my anger into my palm, focusing all my energy and rage into one concentrated burst. The knob electrifies and explodes with a deafening sound, sending shards of metal flying through the air.

I stand there for a moment, thrilled with myself, the realization of what I've done sinking in. I did that. *Me.* I have the power to fight back, to take control of my life.

My hands are still shaking as I reach for the broken knob, but I don't hesitate. I pull the door open and move forward, the scissors clutched tightly in my hand, my mind focused, my body alive with energy. Every step is a battle, every breath a victory. I won't let them win. I won't let them control me. The anger is still there, a burning fire that fuels me, drives me. But it's tempered now by something else, something deeper and more profound. A sense of purpose, a sense of self.

The corridor is silent as I press on, my hand tingling from the celestial power, the raw energy of a living thing inside me. I feel strong, invincible even.

I pause, my eyes catching the glint of another camera. Anger wells within me, and I extend my palm, the camera bursting into sparks as my power obliterates it. The destruction is satisfying, a small victory in the chaos of my journey. But there's no time to dwell on satisfaction.

I turn the corner, met with a new challenge: guards. Three of them, standing tall, their faces masks of grim determination. The first guard, his eyes filled with cold calculation, lunges at me. I strike back, my celestial powers lashing out in a storm of fury, a manifestation of my raw emotion. He falls with a cry, his eyes wide in shock. I reach down and yank his dagger from its sheath, the cold metal a stark reminder of what I must do, stabbing it into his stomach. I feel a pang of guilt but quickly suppress it. This is survival.

The others advance, their movements coordinated, their intent clear. I grip the stolen dagger, its weight reassuring in my hand, its edge glinting ominously. I plunge the dagger into the stomach of the second guard, the sensation both horrifying and empowering. His eyes meet mine, a fleeting moment of connection, of understanding, before the light fades from them. I pull the blade free, my hand stained with his life.

The third guard fights with desperation, his movements wild, his attacks unpredictable. We clash, our blades singing a song of violence, our breaths ragged.

The world narrows, the battle a blur of motion and color. I feel alive, powerful, unstoppable. But also vulnerable, the weight of what I'm doing a heavy burden on my soul. The emotions are a storm within me, conflicting, confusing, driving me forward, holding me back.

I strike, the blade finding its mark, the guard falling to his knees, his life a fading ember. I stand over him, my chest heaving, my body trembling. I look down at the dagger, now a symbol of my strength, my survival. But also a reminder of what I've lost, what I've become.

A sense of foreboding coils around my body as I navigate through the dim corridors, my celestial powers guiding me, fueling my determination to find Henry, Mom, Adip, Ciel.

I approach a seemingly nondescript door, my hand hovering over the handle, dread washing over me. Something pulls me towards this door, a magnetic force I can't resist.

I reach out to touch the handle, and suddenly, a vision flashes before my eyes. *Henry and my mom, together, locked in a dark cell, their faces filled with confusion and pain.* The image sears itself into my mind, and I reel back, gasping for breath, the vision gone as quickly as it came.

I'm shaken to the core but driven by my newfound strength. I force the door open using my powers, stepping into a room filled with darkness and a strange, unsettling hum.

Inside, I find a dimly lit room, scattered with drawings and sketches that are strewn across the floor and pinned to the walls. I kneel down to examine them, my eyes widening as I realize what I'm looking at.

One drawing in particular catches my eye. It's a map, lines crawling under what appears to be the sea. The path seems intricate, filled with twists and turns, and I can't shake the feeling that it means something, that it's vital.

"What is this?" I murmur to myself, tracing the path with a trembling finger. The image is at once haunting and intriguing, a puzzle I feel compelled to solve.

As I dig through the rest of the drawings, I uncover more mysteries, more enigmas. Some depict strange symbols, while others, landscapes and buildings that seem familiar yet alien. The more I explore, the more my mind races, piecing together fragments of a story that seems just beyond my grasp.

The vision of Henry and my mother in the cell flashes in my mind again.

Suddenly, a voice breaks through my concentration, cold and chilling. "So she is immortal."

I spin around, my hand clutching the dagger, my powers crackling, ready to strike.

It's Wes standing in the doorway, his eyes fixed on me, a cruel smile on his lips. "Well done, Covington."

CHAPTER TWENTY-EIGHT

HENRY

THE WEIGHT OF Madeline's revelation hits me hard. Cy's father, Natalie's grandfather, tried to kill her. *Fuck.* As if things couldn't get any heavier.

Before I can form a response, the edges of my sight blur. Suddenly, there's a familiar tug at my consciousness, a sign that I'm plunged into another vision.

Cy—at least it looks like him—is suspended in a tank underwater. He's encircled in thick chains, coiling around him like a python, their weight seemingly trying to pull him deeper into the watery void.

His closed eyes snap open, that electric blue gaze piercing through the water, through the darkness, through me. It's like I'm there, chained up with him, feeling the cold metal bite into my skin. He's screaming, thrashing, but the water swallows everything. His terror becomes my terror.

I'm snapped back to reality with a violent jolt. Now I'm in this dank room with Madeline, not under the sea with Cy, but the darkness clings to me like a second skin, the edges of that vision still scraping at my mind.

"Where's Cy now?" I ask Madeline.

"I don't know. He lied to me. About everything. Amelia told me."

Frustration boils over as I blurt out, "*Amelia's* the one lying."

It's all too much—the betrayal, the confusion, the helplessness.

"She's not your friend. She's experimenting on us, torturing us. She locked you in here, whatever this hellhole is."

Madeline's eyes widen, and her voice trembles as she says, "The last thing I remember was being at Amelia's, one of the homes her family owned, and then it all went dark."

"Then this fortress must be hers." My mind races, trying to piece it all together while grappling with the relentless onslaught of emotions. It's a tangled web, and we're caught in the middle, helpless, manipulated.

I look at Madeline, her face pale, her eyes wide, equally lost, equally trapped. Two pawns in a fucked-up game. My anger burns, hot and wild, but there's something else, too, something like determination.

"Listen to me, we're going to get out of here. We're going to find Cy, find the truth. Amelia *won't* win." But even as I say the words, doubt gnaws at me.

Madeline's face contorts in anger. "No, this is all Cy's fault. We're trapped in this hell because of him." Her voice breaks, but the fire in her eyes doesn't wane. "Whatever he did to my memory, maybe he hoped I'd forget everything. Forget the pain he caused, forget our past. Our daughter…" She chokes on the words, and for a moment, the room is filled with a heavy, heart-wrenching silence.

My mind races, trying to piece together the fragments of the story she's revealing. The weight of her revelation crushes me, adds another layer to this maze of deceit and half-truths.

"He showed me once what it was like to have a normal life. When the authority let me out, he…he took full advantage of it. But it was all a game to him." There's a rawness in her words, the sting of betrayal. The way she speaks about Cy makes my skin crawl, but I can't shake the feeling that it's not all as it seems.

"Madeline, Amelia's the one messing with our heads. It's her game. You can't trust anything she's said or shown you."

She scoffs, her eyes flashing with anger. "You don't get it. Cy's not the savior you think he is. He's dangerous. He's *got* to be the reason we're trapped here."

Before I can reply, the room grows cold. Icy tendrils of darkness snake their way inside, choking the air, suffocating any hope. A power so raw, so terrifying, unlike anything I've ever felt before, permeates every corner. I can hardly breathe. It feels like we're being crushed, watched, judged.

A massive shadow descends, enveloping the room, dwarfing us, making us insignificant. The darkness is so thick it feels almost tangible, as if I could reach out and touch it. The walls, the ceiling, everything is obscured by this immense, looming presence.

Madeline's voice breaks the heavy silence. "He's here," she whispers, hope painting her features.

"Who?" I try to shove down the panic rising in my chest.

"Oman."

Oman. Presumably Adip's father. But her declaration does nothing to alleviate the fear gripping me. I see no one, only the overwhelming shadow that threatens to consume us.

"What are you talking about? There's no one here."

Madeline slowly rises to her feet, her posture straightening, as if she's drawing strength from some unseen force.

"He's close," she says, her voice carrying a strange conviction. "I can feel him. I thought Cy…I thought he'd destroyed him."

I stare at her, my mind racing. Has she completely lost touch with reality? "What do you mean? Where…where is he?"

She turns her gaze towards the inky abyss around us, a serene smile on her face. "He's come to help us."

My heart pounds loudly in my chest, each beat echoing the doubts plaguing me. Madeline's faith in this Oman guy is unnerving. Yet, there's something in her eyes, a spark, a belief so strong it's almost palpable.

But can I trust it? Can I trust her? Can I trust anyone in this twisted nightmare?

The room continues its oppressive hold, the darkness almost alive, pulsating with an energy that feels both menacing and protective. My thoughts are a chaotic whirlwind, and I'm struggling to find solid ground.

"We need to get out of here." If Oman is our way out, then so be it.

Then, without warning, a deafening explosion rips through the room. The force knocks us off our feet, dust and debris momentarily blinding us. The cracked wall collapses, a dark corridor stretching out ahead. A wave of stifling heat washes over us, making my skin prickle uncomfortably. It's not the comforting warmth of a sunny day, but a suffocating, oppressive heat, reminiscent of a furnace.

A blaze of fire catches me off guard. One moment, I'm steeling myself to argue with Madeline, to plead for her to see reason—the next, the corridor is consumed by roaring flames.

Heat sears against my skin, and the stench of burning wood and stone fills my nostrils. Panic grabs hold of my chest, squeezing my lungs, making it hard to think straight.

I lunge for Madeline's hand, desperate to yank her out of this. But she resists, tearing her hand away with a surprising ferocity.

Her voice, when it cuts through the roaring of the flames, is laced with calm. "Trust it, Henry. This is the way out."

Every cell in my body screams at me that this is a trap. The oppressive heat, the choking smoke—all of it reeks of Amelia's sadistic fucking machinations. She's crafted a maze meant for torment, not escape.

And then, just as I'm trying to form a coherent plan, a chilling sight makes my blood run cold. Emerging from the flames that threaten to swallow us, a shadowy figure takes form. Its dark tendrils snake out, wrapping around Madeline's leg.

The hope in her eyes twists into fear. It's clear she didn't expect this. If this is Oman, he's clearly not on our side.

I spring into action. "No, Madeline!" My voice is desperate, hands reaching out, trying to grapple with the shadowy figure, to free her from its clutches. But it's like trying to hold on to smoke—intangible, elusive. Its grip tightens, yanking her farther from me, towards the heart of the flames.

The world narrows to the connection between Madeline's eyes and mine. "This… isn't… Oman," she says with a shaky voice, like she's being strangled by her own fear.

Time seems to stretch and distort, the seconds feeling like agonizing hours. And then, in a swift and cruel moment, the shadow devours her entirely.

Stunned, I barely register the scene shifting before me. The once-open corridor is gone. In its place stands an impenetrable wall. The finality of it all strikes me hard, driving the breath from my lungs.

I slam my fists against the cold, unyielding stone, willing it to give way. My knuckles are raw, my throat hoarse from yelling out, but my rage is pointless.

Amelia will pay for this. Every deception, every twisted game, every ounce of pain she's inflicted—she'll answer for all of it.

CHAPTER TWENTY-NINE

NATALIE

THE GROUND BENEATH my feet lurches violently, causing the papers on the walls to scatter. My heart plummets as the foundation of the building groans.

With the quickness of a flash, the door behind Wes slams shut.

"What are you doing?" My eyes remain locked on his.

Wes smirks, clearly enjoying my frustration. "That wasn't me."

Fueled by those words, I lunge at him, celestial energy coursing through my veins, propelling me forward. But Wes is quick. He sidesteps my initial attack, his own hand flaring with a dark energy I haven't seen before. His palm meets my shoulder, sending a jolt of pain radiating through me. I stagger but catch myself.

Gathering my energy, stars thrust from my palm and I shape them into a whip-like form, lashing it out at him.

My celestial leash wraps around his wrist, and I pull hard, making him stumble forward. Seizing the moment, I snatch the dagger from his pocket, swinging it towards his torso in one fluid motion. But Wes twists, the blade narrowly missing its mark and slicing a line across his arm. Dark blood drips to the floor.

Our dance of aggression and defense continues. I send a surge of celestial energy his way, but Wes manages to block or deflect most of my attempts.

Then, he catches me off guard with a swift kick, making me lose my balance. I tumble backward but quickly roll to my feet, dodging his next strike by mere inches.

My hand glows brighter than ever, and with a forceful push, I send a shockwave of power toward him. Wes is thrown back, crashing into a table littered with research.

Got him.

Gathering all my strength and conviction, I stand over him, the point of the dagger aimed straight for his stomach. I could end him, make him pay for every betrayal, every hurt. But a chilling thought holds my hand: Amelia.

She'll just bring him back.

"What's the point? Even if I kill you now, she'll just revive you."

With my powers at their peak and the blade poised for vengeance, I withdraw the dagger, stepping back, eyes still fixed on him, watching every move, every twitch.

His eyes, a tumultuous storm of emotions—pain, defiance, and something I can't quite place—lock on to mine. Maybe he feels guilty for what he's done to me. Maybe being bound to Amelia's darkness torments him too.

"Why didn't you stab me?" he challenges, the playful glint returning to his eyes. "As much as you deny it, I know you care about me."

I snort. "Like I said, there's no point. You'll just keep coming back, haunting my life again. Over and over. You know, after you knocked over your journal for me to read, I thought you might actually be on my side."

"I *am* on your side, Covington."

"What's your deal?" I demand, frustration evident in my voice. "What do you even hope to achieve? I know Amelia's in your head, reading your every thought, but how long before you break free from her control? I never pegged you as someone who'd willingly bow down to someone. You act so tough, so cocky, but you're really just weak."

"All I've ever wanted is you. You see it as weakness, I see it as perseverance."

"Perseverance? You have a warped sense of what that means, Wes. Perseverance is fighting against the odds, not trying to force someone's hand. That's just plain obsession."

He circles around me. "Semantics, Covington."

"What exactly did Amelia promise you in return for your loyalty? Or did she just hypnotize you with her creepy magic?"

"Well, she promised me you. That was the biggest draw. And she promised me protection."

I cross my arms, narrowing my eyes. "You really believe that? That she'd just hand you protection on a silver platter? Please."

"Some risks are well worth taking," he says. He steps closer, his eyes raking over my body, the familiar scent of him looping around my senses.

I swiftly retreat, putting space between us, disgust churning in my gut.

Thankfully, he doesn't press any closer. He turns his interest to the scattered drawings on the table. "What are these?" he asks, his fingers skimming over them.

My guard instantly shoots back up. "I don't know," I snap, grabbing one of the drawings and crumpling it in my fist before shoving it into my pocket.

Tension hangs between us. Then, from my pocket, a soft glow emerges, piercing the dimness of the room. The ambience changes as the light illuminates my face. I draw out the crumpled paper, the glow intensifying.

My eyes dart across the intricate lines and details. The entire depiction suggests a sprawling metropolis submerged beneath the sea's surface. There's a deeper pull, as if this city, drawn in simple charcoal strokes, resonates with some hidden part of my soul.

Wes, ever the opportunistic asshole, tries to sneak a peek, but I'm not having any of it. I pull the paper back in a sharp motion, holding the drawing possessively against my chest.

As much as the image on this paper intrigues me, something else isn't sitting right.

"Why hasn't Amelia stormed in here yet? She always shows up, and now that I'm back, alive, searching through her things, she's suddenly leaving me alone?"

Wes, though clearly wanting to inspect the drawing more, keeps his distance. "Maybe she's tied up with the mess you made back there with those guards?"

"Or maybe she's playing puppet master, watching from the shadows, waiting for me to dance." Doubt and determination battle within me. "This," I say, gently waving the glowing drawing, "isn't just some random sketch. She must know that."

Clutching the paper, the world begins to blur around me, like someone's smeared Vaseline over my vision. My senses spin, tossing me into an onslaught of memories—fragments, snapshots of my past that bubble up from the recesses of my mind.

A child's laughter—my laughter. The scent of the ocean, the feeling of sand between my toes. Waves crash nearby. I can't resist. I run towards them, feet sinking into the wet sand. My mom stands back, watching with a mix of joy and something else. Fear? Concern? The sea isn't just a place of fun for me. It's an old friend, a constant whisper in my ear. It all feels familiar.

The memories fast-forward a little. *I'm a bit older, playing in the backyard after a rainstorm. Puddles scatter across the ground, and I'm not just jumping in them—I'm controlling them. With a mere thought, the water rises, shaping into whimsical forms, dancing at my command. A crown of droplets floats above my head, as if anointing me as their queen. My laughter is rich and carefree, the kind only a child experiencing magic can muster. But as quickly as the happiness comes, it's replaced by confusion when I spot my mom watching from the window, a worried frown on her face.* I don't recall this ever happening. Surely, such a profound ability—the power to manipulate water—would've been seared into my memory?

My heart races as the vision changes. *It's night, and there's a sense of danger in the air. The very foundation of our home shakes, not from an earthquake, but from a siege. Shadows creep around the corners, formless but very much alive. The water—it's everywhere, roaring in my ears, rising in violent whirlpools, battling these intruders.* But is it defending or attacking? I can't tell.

I hear my own screams, shrill and desperate. Hands, both familiar and unfamiliar, pull at me, trying to shield me, trying to snatch me away. My mom is there—fighting, shouting, using powers I've never seen her wield. The water, my ally, feels both protective and threatening.

And just as quickly as the onslaught of memories began, it fades. I'm back in the dim room with Wes, the crumpled drawing like a lead weight. I blink hard, trying to reorient myself, finding Wes's eyes watching me intently.

"You good, Covington?" he asks, though his voice is more curious than concerned.

"Do I look okay?" I don't wait for his reply.

What was that? Why am I remembering all of this now? Why have I never remembered it before? And did any of that really happen…or not?

Wes looks like he's about to say something, but I hold up a hand to stop him. "Save it. Whatever asshole comment you had ready, I don't want to hear it. I need answers, not your attitude."

He raises an eyebrow but remains silent. Good, because right now, I'm not in the mood for games. The secrets of my past are bubbling up, and whether I like it or not, I'm about to dive deep to find the truth.

CHAPTER THIRTY

HENRY

MADELINE'S VOICE STILL echoes in my ears. She was just here, right here, and then… swallowed by a shadow. This can't be real. Just another cruel, twisted game from Amelia.

Emotions well up inside me in a volatile swarm. I can feel something building within me, something immense and unstoppable. A pressure, an energy. It's a raw, guttural sensation that refuses to be contained.

The ground beneath me rumbles, controlled by my emotions—my powers—heaving like the chest of a living beast. My vision blurs as the tremors grow more violent, feeding off my anger. I watch, almost detached, as the walls around me groan, protesting the immense force that's ripping them apart.

Cracks race across the floor, zigzagging like frenzied lightning strikes, branching out in every direction. The very foundations of this damned place are shaking, and I'm at the epicenter.

Suddenly, with a loud crash, a portion of the wall to my left crumbles, revealing a hidden passage. Dust fills the air, my lungs. Another wall gives way to my right, unveiling another room shrouded in darkness. The sights and sounds of destruction are everywhere, yet a strange sense of clarity cuts through the chaos.

I forge ahead—anger, my thirst for retribution, driving me forward.

My footsteps echo loudly in the stillness as I cautiously approach the entrance. The hidden room to the right seems equally tempting. I'm torn between the two, each path a gamble.

I need to think clearly, act strategically. I opt for the passage. Something about it feels… right. The air grows cooler as I delve deeper, and an eerie red light filters in from somewhere ahead.

I trudge through the debris, each step feeling like I'm dragging through wet sand. Madeline's capture cuts just as deep as the burning need to find Natalie. It's like I'm walking through some fucked-up dream with no way out.

The walls seem to murmur, clawing at my senses. Hollow voices, maybe Amelia's past victims. *"She plays with minds… Beware her illusions… Things aren't what they seem…"*

From the settling dust, a figure forms ahead. Not solid, but not entirely ethereal either. A ghostly woman. Long, jet-black hair flows down her back, her pale skin glowing faintly. Her eyes, a sharp violet, pierce through the dimness. She seems as lost in this world as I am.

I narrow my eyes. "Are you a prisoner here? Or part of Amelia's cult?"

She raises a hand, not in a threatening manner, but almost in a plea. "I'm not on Amelia's side. She tried to kill me before. And if she knew I was here, she'd certainly want me dead."

I proceed with caution. "So, what? Are you here to warn me? Guide me? Trap me?"

"There's been an… opening," she says slowly, a disturbed look on her face. "A portal. It's the only reason I can communicate with you."

My impatience simmers. "A portal? What do you mean?"

She sighs, a sound that seems to drift through decades. "We

managed to crack open the worlds between us. My husband— we got Madeline out, but…she won't be able to come back."

Her husband? What the hell does that mean?

The woman starts to fade, her edges becoming smoky and indistinct. "Amelia's ambitions are different than you think. Control is a part of it, but what she really wants is—" Her voice cuts out before she can continue. Just her mouth moves.

My heart races, frustration and anger bubbling over. "Wait. Then how the hell do I stop her? How do I save Natalie?"

The ghostly figure hesitates, her voice fragmenting like a glitchy radio. "You can't…only—" Her form wavers, slipping away from this realm.

Desperation grips me. "Wait! What's your name? Who are you?"

She tries to speak, but the sound is muffled, lost in the void between us. Her lips move, but no sound reaches me.

"I can't hear you," I mutter in frustration.

With fading clarity, she forms letters in the air with her hand. An F… followed by an E…

"Effie," I voice the name, the syllables tasting unfamiliar yet carrying weight.

As she vanishes entirely, the space she once occupied feels even more desolate and cold. Who the hell is Effie? What portal is she talking about?

These questions cloud my mind, but one thing's clear: she mentioned Madeline won't be able to come back. My chest tightens. Who the hell is her husband and where did he take her? And why? For leverage? For power? For some sick pleasure of seeing me powerless?

Powerless. The word grates against my every fiber. I need to find Natalie. We need to break Amelia's damned device that's playing God with time and space. I'll be damned if I let her keep controlling everything.

Screams of the past reverberate through the walls, whispers of forgotten souls, memories lost in the bowels of this awful fucking place. They're a compass, urging me forward, guiding me through the dark. Anger surges, raw and uncontrollable. I focus it, directing it at the walls of this prison Amelia constructed.

I draw a deep breath, visualizing the earth beneath, feeling its energy, its pulse. With a shout, I release the pent-up fury, channeling it into the ground. The reaction is immediate—the floor trembles, walls groan in protest, shaking violently. Stone and concrete crack and crumble, revealing hidden chambers, each one a testament to Amelia's madness. I advance, causing aftershocks, furthering the destruction.

Chaos follows in my wake. Another roar of my power, another eruption of force. Entire sections of this place collapse, pathways open up, and all the while, the voices grow louder, more distinct. They're not just guiding me—they're cheering me on.

Just as I feel the rush of success, I halt. A hallway stretches before me, dimly lit and lined with guards. The leader steps forward, a smirk dancing on his lips.

"Ahhh, looks like Henry Thorne decided to join us," he says, sneering.

They may know my name, but they don't stand a chance.

Without another word, I draw upon the latent energy, the powers unlocking within me. The air grows dense, the ground ripples, and then a seismic wave erupts, centered on me, radiating outward. The force of it tears the room apart. Pillars crumble, the ceiling collapses, guards are hurled like rag dolls, their bodies shattering against the relentless force of my anger. The room becomes a tomb of scattered, unconscious bodies.

With a focused burst of energy, I blow a hole through the next wall. Behind it, amidst the settling dust, stands Natalie, her eyes wide with shock, her face pale.

And beside her…is Wes.

Rage blinds me. All the pain, the betrayal, everything Wes has done to us—it rushes back. In this moment, nothing else matters. Natalie's figure fades to a mere silhouette against the backdrop of my wrath.

I surge forward. As I close in on Wes, he reacts with surprising speed, as if his powers have unlocked too. A dagger appears in his hand, glinting under the dim lights. Our eyes lock, and in that instant, the weight of our shared past, the battles we've fought, and the betrayals exchanged, all converge.

I swing my fist at him, my intent clear. But he's agile, dodging my strike and retaliating with a sharp thrust of his blade. The edge of it grazes my arm, drawing a line of blood. Pain ignites my anger even further.

His sneering face only adds fuel to my fire. We grapple, each trying to gain the upper hand. His blade comes dangerously close to my throat, but with a quick jerk of my head, I evade its bite and land a heavy punch square on his jaw. He stumbles backward, dazed, but not defeated.

The ground beneath us starts to quake, a manifestation of my emotions. Cracks spread like a spider's web, causing Wes to lose his footing. Seizing the advantage, I send a concentrated tremor right beneath him, throwing him off balance.

I grab him then, my fingers digging into his flesh, and with all the strength borne out of fury, heartbreak, and pent-up rage, I hurl him with everything I've got.

He becomes airborne, his eyes wide in disbelief. With a deafening crash, he breaks through the solid wall, debris and dust marking his trajectory, until he disappears into the void beyond.

Gasping for breath, adrenaline still pumping, I take a moment to absorb what just happened. The room is a mess, rubble everywhere. And there, slightly blurred, out of focus during my rage-fueled battle, stands Natalie. Her face is a mask of shock, eyes wide, lips parted.

Slowly, the weight of the moment begins to settle. Wes is gone. For now.

And Natalie. There she is—the reason I've fought, bled, and nearly died.

I've found her.

CHAPTER THIRTY-ONE

NATALIE

THE ROOM STILL vibrates with the aftershocks of Henry's explosive anger and power. Debris and shattered remains of walls lie everywhere, the aftermath of a battle that seemed pulled from the pages of some dark, twisted fantasy. But in the middle of this destruction, my gaze is focused solely on him: Henry.

Before he can fully react to my presence, I close the distance between us and crash into him. My lips find his, fierce and demanding. It's hot, desperate, a mingling of tongues and clashing teeth. There's an urgency in our actions, a hunger that's been starved for too long.

I don't feel the familiar suffocating tightness in my chest—the oxygen deprivation that always accompanied our previous trysts. Henry, too, senses this anomaly and breaks away, eyes wide and searching.

"You're... breathing," he says, surprise evident in his raspy voice.

"There was some kind of spell," I say, slightly breathless from the intensity of our kiss. "So I couldn't procreate. But Amelia removed it."

His brows knit together in confusion, trying to piece together the implications. "She got rid of it… knowing you were with Wes?"

I nod, but there's a fierce determination in my gaze, a fire that can't be extinguished. "He hasn't laid a hand on me. Not in that way."

Before he can respond, my fingers curl into his shirt, pulling him close. I can feel the hard planes of his chest beneath my fingertips. The heat between us builds again, and it's magnetic, impossible to resist. Our lips crash together once more, a fusion of passion and desperation.

When we finally part, I can see the lingering questions in his eyes.

"What happened? I saw you on the surveillance footage. You were with Ciel and Adip. Where are they?"

He looks pained at the mention of their names, a shadow crossing his features. "I don't know. We got separated trying to get inside this place." The silence that follows Henry's revelation weighs heavy. He looks at me, eyes filled with a cocktail of guilt, pain, and trepidation. "Natalie, there's something you need to know," he says, voice wavering slightly. "I found your mom, but…"

The way he trails off has my heart constricting painfully in my chest. "But what?"

"She's… gone, but not in the way you think." His words are hesitant, like he's treading on thin ice.

I can feel my heart racing, a churning mix of dread and hope. "What do you mean?"

He runs a hand through his hair, a troubled expression on his face. "Her memory has been wiped. She thinks she's nineteen and believes you're still just a baby. She also told me about someone named Oman. That name…I think that's Adip's dad. She said he's helped her before, but that your father nearly destroyed him. She seemed to think everything was your dad's fault. I tried to convince her that this is all Amelia's doing."

The weight of this revelation feels like a punch to the gut, knocking the wind out of me. "I don't understand. What… happened to her? My mom?" The words come out as a whisper, my throat tight.

"Before I could really talk to her, some shadowy figure dragged her away. But then, I met someone else." Henry's gaze grows distant. "She was like a ghost. She told me her name was Effie. Does that ring any bells?"

I shake my head in bewilderment. "No."

He takes a deep breath, looking pained. "She mentioned that her husband got your mom because some portal was opened. But she said Madeline can't come back now."

A chill runs down my spine. "This might be just more of Amelia's bullshit, another illusion," I mutter, partly to myself. A desperate part of me clings to that hope. "I guess one upside is I think I know how to better use my powers now," I say, somewhat proudly. Raising my hand, I summon tiny, shimmering stars. They dance and flicker, illuminating the space around us.

Henry's gaze is fixed on the swirling galaxy in my palm. Tenderly, he takes my hand and presses a soft kiss to it, his lips warm against my skin.

To demonstrate, I aim my hand at a nearby table. The table bursts apart, wood splinters flying everywhere.

"Seems we both have a destructive side," I say. Reaching into my pocket, I produce the glowing paper, the image of an underwater city depicted on it. "Look at this," I say, handing it to him. "Do you think it has something to do with my dad? Why would Amelia have it?"

Henry's eyes scan the image intently. "Your mom said she trusted your dad once but that he betrayed her. I tried explaining about Amelia, but she seemed to think they were allies, friends even."

My father, a stranger to me, now cloaked in even more mystery.

"We should get out of here." I clasp on to his hand, dragging him from the room.

As we dart through the maze-like hallways, anxiety rockets through my veins. "Amelia has to be watching us. But then… why hasn't she stopped us yet?"

He tugs my hand closer, his eyes scanning our surroundings. "Maybe this is exactly what she wants. Leading us further into her trap."

We continue our journey through the corridors, which are oddly vacant. It's almost as if the entire place knows of our presence and is holding its breath.

"Where are the guards?" I ask, the silence only intensifying my anxiety.

Rounding a corner, we suddenly stumble upon a grand entrance, and beyond it, a cavernous room reminiscent of a ballroom. The room's centerpiece, an enormous, opulent fish tank, is impossible to miss. It's filled with the most exotic fish, their scales glinting in the light, weaving through swaying seaweed and corals.

But the joy of this discovery fades as another, far more important, sight comes into focus.

Ciel and Adip. Off to the side of the room, they huddle together, their bodies pressed close in a tight cluster.

Overwhelmed by relief, Henry and I dash towards them, and our reunion is marked by tight hugs and gasping breaths. Pulling away slightly, I look at them, my voice laden with concern. "Where were you guys?"

Ciel forces a weak smile. "I thought we'd seen every creepy corner of this place." She glances at the walls, wrapping her arms around herself.

Adip runs a hand through his disheveled hair, shrugging with a hint of frustration. "Tunnels, more tunnels. We just… ended up in this room."

Henry suddenly takes a deep breath, looking at Adip intently. "Adip, is your dad's name Oman?"

Adip's normally calm demeanor shifts instantly. His shoulders tense, and he fixes Henry with a sharp gaze. "Yeah, why?"

Henry and I exchange a loaded glance, both realizing the potential implications.

"I think he might be here," Henry says cautiously.

Adip lets out a hollow laugh, bitterness seeping through every word. "My dad? Here? That's a good one. He never shows up when it's important, or at all for that matter."

His tone catches me off guard. I've heard bits and pieces about Adip's father before—a businessman with an empire spanning hotels and investments globally. But Adip rarely speaks about him, and now, hearing the coldness in his voice, I start to piece together why.

Pushing the boundaries, Henry ventures further. "Do you know if your dad had any connection to Natalie's mom?"

Adip looks genuinely taken aback. "Not that I know of."

Henry hesitates, but then says, "I think they knew each other, even before she met Natalie's father. And something happened."

Adip's eyes harden, a hint of anger flashing in them. "Look, I don't know what you're trying to get at, but can we drop the dad talk? Nothing good ever comes from discussing him."

We all sense the raw emotion behind his words, a mixture of longing, resentment, and pain. With a nod, we silently agree to move forward, but the revelations hang in the air, adding another layer to our already tangled web of mysteries.

As we catch up, a dark presence enters the room from a door at the far end.

Wes. Infuriatingly untouched, not a single scratch.

"What are you doing here, Wes?" Ciel asks sharply, tension cutting through the air.

Henry's face hardens instantly. "I've got the same question."

Wes's gaze never wavers from me. "I came looking for Natalie after you unceremoniously threw me out of the last room."

Henry steps protectively in front of me, his voice cold. "She's lost to you. Forever."

The atmosphere thickens with tension. The room that was filled with relief moments ago is now a pressure cooker.

With a smirk, Wes says, "You know, Natalie, for someone so intelligent, it's funny how you don't recognize a good deal when it's right in front of you."

Before I can snap back, Henry, fierce and unwavering, interjects. "Don't mistake her intelligence for compliance. She knows a bad deal and a fucking snake when she sees one."

Wes chuckles, a sound that grates on my nerves. "Your attempts at playing the knight in shining armor are cute, but ultimately pointless."

Ciel steps in, eyes narrowed. "Wait a minute—you have a thing for Natalie? Was I some kind of game to you?"

Wes raises an eyebrow, clearly enjoying the attention. "Ah, Ciel. My 'game,' as you call it, is simple—to get what I want. And right now, I want Natalie. I hope you're not offended, considering I was inside of you not that long ago."

Adip launches ahead, ready to punch Wes, but Ciel holds him back. "He's not worth it."

Feeling a familiar rage bubbling inside me, I push past Henry, meeting Wes's gaze with a fierceness that I hope conveys my utter disgust. "What in your fucked-up head makes you think I'd ever want anything to do with you, after everything you've done? To all of us?"

"You don't really have a choice, Covington."

It's then that a soft, chilling voice fills the room. "Ah, the gang's all here."

Amelia.

She steps next to Wes.

Henry's hand grips mine, a silent assurance amidst the uncertainty.

Suddenly, from the ceiling, a massive glass cube descends, enclosing Adip, Ciel…and Wes. A horrific sense of déjà vu hits me. This exact scene played out in the previous timeline.

"No!" Desperation fuels me, my heart racing with dread. Summoning my powers, I direct a burst of stars from my palm right at the cube. But they ricochet off, leaving the barrier untouched, bouncing and flattening defiantly on the hardwood floor.

Amelia's laughter, high and cruel, slices through the room. "Your powers can't fix everything, Natalie."

My heart drops as my eyes rove over to the expansive fish tank. Instead of the exotic fish, my attention is drawn to a familiar face. *My mother.* A much younger version of her, wearing a shimmering gold dress.

She circles the tank, followed by a guy with an undeniable stature. Broad-shouldered, with piercing blue eyes that seem to hold galaxies within them. *My father.*

Are they real? Are they here, right now? But as I take in the scene, their translucent forms tell me otherwise. They seem oblivious to the tension of the room, wrapped up in their own world.

Henry follows my gaze, eyes widening in recognition. "It's… it's him." He sees them too.

I snap my eyes to Amelia. "What is this? What game are you playing now?"

She doesn't answer, her eyes dancing with mischief. Is this some cruel illusion? Or memories from a past that's not mine?

My mom, or the memory of her, exits the room, my presumed father in pursuit.

But there's someone else in this memory. Someone standing on the sidelines, a burning resentment, an unmistakable jealousy in her eyes.

A young Amelia.

CHAPTER THIRTY-TWO

HENRY

THE SIGHT OF Natalie's parents, young and radiant, swimming in and out of focus, is both captivating and haunting. But my gaze immediately shifts to the younger version of Amelia. She has that same dangerous glint in her eyes, only somehow more youthful, maybe even innocent. But I'm not stupid. Nothing about Amelia Collins is innocent.

A sharp rage boils inside me, consuming all rationale. "What the hell is this, Amelia? What sick game are you playing now?"

Amelia simply smiles, her young doppelgänger mirroring her every movement. "Oh, Henry." Her voice drips with feigned concern. "There is no game."

"Then what's all this?" I gesture angrily at the watery vision of Natalie's parents. "Why show us this?"

She smirks, motioning to her younger self. "You keep asking what's going on. Once upon a time, I had an arrangement with someone I loved. But that deal… was broken." She pauses, her eyes narrowing. "Deals, when broken, have consequences. Some more than others."

Fuck this. I'm not in the mood for her cryptic nonsense. "Cut the bullshit, Amelia."

Her predatory eyes lock on to mine, assessing, calculating. "I want to propose a new deal."

Natalie's grip on my hand tightens. Whatever deal she's about to propose is most definitely not going to be in our favor.

Amelia steps forward, her heels clicking ominously on the floor. "Henry, you give up your powers, and I leave Natalie alone."

I can't suppress the bitter laugh that escapes my lips. "You think I'm that stupid? To trust you with any goddamn deal?"

Her devilish smile returns. "It's a simple choice. Your powers or her peace."

Natalie starts to interject, but I can't hold back my rage. "After everything you've put us through, you think I'd let her go? We've faced every fucking trap you've laid out for us. And guess what? We're still here. Together."

Amelia's face contorts, a hint of frustration seeping through. "You're overconfident. I was once too. And that's a weakness, Henry. You should accept that Natalie will never truly be yours. That you two will never be. Trust me. I know what it's like to lose the person you love."

Her words spark something inside me, a surge of power and anger I've never felt before. "Enough!" I shout, my voice echoing across the cavernous room. I focus on the giant glass cube imprisoning Adip, Ciel, and Wes. I extend my hand towards it, but instead of the familiar energy I'm used to, I feel something new, something raw and unrefined. From my fingertips, not a beam, but a ripple of distorted reality emerges, like a mirage on a hot day. The cube's form begins to waver under the effects of the distortion.

The bewildered looks on Ciel's and Adip's faces show they feel it too. Even Wes, despite his eternal cockiness, looks unnerved. The glass doesn't shatter or explode. Instead, it shifts and wavers before dematerializing, as though it was never there.

I withdraw my hand, looking at it in awe, trying to understand what just happened.

"What the hell was that?" Natalie gasps, her eyes wide.

"New power?" I say, still as confused as she is.

Amelia's face is a picture of pure fury. She never expected this, and the thought of her being caught off guard fills me with a perverse sense of satisfaction.

"You think this changes anything?" Amelia sneers, her voice dripping with venom. "The deal I offered was nothing but a test. And since you won't give up your powers, I guess you don't really love Natalie at all." Amelia's eyes dart to the watery mirage of Natalie's parents and the young version of herself, all of them frozen in this suspended slice of time. "I know that better than anyone. The fragility of a heart…and the price of breaking one."

"Your sob story doesn't interest me. I *do* love Natalie. I'm just not stupid enough to bargain with you."

Amelia's cold laugh chills the air. "Your misplaced heroics will be your downfall. Wait and see."

No sooner than Ciel, Adip, and Wes start to move, the room once again reverberates with the same resonating hum—Amelia's power at play. A new cube begins to form around them, its edges sharp and glinting menacingly.

I raise my hand, focusing on my newfound ability. Once again, a ripple of distorted reality forms, causing the cube to waver and disintegrate. The trio inside stumble free, their faces a blend of shock and determination.

Amelia's gaze remains fixed on me, her eyes colder than ever. "You think you're so clever?"

Without breaking eye contact, I wave my hand dismissively at the watery figures of Natalie's parents and the young Amelia, making them fade into nothingness, leaving only a chill in the air.

Her voice shakes with anger. "You cannot just wave away history.

You have no idea what's about to come. Not only will you lose Natalie, but you won't even make it out of this place alive. You have my word on that."

"Your threats don't scare me," I say, all semblance of patience gone. "You can't just take my powers, my life, away."

Amelia's grin returns, but it lacks its earlier confidence. "I've taken more from stronger men."

We stand locked in a deadly stare down, the air between us thick with tension and unsaid words.

But then, the ground gives a violent shake, causing everyone to stagger. It feels like the earth is rebelling, sharing in my fury. Cracks snake across the floor, growing wider, splitting the room in two, ripping Natalie away from me.

I look over in horror as Natalie's side begins to sink, and she loses her footing. Wes lunges forward, catching her hand just in time.

"Natalie!" My scream is raw and desperate. I sprint forward, desperate to get to her, to pull her to safety, but before I can, a force like a gust of wind sends me stumbling backward. It's Amelia and her fucking powers. With a mere gesture, she's locked me in place, my feet glued to the floor.

Flames shoot up from the cracks, roaring and dancing like fiery serpents, their heat scalding. The room turns into a furnace, with Ciel and Adip directly in the danger zone. Another violent shudder, and the floor beneath them gives way, swallowing them whole. Their voices echo eerily as they plummet into darkness.

Natalie's scream pierces through the chaos, full of anguish and pain. I struggle against the force holding me, my body wrought with desperation.

Amelia steps closer, her face illuminated by the dancing flames, making her look even more devilish. "This is just the beginning, Henry."

"Fuck off."

Amelia's magic is a suffocating force, like a vice around my chest, squeezing tighter and tighter. I focus all my attention on the energy pulsing within me. It's the same force that shattered her damn cube, the same energy that's now grown a thousand times over. I visualize the barrier around me as a mere bubble, imagining it popping, the shards scattering into nothingness.

I force all my energy outward, feeling it crash into her barrier repeatedly. On the third try, I feel the protective shield weaken, then shatter. A whoosh of air hits me as I finally break free.

Just as I regain my footing, I see Amelia lunging towards me. Instinctively, I shove her with all the strength I can muster. The force sends her flying backward, smashing her against a distant wall with a sickening crunch.

My eyes quickly dart to where Wes holds on to Natalie, the flame's cruel orange glow reflecting in his eyes. Without a second thought, I bound over to them, my intention to knock Wes out of the way and pull Natalie to safety. But Wes isn't just going to let me take over. He strikes back, a forceful shove to my chest, catching me off guard.

Natalie's scream fills my ears as her grip slips even further. A giant flame roars up, its mouth ready to swallow her whole.

"You son of a—" I growl at Wes, my eyes cold with fury. "I'd love to throw you into those fucking flames right now."

Wes, his eyes equally fierce, snarls back, "Go ahead and try."

The two of us locked in a dangerous standoff would be our doom. But the sight of Natalie, hanging precariously above the flames, acts as a desperate reminder of our real enemy here.

Our gazes meet, a silent agreement passing between us. It's a truce, for now. Both of us leap towards the edge, our arms reaching for Natalie. Working together, in a perfectly timed maneuver, we grasp her arms. It's touch and go. She's slipping, the weight and momentum nearly pulling us all in. But with a last desperate tug, we manage to pull her up and out of harm's way.

I hold her close, her heart pounding against mine, as relief floods over me.

Panting, I look around for Amelia, wanting to end this once and for all. But to my astonishment, the spot where she crashed is empty.

She's disappeared.

Breathing hard, Wes, Natalie, and I are left alone in the room. The flames have settled, but the atmosphere remains heavy with the stench of smoke and singed betrayal. I have no doubt that Amelia will be back.

And when she does, I'll be ready.

CHAPTER THIRTY-THREE

NATALIE

THE HEAT HAS faded, replaced with a chilling emptiness that echoes the void in my chest. My eyes drift to the spot where Ciel and Adip were taken by the ground, by the flames, and I'm stricken with an overwhelming sense of loss. They're gone. Just like that. My heart squeezes painfully, grief threatening to overwhelm me.

Henry, sensing my despair, wraps a comforting arm around my shoulders. "Hey," he whispers, his voice strained. "There's a chance they found a way out. Adip… I think he has some powers we didn't know about. And besides, we can't trust anything in this place. Amelia warps everything. We have to believe they're okay."

I nod as Wes lets out a mocking cackle. "Adip? He doesn't have any powers. Congratulations, Amelia just fried two of your friends. What's your next brilliant move, Thorne?"

Henry's eyes flash with anger, and he lunges at Wes.

But I'm quicker. I dart in front of him, stopping him with an outstretched arm. "No," I say firmly. "Fighting among ourselves isn't the solution. We need to focus on finding my mom, destroying Amelia, getting Ciel and Adip back."

"You think I can't help?" Wes smirks, raising an eyebrow. "Covington, I'm your best bet right now."

I scoff, rolling my eyes. "You expect me to believe you? Last I checked, you were up Amelia's ass."

Wes shrugs, a hint of mischief playing in his eyes. "She's been wildly ineffective. I mean, look at him." He motions towards Henry. "He's still standing. And the deal she offered, to remove his powers for your safety? Pathetically weak."

Henry, his temper flaring again, growls, "You better shut the fuck up before I—"

I interrupt, realization dawning on me. "Wait, Amelia's reading your mind right now, isn't she?" My eyes fixate on Wes.

Wes grins, revealing a glint of sharp teeth. "Most likely. But here's the best part: just because she can read my mind doesn't mean I'm a reliable narrator. Right, Covington?" His gaze lingers on me a moment too long, making my skin crawl.

The air crackles with tension. Henry looks like he's a second away from throttling Wes. "I swear, one more word and—"

I hold up a hand, interrupting him. "Enough, both of you. We need to focus, use whatever we have against Amelia. And if that means using Wes and his shitty mind, so be it." If Wes can be our wild card, I'm willing to play that hand.

The tension begins to swallow us whole. The walls, even with their dreary gray color, seem to pulse with energy. I can't help but recall how Amelia was able to conjure those old memories earlier. Those memories that had my parents in them.

"It's clear that Amelia knows my mom and real dad. But what was she trying to show us?"

Wes shifts, piping up. "I know a spell that might help. It can replay memories of others. I've never tried it before, but no time like the present."

Henry's eyes narrow. "How?"

Wes clears his throat. "Memories are vulnerabilities. So the spell is called the test of trust. To pull it off, you need three people in a similar circumstance. Each of us reveals a truth about ourselves, thus forming a bond and allowing us to conjure the memories from anyone we choose."

I see Henry's hand ball into a fist. "That sounds like complete bullshit."

Wes stares back at Henry defiantly, his chin tilted up. "I wrote everything in that journal for Natalie to find. I've laid out all my secrets for her. I have nothing to hide. Can you say the same, Thorne?"

A storm of anger and jealousy swirls into the room. The mention of his journal makes me uneasy, reminding me of the time I've spent poring over its pages, looking for clues, trying to decipher Wes's intentions.

Henry's lips tighten, but he remains silent.

Wes speaks before Henry can attempt to. "I love Natalie. I have no reason to hurt her." He pauses, eyes flitting over to Henry. "Can you say the same?"

The raw emotion in the room is too much, and I step between them. "Enough! Wes, if this magic can help, we'll try it. But you go first."

He nods, taking a deep breath, locking his gaze on mine. "When I tracked you down at Lockwood, I hid in your closet one day, watching you. It's when I realized we were alike. And when I… when I fell for you."

My stomach churns at his words. "I knew that already. I read it in your old journal, the one you were keeping at Lockwood. Also, you're sick."

It's my turn to share and I comb my mind for a hidden secret. "Okay, when I was ten years old," I begin, the memory making me giggle, even though it shouldn't. "I locked Jack in the basement because he was being annoying. He was there for an entire night, terrified."

Wes tilts his head. "Come on, Covington. Child's play won't work. Give us something more than that."

I inhale sharply, digging to the parts of my mind that I don't like to visit often. Or ever. "Okay, fine. Once, I stood by while someone got hurt because they'd wronged me. I… I could have stopped it, but I chose not to."

The confession hangs heavily in the air, and I refuse to meet anyone's eyes.

Wes simply says, "Petty revenge. That's a good look on you, Covington."

Henry's up next, and as I rake my eyes over him, I notice he's visibly agitated. "This is ridiculous," he says.

But Wes is faster, waving a hand, and an ethereal image plays out before us. It's Henry…with another girl. My heart aches watching him hold her face, fisting her hair, with that same intensity he uses on me.

"Who…who is she?" My voice is shaky.

Henry's voice is defensive. "Someone…insignificant."

Wes's laugh cuts through. "Insignificant? You told her you wanted forever with her."

With another wave, the memory replays Henry's heartfelt confession to the girl. A girl who isn't me.

My heart shatters but I quickly mend it up. This had to be before we met. I can't fault Henry for his past. But because I can't help myself, I ask, "When was this?"

Wes cuts in. "Not that long ago. When he left you at Lockwood to go join the Armory. Right, Henry?"

Betrayal stings, but a larger part of me rationalizes it. I was with Wes then, even if it was a game, even if Henry still consumed nearly all my thoughts. "Why didn't you tell me about this?" I ask.

Henry's eyes are desperate, filled with regret. "It's difficult to explain."

Everything blurs. The memories, the confessions, the heartbreak. But at the center of it all, I realize the truth of Wes's words. Memories are our vulnerabilities. And Henry just laid his bare, whether he wanted to or not.

My heart is pounding so loudly, I'm sure both of them can hear it.

Henry's chest heaves as he grapples with the memory, his voice filled with regret. "When I went into the Armory, I thought I had a way in, but things got complicated, and she was there. She was part of my way in. Gaining her trust, it was part of the plan."

"But not the declarations of love," Wes interjects bitterly, his eyes fixed on Henry. "Seems you were having quite a good time gaining her trust. Just like Natalie did with me."

In a flash, Henry lunges at Wes, and the two are immediately entangled in a fierce brawl. I call forth my powers, and from my palm, bursts of starry light shoot out, spiraling around both of them. The stars pull them apart, suspending them in the air, leaving them powerless and disoriented. As the stars flare and dim, they both crash to the ground, holding their wounded limbs and egos.

But then a different scene plays out before us. It seems Wes's spell worked—we unlocked one of Amelia's memories.

Amelia, younger, her eyes bright with tears, confronts a younger version of my father. "You cannot leave me. If it's not me and you… you know what'll happen."

My father looks at her, guilt and pain evident in his eyes. "I'm sorry. But I'm in love with Madeline."

Amelia looks shattered. "This is a huge mistake, Cy. You'll ruin everything. Not just my life, but yours, and others. There are huge consequences. Don't you see?"

As he turns away, she screams after him, raw pain echoing in her voice.

The memory fades, the room settling back into its previous state. Wes and Henry, now on opposite ends, are panting heavily, the fight interrupted by the shocking revelation.

I clutch my chest, trying to process what I've just witnessed. So Amelia wanted to be with my father. Is this all a revenge scheme? Targeting his daughter to hurt him?

The pieces begin to slot together—but they create an even bigger puzzle.

CHAPTER THIRTY-FOUR

HENRY

Swallowing my pride, I take a step towards Natalie. "I should have told you about her," I say, meeting her gaze.

She looks up, and her eyes, filled with a complex mix of emotions, soften. "It's fine," she says, surprisingly forgiving.

From the corner, Wes scoffs, his anger palpable. "How come you're so quick to forgive him and yet you treat me like the devil?"

Natalie's gaze sharpens. "Because you are."

I can feel the energy in the room shifting, becoming more volatile.

Before I knock Wes in his face, hopefully into the next dimension, Natalie steps in. "We need to focus on what's important. Can we unlock more of Amelia's memories?"

Wes, still smoldering, says, "As long as we keep revealing hidden secrets about ourselves. Personally, I'd like to hear more about this girl Henry fell for." His eyes gleam, teasing Natalie, *my Natalie*, trying to provoke a reaction.

I grit my teeth, temper rising. "I didn't fall for her. I used her as a means for information. Yes, it's fucked up, but no more so than what you've done."

"All I've ever done was want Natalie," Wes snarls, "despite her constantly pushing me away."

"Maybe you should finally take a fucking hint then. She doesn't want you."

Natalie steps between us again, her hand raised as if anticipating another physical confrontation. "Enough! We each need to share one more secret. Let's just get it over with."

I take a deep breath as a memory jolts into the forefront of my thoughts, almost knocking me off balance. I see a younger version of myself, tiptoeing past Oliver's slightly ajar door. He's in his favorite chair, captivated by a locket in his hands. I've caught him in this moment before, heard him mumble something about turning back time. In the memory, I move closer, silently, drawn by curiosity. Over his shoulder, I glimpse the photo within the locket. The face staring back is…Amelia.

Then Oliver's head jerks up, his eyes locking on to mine, snapping the locket closed. "Never tell anyone about this, Henry. Strike it from your memory."

And clearly, I did just that. Until now.

I take a deep breath, feeling the weight of that old memory press against my chest. "I just remembered, when I was younger, I saw Oliver with a locket. Inside, there was a photo of a woman who looked exactly like Amelia."

Natalie's eyes widen in shock. "Amelia and your foster dad?"

I shake my head, just as baffled. "From the way he reacted when he caught me looking, it was something he wanted to keep secret. Maybe he was in love with Amelia, but she was in love with your dad?"

Wes snorts, rolling his eyes. "Honestly, it sounds like all these assholes dragged us into their petty high school drama. All these love triangles and secrets. They couldn't handle their own messes and now it's falling on us to pick up the pieces. Talk about failing the next generation."

Natalie exhales, rubbing her temples. "We need to understand how all of this… this tangled web of relationships… how it affects our current situation." She looks pensive for a moment, her gaze shifting to the floor.

Wes's impatient voice slices through the silence. "Your turn to share, Covington."

She puffs out a deep breath, appearing to comb her memory, her eyes widening as she hits on something. "Once, when I was younger, my mom and I were on a beach vacation. I remember she was wearing this beautiful white bikini, her skin tanned from the sun. As she was applying sunscreen, I noticed a scar on her upper, inner thigh." She pauses, swallowing, her eyes distant as if she's back on that beach. "It wasn't like any scar I've ever seen. And the most bizarre part was… it shimmered. Like it was bathed in glitter. Just faintly, but enough for me to see."

I try to picture what she's describing, the shimmering scar on otherwise perfect skin. The image is haunting.

Natalie's voice breaks my thoughts. "I was just a kid, you know? So I asked her about it. The change in her was… immediate. I remember her eyes darting to the scar. She quickly covered it with her sarong, her face growing more pale." She lets out a shaky breath, looking between Wes and me. "She told me never to bring it up again. To forget it. And for a while, I did. But now…" She trails off, the weight of her memory settling between us.

I turn to Wes. "You're up."

Wes shrugs, offering a smug grin I'd love to knock off his face. "I don't know, guys. I think I'm outta secrets. Like I said, I'm an open book."

I clench my fists, irritation bubbling. "Come on, asshole."

Wes's smug expression fades just a bit, and for a second, he looks distant, lost in thought.

Natalie narrows her eyes. "What is it?"

Wes's usually arrogant demeanor falters. He swallows hard, his gaze distant. "I used to go through my uncle's things. That's how I found the book of magic. But there was something else I found a couple years back. Odd."

I cross my arms. "Spill it."

He takes a deep breath. "It was a shattered piece of a mirror. Pretty random for a guy who had very few possessions. But…when I looked into it, I didn't see my reflection."

"Who did you see?" I ask.

Wes's jaw tightens. "A woman. Exceptionally attractive. Long, blonde hair. Cool, gray eyes. She was hot. Looked like she was in her twenties. Honestly, I kinda wish I'd remembered, tried to find her."

Natalie tilts her head, absorbing the information, trying to piece it together.

I press, "And how is this a secret?"

Wes grimaces. "He caught me. Made me promise not to tell anyone. Tried to beat the shit out of me. But by that time, I had learned a thing or two about defending myself." He rubs his temple, recalling the memory. "I managed to best him. Though the beating I took probably gave me a concussion…must've knocked that memory out 'til now."

As the final secret is shared, the air fogs, and another memory unfolds before us. A younger Amelia materializes, fiddling with the glass contraption—the one we've come to recognize that can reset time.

As she turns a dial, the room around her begins to blur and shift. But then, something goes wrong. The glass cracks, releasing a surge of energy that throws Amelia back. She screams in pain and frustration, scrambling back to her feet.

She's so focused that she doesn't hear the door creak open.

Oliver, my foster dad, steps in, quietly observing her. He's younger also, and his usually stern expression softens, betraying a hint of admiration, maybe even affection.

Amelia mutters under her breath, "It's not working."

Oliver approaches her gently, his voice soft. "Patience."

She snaps at him. "I don't have time for patience!"

He hesitates, then continues. "This is uncharted territory. Your idea is genius, but not something we can rush." He reaches out, tracing a hand along her cheek. He's clearly enamored by her. "Why are you so desperate to bring Cy back?"

She recoils, swatting his hand away, and strides over to the contraption. Her voice is filled with conviction. "Because it's our destiny. We are meant to be."

Oliver exhales. "This device… If it's not calibrated correctly, it might destroy all of humankind. Maybe us too. You know that, right?"

She stares at the contraption. "I'm willing to take that risk."

The memory fades, leaving us all in stunned silence. The weight of what we've just witnessed, the dangerous power of the contraption and Amelia's desperation, hangs heavy.

I break the silence. "We have to destroy that thing. Before she gets another chance to use it."

Natalie, her face pale, nods. "Before it destroys us all."

CHAPTER THIRTY-FIVE

NATALIE

"I KNOW WHERE that contraption is," Wes says, his voice hushed but certain. "I'll lead us there."

I glance at him, skeptical. "How can you be so sure Amelia won't know we're coming? She's in your head, remember?"

"Three against one. I like those odds."

Henry's gaze narrows. "More like everyone here against us."

With a nonchalant shrug, Wes says, "So? You're not confident in your abilities, Thorne?"

Avoiding Wes, I tug Henry's hand over to the doorway. It twists right open, another indication that Amelia has no issue with our plan. Which means we really need to watch our backs.

Wes leads the way as the suffocating silence envelops the hallway. Every shadow in this corridor is a lurking threat. The silence feels so deliberate, so intentional that I can't help but think we're playing right into Amelia's hand. A trap? Bait?

As we proceed, my mind drifts to the contraption. "Assuming we find this thing, we have to figure out a way to destroy it."

Henry nods. "We need to make sure whatever we do doesn't

backfire. That thing can reset time. Imagine the fucking chaos if we mishandle it."

Physics class swells in my mind. "If this device functions on a principle of space-time manipulation, then we have to neutralize that aspect. Disrupt its mechanism. We could use a strong electromagnetic pulse," I say, recalling one of many lectures on electromagnetic fields. "If it has any electronic component, an EMP would fry it."

Wes looks at me, impressed. "This science nerd vibe is working for me, Covington."

Henry grits his teeth as I swallow down my disgust. I squeeze Henry's hand, meeting his eyes as Wes steers us around a corner.

"What if that thing is purely magical? What if physics doesn't apply?" Henry asks, a legitimate question.

"Magic follows its own set of rules," Wes interjects. "Rules that Amelia might be bending with this contraption. If we can find the source of its power, we might be able to counteract it."

Our debate is cut short as Wes signals us to stop. Before us stands a massive door, ornate with intricate designs, and emanating a faint, pulsating glow. This is it.

Pushing open the door, we're met with a dimly lit room. At its center stands the glass contraption, its numerous dials and levers reflecting the low light.

I step forward, inspecting it. The machine hums with a soft vibration, and I can almost feel the raw power radiating from it. But something's off.

"No Amelia. No guards," Henry says, echoing my thoughts.

Wes narrows his eyes, scanning the room. "This is too easy. It's almost as if she wants us to destroy it."

A shiver runs down my spine. "But why?"

Henry gestures to the contraption. "Maybe she realized how dangerous it is. Or it's served its purpose."

"Or this is a trap," Wes adds. "A way to bring us all together in one spot."

The room suddenly feels colder, the weight of our decision pressing down on us. Do we destroy it and potentially play into Amelia's hand? Or do we leave it and risk her using it against us?

I glance at the contraption, my mind racing. If this thing can alter time, then it's a force that shouldn't exist. Despite the potential risks, I feel in my gut that leaving it intact would be the greater threat.

"We have to destroy it," I say, determination setting in my voice.

Henry nods, resolute. "Let's do it."

The hum of the contraption fills the room as I approach it, taking in every intricate detail of its design. The various dials, levers, and fragile glass tubes present a complicated array of connections that seem to dance with an inner light. The physics of it all boggles my mind, but my years of academic rigor help me to focus.

"Energy can't be created or destroyed," I say to myself, reciting the conservation of energy principle. If this device manipulates time, then it must be doing so by redistributing energy from one point in space-time to another.

Drawing a deep breath, I trace my fingers over a series of dials. I remember my studies on resonance and how everything vibrates at a specific frequency. If I could just find the contraption's resonant frequency and disrupt it, the machine would self-destruct.

"I think I've got it," I say. With precision, I adjust a lever, aiming to offset the energy flow.

The machine responds with an angry whir. I hold my breath, hoping that my calculations are accurate. Suddenly, there's a blinding flash, and the machine pulsates with a force that sends all of us flying back.

The deafening explosion leaves a ringing in my ears. I groan, trying to find my bearings, blinking the stars away from my vision. As the dust settles, I see shards of glass hovering in the air, whirling and dancing in an intricate pattern. Before our eyes, the shards come together, forming a large, full-length mirror.

"What the hell is happening?" Henry says, pushing himself up from the floor.

I struggle to catch my breath, my heart pounding. "I… I don't know."

An ethereal glow emanates from the mirror, casting reflections around the room. In its shimmering surface, Amelia comes into view, and we watch as a mirage of scenes unfold.

She's older in this memory, appearing to be the age she is now, and is standing with an older, more anxious-looking Oliver. The weariness of time is evident on his face, and the gravity of their conversation seems to press heavily on his shoulders.

"I've changed my mind," Oliver says, voice tinged with a quiver. "We shouldn't be doing this. It's been years with no luck. It's too dangerous."

Amelia's eyes, filled with determination, lock on to his. "It's the only way to draw him back."

Watching this, it becomes clear to me that this must have been a fairly recent conversation, maybe within the last couple of years.

"If Cy truly loved Madeline, why wouldn't he defy the rules to come here?" Amelia's voice is a mix of frustration and desperation. "After all these years, after everything I've done that should have lured him back…"

Oliver exhales shakily. "He probably feels it's too great a risk. Or hasn't found a way to come back yet."

She stares into his eyes, searching for something. "It's because he doesn't love Madeline. He couldn't possibly . If he loved her, he would have risked everything, done anything to be here. But surely, he must care about something… someone innocent. His daughter, maybe?"

Oliver's eyes widen in alarm. "No, Amelia. That's going too far. We can't involve children in this."

She tilts her head slightly, her gaze sharp and calculating. "Aren't you taking care of a boy? Henry, was it?"

The mention of Henry makes my blood run cold.

Oliver visibly swallows, hesitating for a moment before admitting, "Yes, he's under my care. He's... special. I can't put my finger on why, but..."

A predatory smirk plays on Amelia's lips as she cuts him off. "Special? Well, then I have an idea..." Her voice drips with malevolence. "I will turn my attention to Natalie," she says. "If the threat to his own daughter doesn't draw Cy here..."

I can hear the weight of years, the strain of a thousand sleepless nights in her voice. This is more than just a plan. It's an obsession. *With my father.*

The reflection in the mirror suddenly shatters, like a screen losing signal, and the glass explodes, littering the floor with razor-sharp shards. I'm left staring at the mess, breath ragged and fury clouding my vision.

It hits me then, like a thunderbolt. "He could have helped?" My voice is raw, disbelief evident. "My own father could put an end to all this suffering, and he's just been... what? Watching? Hiding? Like a coward?"

Without thinking, I race over to the contraption, summoning energy I didn't know I had. From my hands emanate brilliant stars, their luminescence a stark contrast to the cold machinery. I shoot the power straight at it, not caring about the consequences anymore.

The room reacts violently. The walls blur, the ground seems to tremble, and the air is thick with electricity.

Henry is shouting, his voice distant and distorted. "Natalie! Stop!"

But I can't. Not now. Not when the possibility that my father could end all of this looms in my mind.

Henry's strong arms circle around my waist, trying to pull me away, but I channel more energy, stronger, fiercer. Henry goes flying, his body slamming against the wall with a thud. I hear glass breaking, embedding itself into the walls, the ground, everywhere.

"Covington, enough!" Wes is shouting now, desperation in his voice.

But my powers are too strong, my anger has swelled too large to shove it away.

The ground, angry and pulsating, cracks open beneath him. I watch as the floor swallows Wes whole, leaving only a gaping hole behind.

Henry grabs hold of me, taking me down to the cold, hard ground. My powers dwindle. I'm drained. As reality comes crashing back, all I can do is sob into his chest.

"All of this…" I choke out between sobs, "…is because of my father."

CHAPTER THIRTY-SIX

HENRY

I GENTLY LIFT Natalie's chin, gazing into her eyes, which now seem distant and empty. Her breaths come in shallow gasps, fragile as glass, like she's on the brink of splintering.

"Let's relax for a minute," I suggest, pulling her into my arms. "You're going to need your strength."

She looks up at me, the weight of everything we've been through resting heavily between us. Every moment of fear, loss, and uncertainty pushes us towards each other. Our gazes lock, and in that moment, the world fades away. Mentally, we're no longer in this broken room, haunted by Amelia and her machinations. It's just us. For now, this shattered space is our world.

Our breaths mingle, the intoxicating scent of her filling my senses. She leans into me, lips parted, eyes fluttering shut. I close the distance, capturing her lips with mine. It's a desperate kiss, full of raw emotion, pain, and an overwhelming desire to drown out the chaos around us.

The heat of Natalie's breath, ragged and uneven, brushes against my neck. The scent of her—earthy and cinnamon with a touch of something indescribably her—overwhelms my senses, pushing every other thought out of my mind.

My hands move to her waist, pulling her closer. She gasps into the kiss as I deepen it, the world blurring out completely.

"Natalie." I breathe into her neck, tracing my lips to her ear. "No matter what happens, I'm with you. Always."

She pulls me back to her lips, kissing me deeper, more urgent. A low moan escapes my throat as I press her down to the ground, her legs curling around my hips. *Fuck.* This isn't what we should be doing right now, but it's exactly what we both need.

"What if this is the last time we're together?" she asks.

"It won't be," I say, even though I'm not exactly sure that's true.

Her hands fly to my shirt, tearing the fabric from my body, clawing her hands over my back.

With her body splayed out before me, I pull off her tank top and run my hands down her skin. She lets out a groan as I trace a hand up to her neck, my ache for her building. My lips trail down her chest as she whispers, "I want you, Henry."

Not all that long ago, my kiss could render her unconscious. But now that Amelia's spell is broken, there's nothing holding us back. Having her lying beneath me fuels my urgency. I'm fucking desperate for her.

Her gaze never leaves mine as I brush a thumb over the curve of her collarbone, tracing my palm down her chest, pausing to cup her breast before tracing it down to her waist, her body writhing under mine.

She begs, "I need you, please."

Her words, breathless and wanting, drive me to brink of madness. I grip the top of her pants, yanking them down her hips. She tugs me closer, her own fingers pulling down my pants, our lips meeting in a dance of raw need and longing.

"Please, Henry."

Her words drive me feral and I press myself inside of her. I need her so fucking badly it hurts. She moans, raises her hips, and buries her head into my neck, biting into my shoulder as I drive into her. She eagerly meets me with each thrust, nails digging into my back, both of us desperate to escape—even if it's just now. Even if this is it.

Just as the heat between us is about to cross the point of no return, a sudden noise shatters the moment—a distant crash, like a door being thrown open and the unmistakable shouts of guards.

We break apart, panting, throwing on clothes.

"Come with me." I grab her hand and lead her into what seems to be a storage closet. We shove the door closed behind us, locking it just as the footsteps enter the room.

Pressed against the cold wall, the air between Natalie and me crackles with electricity. Every inch of her seems to swallow the confined space, her warmth teasing against the coolness of my skin. I press my lips into her neck, trailing my fingertips across her chest, feeling her heart hammering against her soft skin.

Outside, the footsteps grow louder, guards speaking in hushed whispers, hinting at the chaos Natalie unleashed upon Amelia's device. How long before they realize we're here, hidden just out of reach?

The jarring sound of the closet door jolts me from my thoughts. Someone tries to force their way in, the locked knob resisting with every twist.

In the middle of the threat, I find solace in the curve of Natalie's neck, leaving a trail of heated kisses. Her body arches back into me in response. Her fingers entwine with mine, urging me to grip her even tighter.

I catch the guard's voice, a sharp whisper piercing through the door. "Amelia won't let them live after this."

The reality of our situation descends upon us—a death sentence hanging over our heads, guards with a singular mission just beyond the door, and yet, the danger is intoxicating.

Natalie shifts, spinning around to face me. Our gazes lock, twin pools of emotion holding a silent, charged conversation. The distance between our lips disappears as the world outside seems to both slow down and race forward at the same time. The sensation is like a dam breaking, unleashing torrents of pent-up desire.

I deepen the kiss with feral intensity—pouring a mixture of everything we've been through, of desperation born from danger. Our hands search and cling to one another, trying to pull each other even closer.

A sudden jerk at the door propels us back to reality. Our foreheads press together, breaths mingling.

Miraculously, the danger outside diminishes, the voices fading as the guards seem to move on. We remain in our makeshift haven, wrapped in each other, every fiber of my being screaming for us to stay…to finish what we started.

"We need to go," I say, trying to make the rational choice.

She pulls away, nodding, and it's like an icy blast overtakes the cramped space. With our lives teetering on the edge, and within Amelia's fucked-up experiment, all I want is her.

Natalie turns to open the door, her fingers grazing the lock. Acting on impulse, I seize her wrist and press it above her against the wall. The world becomes a blur, a whirl of sensations and overwhelming desires. She's panting, blinking up at me, everything about her feels frenzied and urgent, making me lose control, but no, we can't…

This isn't the time.

"We should go," she says, echoing the logic that both of us should cling to now. But relief doesn't settle in as it should.

I free her hands and she responds immediately, her palms cradling my cheeks, drawing me in. Her kiss is fervent, charged with desperation. There's an unsettling undertone, a sense of finality that gnaws at my core. My fingers lace through hers, our mouths moving in a heated dance.

"Stay here, just for a bit longer." I mumble the words against her lips.

She pulls away with gentle force, twisting away from my mouth. I release her hands, and suddenly, everything is fucked, reality crashing down on both of us.

"You heard the guards. Amelia's got to know by now that I destroyed her device. Maybe we were just pawns in her game before, but now? The stakes have changed."

Silently agreeing with her analysis, I follow her out of the closet. My gaze drifts over the room and back to the closet, and that's when I spot them: uniforms. Folded neatly, identical to those worn by the guards.

"Put these on," I say, pulling out the black-button shirts and pants.

Natalie's eyes widen in realization. "Disguise ourselves as one of them? There's surveillance everywhere, she's going to know."

"It could help us blend in. It's worth a shot," I say, swiftly pulling the baggy uniform over my own clothes. The material feels rough against my skin, foreign and heavy. I watch as Natalie does the same, fumbling with the buttons, her fingers shaky.

Draped in the fabric of our enemies, I clasp Natalie's hand. "Find your mom, Ciel, Adip…get out of here."

She nods as we move into the hallway, releasing hands and keeping our heads lowered. A group of guards linger at the far end of the hall-way. A large set of double doors looms ahead in the opposite direction.

We head away from the guards. But as I'm about to push the door open, it swings inward, and there, standing in the dim light… is Oliver.

His piercing eyes settle on mine, an amused smile tugging at his lips.

"Well, you two are full of surprises."

CHAPTER THIRTY-SEVEN

NATALIE

Every instinct screams at me to fight off Oliver, to protect Henry, us…to survive. The dimly lit room casts dark shadows around us, with Oliver's smug face illuminated, challenging me.

Before I can mentally process my next move, an intense warmth spreads from my chest to the tips of my fingers. Without hesitation, a shower of twinkling stars bursts from my hands, directed straight at Oliver. The force knocks him backward, sending him sprawling on the floor. My power, the celestial force inherited from my mom, courses through me, unstoppable.

Oliver's face contorts in a mixture of awe and fear. He tries to scramble to his feet, but I'm faster. Another wave of my hand, and the stars merge to form a shimmering barrier around him, pinning him down. My powers are growing…*working*.

"You *are* going to start talking," I hiss at him. "What does Amelia want with us? How are you connected to all of this? And what do you know about my real father?"

Oliver struggles against my barrier, trying to stand, but the celestial forcefield holds him down. His eyes dart around the room, searching for an escape, but finding none. "I… I don't want anyone to get hurt." There's a desperation evident in his voice that sends a surge of satisfaction through my heart.

Henry scoffs, stepping next to me in a flash of anger. "You're full of shit. After everything you've done, how can we believe a word you say?"

Oliver's gaze remains locked on me, his eyes filled with an odd mixture of respect and trepidation.

"You need to ask Amelia these questions," he says, almost pleading. "She should be the one to tell you."

My fury builds and the stars erupt from my hands once more, this time forming luminescent tendrils that coil around Oliver's neck, tightening their grip, choking the breath from his lungs. It's intoxicating, the pure, raw power flowing through me. The stars react to my emotions, growing brighter, squeezing tighter with my rising anger.

Oliver sputters and gasps, his eyes bulging, his face turning a shade of purple. I can see the fear in his eyes, the realization that he might meet his end.

Henry steps forward, glaring down at his foster dad. "Does it even matter that you can't breathe? You always seem to come back, no matter how many times you're taken down."

Oliver's strained voice breaks through, gasping, "Not… anymore. You…destroyed the device."

My powers falter for a moment. I wave my palm, and the leash of stars around his neck retracts, releasing the stranglehold.

Oliver coughs violently, wheezing, his hands clutching at his reddened throat. He stares up at me with a look that shows he's aware the tables have turned.

I keep my eyes trained on him, the remnants of my power still crackling in the air, still holding him down. "What's that supposed to mean? Magic no longer works because I destroyed that device?"

He coughs again, wincing. "The device made it possible for us to access and harness it."

Confused, I continue prodding. "I thought magic was forbidden for your kind anyway."

Oliver nods, eyes heavy with secrets. "Yes, but there was another layer, a protective field stopping us from using it. It's the same kind of force Amelia put on you, to ensure you couldn't bear a child with any supernatural creature. The device allowed us to override that force."

The words send a shiver of disgust down my spine.

Henry's face darkens, a protective fire burning in his eyes. "Why are you helping Amelia? Is this just some sick game to you? Take in precogs as foster kids and torture them?"

Oliver hesitates, his gaze drifting. "No, Henry. I never intended for all of this to happen. I met Amelia the summer after she finished high school. Circumstances for her...changed. She had to act."

Henry steps closer, eyes fixed on Oliver. "What circumstances?"

True to his nature, Oliver remains evasive.

I summon the stars again, forming them into a tight leash that wraps around his chest. His face goes pale as it tightens, and I can see the strain in his eyes, my threat evident.

"Start talking."

"Alright, alright!" Oliver gasps, catching his breath. "Amelia was arranged to marry your father, Natalie. He chose Madeline. A lot of bad things happened because of that decision. A lot of people got hurt. Amelia thought using magic was the only way to lure him back. Her obsession with him grew, and I...I became equally obsessed with helping her. Or at least, making her believe I was."

My mind reels at his admission. "So my father fell in love with my mother, dumped Amelia, and she thought she could use magic to change that?"

"It's a lot more complicated than that."

My patience wears thin. "Then enlighten us." I channel my power once more, squeezing Oliver's chest for emphasis.

"It's beyond my understanding," Oliver says, his eyes darting between Henry and me. "It all stems from Cy's family. Their lineage. They operate on a much different plane of existence than we do."

Henry's face contorts with frustration. "Why the hell were you helping her then? You told me before that you believed Amelia was some kind of progressive innovator. Is that it? You're just power hungry?"

Oliver's face falls, guilt shadowing his features. But he remains silent, prompting me to tighten my celestial grip on him once again.

"No!" Oliver finally gasps. "It wasn't about power. I…I was in love with Amelia. Always have been. It's clear Cy is not coming back. And I thought if I helped her build that device, she'd eventually give up on him and see that I was the one she needed all along."

A heavy silence fills the room as the depth of Oliver's confession sinks in. All this chaos, all the destruction, driven by unrequited love.

Hot, blistering rage surges through me, leaving me trembling with the force of it. "It's just like Wes—trying to use magic, manipulation, anything to override true love, to get what you want."

Oliver takes a breath, eyes haunted. "Wes isn't a Cambion. He was made to believe he is by the authority, to try and keep him somewhat in line. If we don't control him to some extent, he'll devour everything in his path."

"He's an assassin," I say, confusion muddling my thoughts. "Your authority made him one. He's never shown restraint or control."

"The authority knew what he needed—a fixation," Oliver says. "Something, or someone, to focus his thoughts, to prevent him from spiraling."

Bile rises in my throat as I realize I was—I *am*—that fixation. "If he's not a Cambion…what is he?"

Oliver shifts his gaze uncomfortably. "There's another plane of existence besides ours, Natalie. It operates by rules far more ancient, far more powerful. Rules that… overshadow anything we know. Wes has fallen from that world."

I'm momentarily taken aback. Desperation edges my voice but I steel myself. "Forget Wes. Where's my mom?"

Oliver hesitates, seeming to choose his words carefully. "I believe she's there, in that different plane of existence. Perhaps with Cy now, or not."

A fusion of fury and grief boil within me, confirming my worst fear—I'll never see my mother again. Without thinking, I tighten the celestial leash around Oliver, hoping to make him feel a fraction of the pain inside me.

He grimaces, clutching at the celestial rope. "There's nothing I can do, Natalie. Amelia won't stop this until Cy returns for her."

"If my father was coming back, he would have by now. All this pain. All this torture."

"He can't," Oliver croaks. "That's the thing. It's forbidden. It will tear apart the barriers between our worlds. We can't even begin to fathom the horrors that would be unleashed, let in."

My mind races, attempting to piece together the fragments of information, desperately searching for answers about my father. "Where exactly is my father?" I demand, eyes never leaving Oliver's.

Oliver shifts uncomfortably, his gaze flickering briefly away from mine. "We think he's imprisoned. It's… complicated."

"Oh, how convenient!" I snap, letting the stars materialize around my fingers again. "Unless you want my powers strangling the life out of you, especially now that Amelia can't use magic to resurrect your kind, I suggest you start explaining. Clearly."

His eyes widen in genuine fear, knowing that his lifeline has been severed, the weight of his own mortality finally sinking in. "Alright, alright!" he stammers. "Cy… he had responsibilities, duties, to his family. When he failed to meet them, he faced consequences."

"So what, my father is in some sort of… underworld prison?"

Oliver nods hesitantly. "Yes. The Black Sea."

Henry's face contorts in rage, stepping in. "So you really hoped that, in time, Amelia would give up on Cy and turn to you instead? What an asshole."

With a weak nod, Oliver admits it. "Yes. You're right. Naïve and foolish, but I clung to that hope. But now, I fear what comes next." His ominous words hang heavy in the air. Oliver looks between us, his expression grave. "I shouldn't be telling you this, Natalie, but your lineage grants you immortality," he says, pausing as if the next words are harder to utter. "But Henry, you don't share that lineage. You're vulnerable." He meets Henry's gaze, the weight of past decisions swirling in his eyes. "I know I've failed you in so many ways. But please, be careful. Without that device, magic doesn't work anymore."

Suddenly, the room shudders violently, causing us to stagger. The room's doors burst open with such force, they almost unhinge. Through the disarray, a figure emerges from the billowing dust and shadows—Amelia.

The air around her crackles with an electric energy, like a malevolent goddess, exuding dominance and raw power. Those eyes, usually cold and distant, are now blazing with such intensity, I can feel the heat from where I stand.

Henry shifts to shield me, a protective grip on my hand. But for all his bravado, I can feel the tremor in his body, the uncertainty that Amelia's presence brings. She steps forward, the ground responding to her every move, pulsating like the heartbeat of the room.

A swirl of dark, ethereal energy manifests around Amelia's outstretched hand. From it, hissing tendrils emerge, like shadowy snakes, moving their way towards us. Henry and I stand firm, but just as swiftly as they approach us, the tendrils divert their course, targeting Oliver instead.

He barely has time to react. The snaky appendages wrap around him, constricting tighter and tighter.

Oliver's eyes, once prideful, now mirror sheer terror. "Amelia, no!" he screams, but his plea falls on deaf ears.

She's unwavering, her expression devoid of any emotion.

As the tendrils tighten their grip, Oliver's form begins to disintegrate, turning to dust.

CHAPTER THIRTY-EIGHT

HENRY

THE SILENCE THAT follows Amelia's entrance is shattered by her biting words. "You think you're so smart, destroying what I've worked so hard to build," she hisses, her eyes fixed on Natalie.

Natalie meets her gaze head-on. "What are you even trying to accomplish? My father doesn't want you. Why destroy all these lives?"

With a graceful yet menacing wave of Amelia's hand, the room begins to fill with water. I feel the cold liquid seep into my shoes and drench my pants. Clenching my fists, I grip Natalie's hand, the touch grounding me. What the hell is Amelia planning now?

With another flourish, she morphs the water into a shimmering mirror. Nerves claw down my back as we see Adip and Ciel in the reflection, in some other room, huddled together.

"They're alive," Natalie says, her voice breathy.

A rush of relief courses through me, but the sensation is short-lived.

Amelia's voice takes on a mocking tone. "Take a closer look."

Drawn in by Amelia's ominous words, we step forward. The horror becomes clear—their room, too, is filling with water, far more rapidly than ours. Ciel's desperate cries for help echo in our ears while Adip frantically searches for an escape.

"Stop!" Natalie screams, anger simmering.

The water is already at their knees.

"We have to find them," I say, pulling Natalie by the hand.

Amelia gives us a chilling laugh. "It's no use. You'll never find them. Not in time."

The sight of the water reaching their chests, drowning the hope from their faces, threatens to break us.

Natalie shouts, "This is an illusion! It's not real. It can't be."

"No, Natalie. I can no longer use magic, remember? This is just one of my abilities—to manipulate the elements."

My anger boils over. "Why are you doing this, Amelia? All this pain, this destruction? Ciel and Adip are innocent, they're not even part of this."

She just stares at us, cold and unmoved.

Natalie, blazing with rage, channels her power and unleashes it upon Amelia. A torrent of radiant stars rushes towards her. But as they make contact, they ricochet off Amelia's body as if they've struck an invisible, unyielding barrier.

Natalie concentrates harder, hurling another barrage of her celestial might towards Amelia. Just as before, her power is rendered ineffective, the stars scattering in all directions, their luminescence dimming as they hit the ground.

Amelia, eyes cold and mocking, smiles ever so slightly—a chilling smirk of victory.

Before we can process this hell, or even regroup, Amelia retaliates. She thrusts her hands forward, and a towering wave of water, monstrous in its size and intent, barrels towards us. There's barely a split second to react, to brace ourselves, before we're engulfed, the sheer force pinning us mercilessly against the cold, unyielding wall.

The chilling embrace of the water, combined with the shock of Amelia's unexpected power, leaves us gasping, struggling, and vulnerable.

Sputtering and struggling for breath, I try to locate Natalie through the torrent. "Natalie!"

Another wave knocks me off my feet. But I, too, can control the elements.

That's right, Amelia. Prepare for a fucking storm of your own making.

With every ounce of will and anger, I force the water back, sending it crashing into Amelia. Overwhelmed, she stumbles as I hit her with wave after wave.

Crawling through the waterlogged floor, I finally locate Natalie, half submerged, her curls plastered to her face, her breaths coming in short, desperate gasps.

I grasp her, pulling her fiercely to my chest, trying to shield her from the madness around us. But despite my efforts, there's one thing I can't protect her from—the cruel reality reflected in the water mirror.

There, in heart-wrenching detail, float Ciel and Adip. Their bodies are still, their faces frozen in the throes of panic, a snapshot of their tragic final moments. The silvery surface of the mirror doesn't just show the scene—it amplifies the horror, making it impossible to look away.

I can feel the tremors racing through Natalie's body, the raw anguish in every shuddering breath she takes. She clings to me, her fingers digging into my arm, but her gaze remains locked on the haunting image of our friends.

Tears spill down her cheeks, merging with the water that's already soaked us through. The sheer enormity of the grief threatens to drag us under. Watching her suffer, seeing that profound pain in her eyes, is a blade twisting in my chest.

As Amelia moves her hand, the water in the room rapidly evaporates, leaving only the damp remnants on our clothes and the coldness that settles deep in our bones. Soaked and shattered, we're left dripping and disoriented in the dry aftermath.

Amelia steps forward, every ounce of her posture radiating a triumphant arrogance that makes my blood boil. Her voice, thick with disdain and brimming with dark satisfaction, seems to reach from all corners of the room. "If you hadn't destroyed my device, they could have been resurrected. It's no one's fault but your own, Natalie. It's because of you that your friends are dead."

The ground trembles beneath me, but it's not from any powers—it's the visceral, rolling tremor of rage building up inside. I shoot a look towards Natalie, and in her eyes, I see the same unrestrained fury that must be blazing in my own.

I charge at Amelia with a roar, raw emotions acting as fuel. Our powers clash, but hers are sharper and more refined, forcing me to the ground with brute force. Each blow she deals feels like a sledgehammer, breaking down my defenses.

Natalie takes her turn, celestial powers colliding with Amelia's. For a moment, it seems Natalie might succeed where I failed—the stars forming from her palms into aggressive bolts.

But Amelia summons a force we've never seen before, some deep-crimson energy that seems to sap the strength from everything it touches. With a sweeping motion, the force crashes into Natalie, sending her tumbling backward, gasping for breath.

With Natalie momentarily incapacitated, Amelia slowly reaches into her pocket, producing a dagger. Panic sets in as I watch her advance towards Natalie.

"That won't kill me," Natalie spits out defiantly, trying to stand but struggling. "I'm immortal."

A sinister smile spreads across Amelia's face. "I know."

Adrenaline ripples through my core as I force myself to move, lunging at Amelia in one last desperate bid to protect Natalie.

But she anticipates my move.

She turns, driving the dagger backward, piercing straight into my stomach.

Pain, sharp and blinding, radiates from the wound, and I crumple to the ground, the cold blade still lodged within me. The metallic taste of blood fills my mouth, and the edges of my vision start to blur. Through the haze, I see Natalie's face, stricken with horror and grief, as she rushes over to me, crying out in despair. A silent scream builds from my wound, trapped behind my clenched teeth as I grit through the pain.

"No, no, no, no…" Natalie says, each repetition a dagger in its own right.

My ears ring with a high-pitched whine as she cradles my head in her lap, her tear-filled eyes locked on to mine, searching for a sign that I'll be okay.

But deep down, we both know the gravity of this situation. She won't be able to bring me back.

A cold sweat breaks out on my forehead, her voice a distant echo as she assures me, "It will be okay. It will be okay." But everything else is fading, the room, Amelia, the pain—all except for Natalie.

With every ounce of my dwindling strength, I force my heavy eyelids open, needing to see her, *really see her*, one last time.

Her eyes, shining with tears, meet mine. "No," she whispers, gripping my hand tightly. "This isn't it. I'll fix this."

"We destroyed the device," I say, the weight of realization crushing me. "There's no magic to undo this…"

Her face contorts with anguish, tears spilling down her cheeks.

I take a shuddering breath, cold tendrils of death spidering through my veins. "Promise me, do whatever you have to. Stay safe. For both of us."

She clings to my hand, her grip fierce and desperate. "I can't lose you."

Holding on to the last shred of consciousness, I muster up the strength to speak, my voice ragged and weak. "I love you."

Her voice breaks as she responds. "No, this isn't the end. We can find another way."

But the dark tendrils wrap tighter around me, and the world dims. With the last of my consciousness, I wish for more time, more moments with her.

As the void claims me, I hold on to her touch, our shared moments, no matter how brief—letting them comfort me as I take my final breath.

CHAPTER THIRTY-NINE

NATALIE

MY SCREAM RIPS through the silence as I stare down at Henry's body, echoing the cavernous void in my heart. The sound of my own voice terrifies me, but the pain is far worse.

Suddenly, the ground beneath us trembles, and I feel a vertigo-inducing shift. The walls fall away like an illusion dispelled.

The cold wind bites at my skin, the taste of salt on my lips. We're now on a cliff's edge, shrouded in darkness. Amelia's fortress looms in the distance.

Amelia's mocking laughter pierces through the night, a cold reminder of the cruelty of our reality. "Once again, Natalie," she says, stepping out of the shadows, her silhouette menacing against the pale moonlight. "This is your fault. You destroyed the device. You could have brought him back."

My heart thunders as I push to stand, anger building, every fiber of my being straining against the desire to crash down in sobs. But I won't give her the satisfaction of seeing me broken.

"I'll just find a way to remove the damned shield that prevents us from using magic. Whatever it takes."

She chuckles in response. "Good luck. Removing the shield? That could take years, decades, even centuries. All without your precious Henry by your side. His body will rot into nothing by then. Now you know what it feels like to lose someone you love."

Rage surges within me, but I tamp it down, refusing to be baited so easily. "You've already taken everything from me. My mother. My friends."

Amelia tilts her head, her eyes gleaming. "You're right. All of them are gone thanks to your choices. And Wes could've been a great asset to you. Now, it seems he's gone too. All this devastation you brought upon yourself."

Tears prick my eyes, but I refuse to let them fall. "You gave me no choice. You offered me a prison, not a life."

Amelia steps closer, her voice dripping with false sweetness. "It's all about perspective. I gave you an opportunity. A life with Wes. A chance at happiness. And yet, you chose chaos."

I take a deep breath, my resolve hardening. Amelia may have won this battle, but the war is far from over.

"You made your choice. And choices have consequences," she says.

Our gazes lock, two fierce warriors in an unending battle. The weight of my loss anchors me to the spot, but I'll rise, fight, and take back everything Amelia has stolen from me.

The tense stillness is shattered by a pulsating darkness that engulfs the moonlight, like a shadow rushing to cover every last beam of light. My eyes dart upwards, the ground beneath me vibrating with the thunderous whoosh of wings.

Goosebumps scatter across my skin as I attempt to make out details of the colossal creature overhead. The rhythmic beating of wings returns again and again, each pass making my heart speed faster.

On one pass, the moonlight catches something—a fleeting glimpse, but enough for my eyes to capture a terrifying detail. A vast expanse of leathery skin stretched tight over powerful bone structure, veins pulsating with life. The wing is etched with patterns, maybe even scars.

Is it a dragon? The thought seems preposterous, the stuff of fairy tales. Yet, in a world where all sorts of beings exist, where even I am not human, maybe dragons aren't too far-fetched.

Suddenly, the monstrous being swoops low, its immense presence creating a powerful downdraft that pushes me to my knees. The gusts whip my hair around, dust and debris stinging my eyes, but I force them open, desperate to glimpse more of this creature.

Turning my gaze to Amelia, I find her watching the beast, but her expression doesn't mirror mine. She appears to be in awe and maybe even…recognition. It's as if she's been expecting this creature, summoning it, welcoming it.

Just as suddenly as it arrived, the beast ascends into the night, its shadow dissipating.

Panting, I stagger to my feet, my gaze locking on to Amelia's. "What the hell was that, Amelia?"

Her eyes glow with anticipation. "It's finally happening," she says with a tinge of awe.

Before I can even brace myself, Amelia's fingers curl into claws as she lunges for me. I dodge to the left, barely avoiding her first swipe.

We circle each other, our heavy breathing meeting the sound of turbulent waves crashing against the rocks. I surge forward, driving my elbow towards her face. She dodges just in time, but I use the momentum to swing my leg around, aiming a kick at her midsection.

Suddenly, she dodges to the left and then comes in from the right, grabbing my wrist and twisting it viciously. Pain shoots up my arm as she delivers a powerful kick to my midriff, sending me staggering back.

Gasping for breath, I catch a glimpse of triumph in her eyes. But it's a fleeting moment. With a burst of energy, I tackle her to the ground. We roll, each trying to gain the upper hand, but her strength is unnerving. With a swift move, she pins me down, her fingers closing around my throat.

I tap into my celestial powers, concentrating my energy to release a cascade of stars from my palms. They shoot towards Amelia's face like a meteor shower, knocking her away.

I shove to my feet just as Amelia summons her own energy force, an invisible shield forming around her, repelling the onslaught of my starry attack. Each star collides with the shield, erupting into dazzling bursts of light before dissipating into the air.

Frustration builds inside me. If this power won't work, I need to dig deeper, to uncover another layer of my power that she doesn't expect. Closing my eyes, I focus on my energy, my uncovered powers, feeling the threads wrap around my fingers. With a determined shout, I release the energy. It manifests as a spiral of glowing golden light, winding its way towards Amelia.

Caught off guard, she attempts to block it, but it entangles her. The spirals wrap around her limbs, slowing her movements as if she's caught in a web.

Amelia struggles against the chains of my power, letting a smidge of fear pass over her expression. Using this momentary advantage, I gather my strength, and with one more powerful push of energy, knock her down. She crashes to the ground, still ensnared by the golden coils.

My victory is short-lived as the sound of snapping coils breaks the silence. My eyes widen as Amelia shatters the golden bindings, each fragment dissolving into sparkling dust. She doesn't even pause to catch her breath—in a flash, she's on me.

I try to dodge, to summon more power, but everything happens so fast. Amelia's hands find my throat, squeezing with immense strength.

The ground falls away beneath me as she lifts me effortlessly off the cliff. Panic overtakes my senses, my fingers scrabbling desperately at her grip.

Through my dimming vision, I see the dark abyss below, the roaring waves waiting to claim my body. My celestial powers pulse within, desperate to be unleashed, but Amelia's grasp is relentless.

Drawing from deep within, I tap into the core of my human emotions. Love, anger, sorrow, hope. Henry, my friends, my mom, every moment, every emotion, comes flooding back. It's a raw, uncontrolled energy, and it's my last hope.

I channel all of it into a scream, a primal cry that emanates from my core. The sound waves ripple outwards, a tangible force that rocks the air around us. Amelia falters, her grip on my throat loosening ever so slightly.

Using the split second, I kick out, my heel connecting with her midsection. The force pushes her backward, releasing her grip entirely. I fall to the ground, gasping for breath, my throat burning from her chokehold.

Amelia stumbles backward. We're both on edge, each waiting for the other to make a move. All I can think of is how this has to end, once and for all.

"You may be immortal, Natalie, but I'll let the Black Sea tear your body into pieces that can never be put back together."

With that, she crashes into me, sending me soaring off the edge of the cliff. The wind screams in my ears as I plummet, the cold and cruel embrace of the water rushing up to meet me.

The impact with the water is jarring, and I'm immediately engulfed in the dark, tumultuous depths of the Black Sea. Waves toss me about like a rag doll, and sharp rocks loom out of the darkness, bruising and battering my body. Every time I try to swim to the surface, another wave crashes down on me, sending me spiraling deeper.

Clumsily, but with determination, I begin to shed the heavy layers of the uniform I have on over my clothes, tugging at the waterlogged fabric that clings to my frame. I shrug off the top and pants, watching as they sink into the watery void below. Free from the restricting weight, it grants me a few precious seconds.

Unfortunately, it's not enough.

Despair gnaws at my heart as oxygen leeches from my throat. Maybe Amelia was right. Maybe this is it. With everything I love gone, what's the point of fighting anymore?

Salt water fills my mouth as I scream in frustration and anguish. The weight of my grief, combined with the relentless force of the sea, pushes me towards surrender.

Just as darkness threatens to consume me completely, an ethereal blue light pierces the depths below. It's gentle yet powerful, drawing me towards it with a magnetic pull. The chaotic currents seem to lose their grip on me, and I find myself being guided down, down to the source of the light.

My lungs scream for air, but instead of succumbing to the suffocating pressure, a rush of adrenaline spikes through me. Fear gives way to determination as the blue light below grows more radiant.

No. This isn't how it ends. Not here, not now.

With that singular thought driving me, I kick my legs with newfound vigor, my arms slicing through the icy water. But no matter how hard I try to ascend, the currents seem to tighten their grasp, pulling me deeper. The sharp coldness feels like a million needles pricking my skin, each tiny puncture reinforcing my desperate need for air.

The blue light below spirals faster, its whirlpool force dragging me closer. The world blurs, sounds become distant. Hope pours from my body as I have no choice but to surrender to the inevitable pull.

But then, out of nowhere, there's a presence—a strong, undeniable force. Arms encircle my body, locking me in a vice-like grip. Shocked, I look to see who it is, but my surroundings are too dark, the figure too obscured.

Our bodies shoot upwards to the surface, my pounding heart mingling with the roar of the ocean. As I break through the surface with this stranger, I gulp in lungfuls of air.

Coughing and gasping, I blink away the stinging salt water from my eyes, eager to see the face of my rescuer.

But when my vision clears, I'm met with a sight I hadn't expected, leaving me with more questions than answers.

"You're…my father."

CHAPTER FORTY

NATALIE

THE SALTY WIND tugs at my hair as I find myself staring intently into the face of the man before me, my supposed father. His eyes, a piercing blue, seem to search my face, as if trying to find traces of a past he once knew. His sandy-brown hair is tousled, dripping wet, and a faint scar runs down his cheek.

Following his gaze, I look up. There she stands, at the mountain's precipice, the villain in my story—Amelia. I'd expect a triumphant smirk or a vindictive glare, but she looks… elated. Pleased, as if she's just won some coveted prize.

I feel a tug, and I realize he's still holding my hand, our fingers intertwined. The weight of his touch is both foreign and invasive.

I wrench my hand away. "Don't touch me," I say, voice quivering with anger and confusion.

He swallows hard, eyes glistening. "Natalie, I… I'm so sorry."

His words hang in the air, but they bring me no comfort. "Sorry? After everything that's happened, that's all you can say?"

He glances back at Amelia, who still watches us like a raptor. "Look, it's complicated."

I let out a scoff. "Of course, it is. 'Complicated.' I'm so sick and tired of hearing that word."

He hesitates before speaking again. "When I was eighteen, my father revealed my true nature. I'm a God, Natalie. My life is dictated by duty. Then I met your mom and I fell in love with her. I didn't want any part of the world I was destined for. But I was reckless. I put you both in danger."

"So, what? You just bailed on her? Me? Because you're… scared?"

His face twists in pain. "I've made so many mistakes. Mistakes that haunt me. I wanted to shield you both from any of that, from any danger that my existence brings."

I slowly lift my gaze to the top of the cliff where Amelia stands, still watching us like a hawk eyeing its prey. Her eyes remain inscrutable, her face betraying nothing. For a split second, our eyes lock, and I try to decipher the twisted thoughts behind that cold, calculating stare. What is she planning now?

A chill runs down my spine, and I return my attention to this strange man…my father. "And Amelia? How does she fit into all of this?"

He gazes out into the distance, seeming to grapple with a deluge of memories. "In the realm I come from, lineage is everything. The Gods believe in cementing alliances through unions, marriages designed to strengthen power and maintain order. Amelia…she was chosen for me. A strategic match. But everything changed the day I met your mother." His voice trembles slightly as he continues, "The connection, the love I felt for her… It was something I had never anticipated. It defied every rule, every expectation."

My mind races, trying to process this revelation. "So all of this," I gesture around, the weight of everything we've faced pressing in, "was because Amelia wanted you? By going to such horrifying lengths? By tormenting my mother? Bringing such pain to me? To the people I love? Establishing an entire reign of terror?"

He nods slowly, a heavy burden evident in his eyes. "Amelia's desire for power and control knows no bounds. Losing me to your mother was an affront to her, a blow to her pride and ambitions. In her twisted logic, if she couldn't have me by love, she'd make sure she got me another way—by making sure that every path led back to her."

The weight of his admission sinks in, thickening the tension between us. "So everyone suffered for your arranged marriage gone wrong?"

Cy nods, his jaw tight with regret. "She won't rest until I'm with her."

I try to make sense of it all. "But 'with her' where? What does that even mean?"

Cy motions out towards the sea, its waves crashing angrily against the cliffs. "There. The Black Sea."

"You live… underwater?" My voice quivers, still trying to grapple with the surreal reality of it all.

Cy shakes his head, eyes clouded with a mix of sadness and nostalgia. "It's not just underwater. There's a realm, an entire universe beyond what you see. There's so much you don't know, so much I wish I had the time to explain. But right now, I just need to make sure you're safe."

My frustration boils over and my voice rises. "Safe? Everyone I love has been taken from me! Mom was ripped away, Amelia murdered my friends, killed Henry. Tell me, what is there left for me here?"

He looks at me with earnest eyes, full of a sorrow I can't quite place. "You have a purpose, Natalie. You can change things. You can make a difference in ways you can't yet understand."

My chest feels tight, the pain almost unbearable. "Then make me understand."

His voice drops to a whisper. "Do you want to bring Henry back?"

The mere thought takes my breath away. I nod, struggling to find words. "But it's impossible… The device, I destroyed it. The magic is gone."

Cy inches closer, extending a hand. "Hold my hand."

I hesitate, fear bubbling up, but the promise of hope, however slim, makes me relent. As soon as our hands touch, a rush of ice-cold energy surges through me, sharp and relentless. Pain lances every nerve, every cell. It feels as if a thousand needles are piercing my very soul.

"Hold on to me," he says, his grip firm. "Don't let go. It'll be over soon."

The world blurs, wind howling around us, the sea frothing and roaring in response.

"What are you doing to me?" I gasp, feeling overwhelmed.

A tear escapes his eye as he says, "I'm giving you a gift, one I should have used differently. A power I believe you won't misuse. Because you, my daughter, are special. You can make things better on this plane of existence. And maybe others one day."

The pain starts to ebb, replaced by a warmth, a strength I've never felt before. As the wind dies down and the sea calms, I'm left staring at my father, trying to process what he's just given me. "What did you do?"

"I transferred some powers to you," he says, his voice filled with a raw pain, making it clear that this act was one of great sacrifice.

The gravity of his words crashes over me, the weight of it pulling at my heartstrings.

Cy's tone shifts, urgency shining through. "Listen closely. If I don't go back now…" His voice falters, a shadow of regret passing over his face. "I'm going to take you up there to Henry. Once you're with him, hold his hand and don't let go. Do you understand? I let go of your mother once, and it's a regret I've lived with every single day. Don't make the same mistake."

A surge of anxiety tightens my chest. "What's going to happen to you? Will I see you again?"

His eyes become distant, reflective. "No. I've already broken so many rules, breached our planes of existence, and defied the treaty. There are consequences, and I don't know all of what they'll be. I'm in uncharted territory."

I grasp at any shred of information, any clue to make sense of it all. "What about Mom?"

"Effie and my brother have her in another realm—your aunt and uncle."

My eyes dart to his, searching for a deeper understanding. "But if they're my family, why can't I see them? Why can't I be with them?"

He hesitates. "Every time we open the portal between our worlds, we risk ultimate destruction."

I push away the frustration that threatens to overwhelm me, taking a breath. "Okay, but what about you? And Effie? How is it possible that you could come here, in this world?"

His jaw tenses, clearly grappling with how much to reveal. "Navigating between realms is forbidden, complex, risky. Effie and I, for the longest time, didn't have the knowledge to even attempt it. We were trapped, powerless to intervene in a world we once called home."

My heart races, each revelation causing a cascade of emotions. "Then what changed? Why now?"

His eyes soften with a protective edge. "When the news reached me about the danger you were in, about Amelia and what she was doing, I had to do something. I reached out to Oman, an old friend, a guardian angel. He has the ability to traverse realms, and I was lucky he was willing to help, despite everything I'd done to him in the past. It was a shot in the dark. We weren't even certain it would work."

My memory jolts with recognition. "Oman? Adip's dad?"

He nods. "Yes, his father is a guardian angel. Initially, I could only reach Adip, and only as an apparition. But each time I tried, I managed to manifest more solidly. The longer we stay away from this plane, this human world, the less tangible we become. But our repeated breaches, opening the portal between our realms, may have opened a path for other beings—ones we don't want here. Ones who might destroy everything."

A shiver of dread runs down my spine. "So others got in?"

Cy's gaze is grave. "I don't know. But if they did, it's up to you now. With the power I've given you, you have to be the one to stop them."

With the sea's roar echoing behind us, my father hoists me effortlessly, and a surge of water propels us upward. As we ascend to the top of the mountain, my heart thunders. Is this another part of his godly powers, or mine? Or both? The winds shriek around us, tangling my hair, before we land gently on the mountaintop.

Amelia stands there, her presence commanding and sinister. "Cy," she purrs, her voice dripping with mock sweetness. "Took you long enough."

My father doesn't respond, his gaze piercing as he looks at her. There's a deep history there, a history I may never know.

Without taking his eyes off Amelia, he whispers softly to me, gesturing to Henry's body. "Hold his hand. Don't let go. No matter what." His voice trembles with urgency, making it clear that this is my last chance to bring Henry back.

Swallowing the lump in my throat, I kneel beside Henry. He looks almost peaceful, as if he's just asleep. But the coldness, the stillness, the blood staining his clothes, speak a different truth. Tears blur my vision as I take his hand, the chill of it stinging my palm. I squeeze, hoping against hope for a sign. A twitch, a breath, anything.

Yet, nothing comes. It's silent, except for the crashing waves and my own ragged breaths. My mind screams at me, to rage against this cruel fate. I think of his smile, his warmth, the way he made everything seem brighter, even in our darkest moments.

Desperation crashes over me. "Come back to me," I whisper, my voice breaking. "Please."

Seconds tick by, feeling like an eternity. My hand never leaves his. I don't care if the world collapses around me. I'm not letting go. Amelia and my father seem to fade into the background, my entire universe narrowing down to the guy lying beside me. The guy I love.

The pain becomes unbearable, and a sob wrenches free.

I don't want to do this alone.

CHAPTER FORTY-ONE

CY

I'LL NEVER FORGET the first night I saw Madeline.

Every damned memory of her golden silk dress, her captivating green eyes, her chestnut hair. She was my only love…and my destruction. And now I face the aftermath—a daughter, *my daughter*, whose very existence screams the repercussions of my choices.

I see the tears, the rage, the confusion in Natalie's eyes, and it stings. That look, it's like a mirror, reflecting back all my regrets, all my failings. I'm no hero in her story. To her, I'm just another monster, or worse. And maybe she's right. After all, what kind of man—no, what kind of God—forsakes his own blood?

This is the price I pay, a hell of my own making. All the pain, all the agony I've inflicted, not just on Madeline, but on my own child, and others. What was I thinking? That I could defy my destiny without a cost?

Amelia's triumphant gaze feels like a slap. She loves my misery, drinks it in like a fine wine. To think, all this could've been avoided if I'd just done what was expected of me. But no, I had to chase what I couldn't have, what I shouldn't have.

As the wind whips around us, my emotions move with it. Anger. Shame. And the disturbing realization that, given a chance, I wouldn't change a thing. It's monstrous, really, to admit that those fleeting moments with Madeline, those memories, still outweigh this devastation.

"Nearly two whole decades, Cy." Amelia's voice is like a whip lashing in the salty air. "All that time wasted."

Her eyes still hold a dark gleam I recognize from our youth—a time when life was just a series of high school challenges to overcome, not this tangled nightmare.

"Those wasted years are only in your head," I growl, letting the wind carry away my words.

Her smirk falters, but only momentarily. She reaches out, her fingers wrapping around mine, and memories of our twisted past come rushing back. Her threats, her games, the lure of a shared life—a trap I'm all too aware of.

"The Black Sea," she says with a dreamlike wonder. "Our home."

Her fairytale vision of an underwater kingdom is far from the truth. She dreams of us reigning the sea, side by side, but she's completely oblivious to the cold reality.

My father is the almighty tyrant. And I was never an heir, but a thorn in his side. My defiance, my insubordination, always kept me caged, out of reach of true power. Instead, I found myself imprisoned in an endless void.

Most days I spend caged in a watery tomb, left with my thoughts, my regrets, my shame, my anger. It's torture of the worst kind, a relentless cycle of reflection and self-loathing.

My brother Hayden carved out his own kingdom in the pits of hell. Rumors of his so-called heated paradise even reached my desolate chamber, making my confinement all the more unbearable.

And my audacity—escaping into this realm, meddling in mortal affairs, and transferring some of my powers to my daughter—will unleash my father's fury.

He'd surely kill me if I wasn't immortal.

I look over at my daughter, a shred of hope in this sick world. She deserves better than this, better than me. And I'll drown the whole fucking world for her if I have to.

I glance at Amelia as she speaks, her voice dripping with anticipation. "Finally, we'll be together, married." She trails her finger along the contours of my chest.

My blood simmers, and I get a familiar yet haunting urge to inflict pain. Memories of every person I've wronged flash before me: the betrayals, the disappointments. My brother. His wife. Friends like Oman. I may have never set out to hurt Madeline and Natalie, but intent doesn't matter when the damage is done.

And Amelia? Well, I've wronged her in ways both deliberate and inadvertent. And now? Every fiber of my being screams to lash out at her, especially knowing the fate that awaits her beneath the Black Sea.

Glancing over at Natalie, I let her innocence give me strength. I steel myself, biting back my venom, offering Amelia only silence.

Amelia's hands grip my face, forcibly turning it towards her. "Soon, you'll forget all about Natalie. She's nothing like you, Cy. A shadow of her mother."

Rage courses through me, almost blinding in its intensity. My gaze drops to Amelia's forearm, spotting the psi symbol there.

"Playing the role of a precog, are we?" I spit out.

Her nonchalant shrug only fuels my anger.

"*That* was your trick? Your way to climb the ladder of power here?"

She grins, probably thinking I'm enjoying this twisted charade. Maybe once, I might have relished in her games, but those days are long gone.

Seized by an impulse, I grasp her wrist, trying to rub away the marking.

"Stop it, you're hurting me!" she cries out.

"Do I look like I give a fuck?" I snap, rubbing her forearm raw.

"It's branded, Cy. It's real. I did it to myself."

I thrust her arm away, disgust and fury mingling. I battle the urge to enact punishment on her, here and now, rather than wait for the cold embrace of the sea to do it for me.

With a jolt, I seize Amelia by the nape of her neck, forcing her eyes to lock on to mine. At first, she seems to enjoy the roughness, but she doesn't know the storm that's about to be unleashed.

As much as I despise acting like this around my daughter, a part of me wants Natalie to witness it. Maybe then, she'll understand what a monster I am, why our paths should never cross again.

"You know what's really beneath the Black Sea, Amelia? Pain. Unending pain. And let me be clear: we won't be in this together. It's no royal haven, no paradise."

She flinches, disbelief in her eyes. "You're lying."

"You'll be confined, isolated, left with nothing but the weight of your choices. Your thoughts."

Her voice cracks in a rare moment of vulnerability. "I don't care. I did everything for you, Cy. When I'm down there, the only thing occupying my thoughts will be you. It's always been you."

"Then I hope you savor the misery. Spend an eternity thinking about a man you can never have. There's nothing in any world that could make me feel anything but disgust for you."

She takes a step back, anguish and desperation written all over her face. "You don't mean that. I know you better than anyone."

"You only know the version I chose to show you. Both of us are cursed with immortality, Amelia. An endless loop of thoughts and suffering. And trust me, you've earned every excruciating moment."

"You're lying," she chokes out, tears leaking down her face. "Deep down, you love me. We belong together, we always did."

"I've lied to you many times. This isn't one of them."

I maneuver the waters around us to rise and rage, threatening to rip apart the mountain we stand on.

In the chaos, my eyes find Natalie's, her figure being battered by the violent waves as she clings desperately to Henry's lifeless hand.

I mouth to her, "Don't let go."

She nods, her eyes wide with fear and determination.

Amelia's courage falters as the monstrous waves threaten to sweep her away. She starts to retreat, but it's too late. Without a moment's hesitation, I grip her tightly around the waist, dragging her into the dark, icy sea below. The Black Sea isn't just water—it's another realm, one she's wholly unprepared for.

She thrashes and fights against my hold as we plunge deeper, but her resistance is pointless.

Before long, we cross the realm, and she's locked in a crystalline prison, suspended in the waters, alone with her endless thoughts. Some part of me should feel remorse, maybe even a hint of pity.

But all I feel is satisfaction.

Maybe I've done right by my daughter, for once. But there's something broken in me. Something that's undone and can never be pieced together.

Staring at Amelia's imprisoned form, my words move through the frigid water. "Goodbye, Amelia. I hope you rot forever in the silence of your regrets."

CHAPTER FORTY-TWO

NATALIE

Giant waves assault us from all sides, each forceful crash threatening to tear Henry's hand from mine. I grit my teeth, fighting against the onslaught, using every ounce of strength I have to keep our fingers intertwined.

And then, as suddenly as it began, the waves subside. The night air turns frigid and biting, wrapping around me like a cloak of memories.

Silence follows, deafening in its emptiness.

My gaze fixes on Henry. "Henry," I plead, my voice trembling, but he doesn't respond.

There's no rise and fall of his chest, no warmth in his skin. Maybe this is all a twisted game. Maybe my father and Amelia are two sides of the same cruel coin. I can't know. I can't trust.

Tears blur my vision as I shake Henry, willing him to wake. But he remains motionless. Despair wells up inside, choking me. I thought I'd reached my limit of pain, but this—this raw, unbearable heartbreak—surpasses everything.

Suddenly, a tender warmth blossoms from where our hands are

interlocked. My breath hitches, and I glance at Henry's face. A subtle pink flush spreads across his cheeks, and the gentle rise and fall of his chest mirrors the ebb and flow of hope inside me.

Eyelashes flicker, revealing those deep-green eyes that hold a universe of shared memories, pain, and love.

"Natalie?" His voice, weak and raspy, sounds like the most beautiful melody. All my focus, all my world, narrows down to the guy before me.

Our tears mix as the dagger, once impaled in his torso, simply evaporates. And as if by some miracle, the deadly wound knits itself closed.

Without hesitation, Henry pulls me close, and our lips crash together in reunion. The world narrows to just the two of us, the horrific night momentarily forgotten.

We part as he gazes into my eyes, a hint of astonishment in his. "Your eyes… they're bright blue, like your father's."

A rush of emotion sweeps over me. I have…my father's eyes. "He shared something with me. Some sort of power. I think it's why you're here with me now."

"And where's Amelia?"

"He took her with him, to some other plane of existence. Apparently, for good."

Seemingly still trying to wrap his head around everything, Henry says, "So, are we safe?"

I glance towards the looming entrance of the building. "This is Amelia's place. Her guards are still lurking inside. And with her gone, they're probably not going to be happy."

Henry grips my arm. "We need to go. Now."

We sprint to the only way out of this place—the cliff's edge—but our path to escape falls short. It's a dizzying plunge, impossibly steep and straight down. I gulp down my fear, trying to figure out how we can possibly escape this way.

"You said you had some of your dad's power now."

"I don't know. I'm not sure diving us both off a mountain is in my new arsenal."

Our dilemma intensifies when a vast shadow spreads across the mountaintop. I instinctively step back, as Henry grips my hand.

"What the hell is that?" he asks. "Is that…wings?"

I squint into the shadow, and the memory of a similar darkness surfaces, the same one that happened right before my father's arrival.

"I think it might be…an angel. Adip's father."

Henry looks skeptical, and I have to agree. Something feels off. The ominous nature of the shadow feels heavier, less in control than before. The figure swoops down with such intensity that one of its wings clips me, sending me sprawling backward. In a heartbeat, Henry's over me, forming a human shield against the advancing threat.

"If it's an angel, I don't believe it's on our side!" he shouts.

Adrenaline courses through my veins, and I thrust out my palm, releasing a torrent of shimmering stars. But they ricochet off the wings, spiraling back towards us, nearly burning our skin in the process.

Henry pulls me closer, our faces inches apart as the stars, my power, rain down, hissing and sparking.

"We can't stay here!" I shout over the chaos.

Henry nods, desperation in his eyes. "We need a plan. Fast."

Taking a deep breath, I focus on the power within, the energy my father transferred to me. If there ever was a time to understand and wield it, it's now. "On three, we make a break for the cliff. I don't know if I can do this, but we have to try."

One.

The wings arc for another pass, the shadow growing darker.

Two.

The wings whip dangerously close again, nearly knocking us both down from impact.

Three.

Hand in hand, we sprint for the cliff's edge, a leap of faith in the face of imminent danger.

But before we can jump, the force of the wings snatches both Henry and me off our feet, our bodies dragged backward across the rough, gravelly ground. Grit fills my mouth as I struggle to free myself, the air compressed from my lungs.

As I spit out the earth and try to regain my bearings, my eyes catch the shadow of the wings coming closer, poised to strike. I instinctively lean back, my heart pounding, fully expecting to be impaled or swept away again. But then—

A human silhouette lands before us. As the wings gracefully retract into its back, the moonlight reveals the all-too-familiar face of Adip.

I can't contain the relief that washes over me. "Adip? Oh my God. You're alive!"

I surge to my feet, hoping for a warm hug from a friend I thought I'd lost. But he recoils, cold and distant.

Henry, equally relieved but wary, steps closer, his hand resting protectively on my shoulder. "Hey, man."

Brow furrowed, I try to reconcile the Adip I knew with this new version. "What happened to you? I thought Amelia—"

He cuts me off, his voice laced with bitterness. "Turns out, I grew wings and survived. That's it."

"Is Ciel okay? Where is she?"

He snorts, the sound harsh and grating. "I got her out too. Given what we've been through, she's probably in some psych ward by now."

Struggling to understand his attitude, I ask, hesitant, "So, you're a… guardian angel? Like your dad?"

His eyes flash with a mix of rage and despair. "Just another thing my father kept from me all my life."

I try to lighten the moment. "Join the club."

Henry nods in agreement.

Adip's gaze hardens. "I never wanted this. Any of it."

"We didn't ask for this either," I say.

He looks at me with cold fury. "I just wanted a normal life. And now, I'm supposed to protect people? How the hell am I going to do that?"

"I don't know," I say, searching for the right words. "Maybe we can all figure it out together."

He laughs, the sound empty. "No, I'm leaving. I'll cut these fucking wings off my back if I have to."

"Why are you mad at *us*?" I say, genuinely baffled.

His voice drips with venom. "Because I'm not that naïve teenager everyone, including you, thought I was. Because you and your family, Natalie, caused all of this. And apparently now, I'm stuck guarding you. But guess what? I don't want the job. You're on your own."

As he turns to leave, my heart breaks. The world continues to shatter around me, and the people I once knew are drifting further and further away.

With his back turned to us, Adip shouts over his shoulder, "Don't jump off that mountain!"

The suddenness of his words against everything else he's said, so practical yet tinged with concern, hits me. It's a welcome whisper of the old Adip, the protective, brother-like friend—a stark contrast to the cold detachment he showed moments earlier—and it tugs at my heartstrings.

His posture stiffens, and for a moment, his silhouette appears vulnerable against the moonlight, like a boy lost. But then, a majestic span of wings explodes from his back. Feathers, shimmering silver in the dim light, stretch out, creating a glow around him. The sight is both beautiful and heartbreaking.

He glances over his shoulder one last time, and I catch a fleeting glimpse of remorse in his eyes. But it's gone in a flash, replaced by that cold, distant look that feels so alien to me. He doesn't say a word—no goodbye, no explanation, only the weight of our shared past and the gulf that now separates us.

With a powerful beat of those incredible wings, Adip soars into the night sky, leaving a trail of turbulent air in his wake. I reach out involuntarily, as if I could somehow pull him back to earth, back to the Adip I once knew. But he continues to rise, becoming smaller and smaller until he's nothing more than a distant speck.

Henry wraps an arm around me, trying to offer some comfort, but the hollow feeling inside is too big to be filled. Our world has become a place of rapid shifts and unstable ground, where nothing is as it seems. Where best friends become strangers.

I lean into Henry's arms, but my gaze remains locked on the point in the sky where Adip disappeared. It's as if someone snatched his very soul, replacing him with this... this other being.

"That's not the Adip I know," I whisper, more to myself than to Henry.

The wind carries my words away, but the sting of betrayal, the rawness of the wound, remains. The world continues to crumble, and as the fragments of what I once believed scatter to the wind, I'm left reeling in the wake of it all.

CHAPTER FORTY-THREE

HENRY

THE AFTERMATH OF Adip's sudden transformation and even more abrupt departure hangs in the air like a thick cloud. We're standing on the edge, both figuratively and literally. Adip's warning still echoes in my mind.

We can't jump.

There's a shuffling sound, like feet dragging over gravel, and my instincts kick in. I step in front of Natalie, trying to shield her from whatever's coming. I can feel the power radiating from her—a new, unfamiliar force I'm still trying to understand. But that doesn't change my primal need to protect her, to make sure she's safe.

A group of guards emerges from the shadows, their intentions clear in their fierce eyes and tense postures. I tighten my grip, preparing for a fight. I'll give them everything I've got, even if it's not much compared to the power Natalie wields. I will be her shield, her barrier.

But then, the guards drop to one knee, one by one, their heads bowed in a show of submission. Completely shocked, I steal a glance towards Natalie. Her blue eyes mirror my own confusion, widened in pure disbelief.

Two figures detach themselves from the group and approach us, a man and a woman. The man is tall, with a chiseled face, while the woman has salt-and-pepper hair, her gaze sharp and assessing. They're both familiar—Amelia's trusted lieutenants.

"I'm Torin," the tall man says, his voice as rough as gravel. He bows slightly.

"And I am Elara," the woman chimes in, her voice dripping with command. She, too, gives a respectful nod towards Natalie. "We are here to serve you now."

I can hear the surprise in Natalie's voice as she responds, "I don't understand. What do you mean?"

Elara straightens, her gaze never wavering from Natalie's. "You defeated our ruler. By the ancient laws, we now serve the one who holds power over the defeated. That is you—the new head of the authority."

I can almost feel the weight of this unexpected responsibility settling onto Natalie's shoulders. "No," she says, her voice trembling. "I don't want it. I don't want any part of this."

I lean closer to her, whispering so that only she can hear. "We might not have a choice right now. Play along, at least until we find a way out of here."

She nods slightly, a subtle agreement, then takes a deep breath, steeling herself. "Alright," she says, her voice now firm. "But know this: I don't just want full loyalty. I want peace. Help us leave, and then find a way to live without causing harm."

Torin and Elara exchange a look before nodding. "As you wish," Elara says.

I can't shake the uneasy feeling settling in my gut. Trusting these two might be our biggest gamble yet, but for now, it's the best play we've got.

The guards encircle us like a pack of wolves. The oppressive walls close in as Torin and Elara lead the way. Each step feels like a commitment to the unknown, and I grip Natalie's hand tighter, ready to kill every last one of them if they dare touch her.

We step over the threshold and into the house. As we move forward, the hallway opens into an expansive dining space. A grand chandelier hangs above, casting a warm, golden glow over the room, the air perfumed with the aroma of cinnamon tea.

Elara gestures for us to sit, her eyes never leaving Natalie.

After a moment's hesitation and a shared glance with Natalie, we both take a seat. The warmth of her hand in mine is the only reassurance I have in this moment.

Elara and Torin move to sit opposite us, placing teacups filled with the aromatic beverage in front of us.

"Drink," Torin encourages. "We mean you no harm."

"No," Natalie says.

I shake my head as well. "We're good."

Elara's gaze hardens slightly as she looks at Natalie. "Our allegiance is to the current leader. Your choices, your desires are respected."

Natalie tilts her head, her blue eyes piercing. "Even if that leader is evil, inhumane?"

Elara sighs, her demeanor showing a hint of weariness. "We are not human, Natalie. We don't operate within the bounds of humanity or its morals. We don't truly understand what that is. Amelia was once our leader, and we followed."

Natalie and I sit with our fingers interlaced, drawing strength from each other.

Torin clears his throat, breaking the silence. "What do you want, Natalie?"

She hesitates, then meets his gaze boldly. "I want to leave. I want a life with Henry, away from all this."

Elara leans forward. "That might not be as simple as you wish. You now have duties, responsibilities."

"I won't be some puppet leader," Natalie says, anger lashing out. "I won't do what Amelia did, continue how the authority has operated."

"You can shape the authority how you see fit," Elara says calmly. "You have that power now."

This seems too good to be true. A trap? My gut churns with unease.

"I'm only eighteen," Natalie says. "How am I supposed to lead an entire organization of supernatural beings?"

"No one else knew how when they started," Torin says. "There's no definitive playbook. You make your own rules."

Natalie looks down, conflicted. "I still want to leave. All I want is a normal life."

Elara's eyes flash. "There's one more complication you might want to consider before you decide—Wes."

My heart rockets into my throat. "Wes is alive?" The guy's like an immortal cockroach.

"Of course," Elara says. "Wes won't be easy to defeat. Maybe impossible."

"So what is he?" I ask.

Elara glances at Torin, a silent exchange happening between them. "We went deep into his lineage," Torin begins, choosing his words carefully, "and while it's still a bit murky, we have reason to believe he may belong to a group referred to as 'the Fallen Ones.' They're remnants of angels who lost their grace. Deceptive. Relentless. Obsessed."

The description certainly tracks.

"So you're telling us Wes is a part of some ancient group of exiled angels?"

Elara nods gravely. "They were apparently extinct, but some things, as we've found, refuse to be extinguished."

Natalie's hand tenses in mine, her anxiety palpable. "That tracks with what Oliver said. And what do you suggest we do? Hunt him down?"

"We believe he can be neutralized," Torin says. "Made subservient even. Primally, he needs to fixate on something, or some*one*." His eyes flit to Natalie, and a pang of protectiveness surges within me.

Natalie pulls her hand away and crosses her arms, looking defensively at the pair. "I don't want his loyalty or anything to do with him, for that matter."

Elara raises an eyebrow. "Then we may need an alternative strategy."

"Which would be?" I say, feeling a sense of urgency.

Torin leans forward, resting his elbows on the table. "From what we understand, Wes was initially transported as a child to our realm through a breach."

Natalie's eyes widen in surprise. "My father said breaches weren't possible before. I mean, except if a guardian angel…" Her voice trails off, a look of realization crossing her face.

Torin nods. "Indeed. Which means someone—or some*thing*—found another way to pierce the veil between our realms. And they delivered Wes to our world."

An unsettling chill slips through my veins. "So a guardian angel brought him in?"

Elara and Torin share another of their wordless exchanges, deepening the unease I feel. "We don't know for sure," Elara finally admits, "but whoever or whatever it is, they wield power beyond comprehension."

Torin sighs, rubbing his temples. "But his presence here, in our realm, combined with his unique lineage, indicates he might be a pawn in a much larger game."

The room feels colder, the weight of their revelation suffocating. In this world of gods, angels, demons, and apparently now, fallen angels, how do we even begin to navigate this?

The room's ambience seems to fade away as a vision consumes my senses. *Wes, towering and commanding. The guards, including*

Torin and Elara, line up behind him in perfect order, their expressions vacant, suggesting allegiance. How did this happen?

Wings sprout from Wes's back—not angelic like Adip's, but decayed and bloodied. They spread out, casting a shadow that seems to suck out the remaining light.

Natalie stands beside me, her hand gripping mine.

Wes growls at Natalie. "Miss me?" A twisted smile curls his lips. "Looks like there's someone new in charge now."

The vision dissolves as swiftly as it appeared, yanking me back to the present. I blink fast, momentarily disoriented, the edges of my vision blurred.

My heart thunders against my ribcage, the taste of fear bitter in my mouth. I meet Natalie's gaze, a silent plea in my eyes, hoping she'll somehow know, somehow understand what's coming.

CHAPTER FORTY-FOUR

NATALIE

A HEAVINESS SETTLES over me. Not just from Henry's clear distress, but from the weight of the past—the past I've only ever known in disjointed fragments.

"I need some time alone with Henry."

Elara nods understandingly, her gaze lingering on me for a moment. "As you wish." But just as she and Torin start to turn away, she gestures to a trunk sitting in the corner of the room. One I recognize. "We thought you might want to see this."

I stiffen, my gaze turning sharply to her. "I've seen it before. I don't want anything from Amelia. Nothing."

Elara holds up a hand, her expression gentle. "It's not Amelia's, dear. It's your mother's. Memories from her past. Memories Amelia boxed up."

It's like the wind has been knocked out of me. I'd assumed when I saw it before that the box—the contents—belonged to Amelia.

Drawing in a shaky breath, I muster a nod of gratitude. "Thank you."

With a last lingering glance, Torin and Elara make their way out, leaving Henry and me alone.

The room becomes a vacuum of silence. Hesitantly, I approach the trunk, Henry by my side. Every item within it holds a story, a piece of a puzzle, a part of my mother's history with my father.

The initial lift of the lid sends a rush of nostalgia into the air, a mix of old paper, dried flowers, and a faint hint of perfume. The world falls away as I lose myself in the contents.

The varsity jacket from before immediately catches my eye—deep hunter green with bold white letters spelling out "Lockwood" across the front. Its size, unmistakably men's and XL, makes me think of a younger version of my father, perhaps wearing it with pride during his school days.

I trace the embroidered letters with my fingers, feeling the texture. Why did my mom have it? Did he give it to her? Wrap it around her shoulders one night when she was cold? My mind races, wondering about the moments this jacket witnessed. Moments I'll never truly know.

The photos catch my attention next—an envelope of them I didn't see before, old Polaroids, slightly faded, but the emotions captured are as vivid as ever. One shows a younger version of my mom, laughing, nuzzling into my father's chest. Another shows them at some kind of fair, cotton candy in hand, the bright lights of the Ferris wheel illuminating their features.

Then there are the ticket stubs. Each one is a small gateway to a memory. An old cinema ticket from a local theater, dated two decades ago. There's no movie name. What did they watch? There's another stub from a carnival, perhaps the same one from the photo.

My fingers wrap around a dried flower corsage. It's fragile, the petals delicate to the touch. I imagine it wrapped around my mother's wrist at a dance, both of them lost in each other's eyes as they swayed to music.

There's a jar of sea glass—it's filled with smooth, rounded pieces, tumbled by the ocean, each a different shade and size. I can picture them, walking hand in hand along the shoreline, during happier times, occasionally bending down to pick up a piece.

Every item tells a story—a snapshot of their love and a glimpse into their world. A time before the chaos, before the pain, and before me.

Tears prick my eyes as Henry's arms wrap around my body, his chin resting on my shoulder. "They had a whole life before me."

He squeezes me tighter. "They did. It looks like a beautiful one."

We stay like this for a moment, surrounded by remnants of my parents' past. The weight of their memories presses against my skin, like a physical burden on my chest.

"I want to get out of here."

Henry hesitates, spinning me to face him, then slowly starts, "About that… I had a vision." His eyes are heavy with worry.

"What was it?"

"It was Wes. He… he seemed to have taken over the authority. The guards—Torin, Elara, everyone…they were behind him. And he had wings—rotted, torn wings."

I stare at him, trying to process his words. "So what do you think that means? If we leave, Wes will build an army against us?"

Henry nods. "They said Wes, whatever he is, needs something, or some*one*, to fixate on. If we leave, we might just give him the opportunity."

"So what are we supposed to do? We can't exactly go back to Lockwood. That school is nothing but a puppet for the authority. It shouldn't even exist in the first place."

"All of it should come crashing down. Lockwood, that fucking prison they held me in, this place… Everything should be ripped apart."

I find myself staring down at the photo of my parents. The

smiles on their faces, the happiness, the love—it all feels distant, yet somehow right within my grasp.

A strange sense of purpose begins to grow within me. "What if there's another 'me,' Henry? Another 'you'? Someone out there who's just as lost, just as tormented. Someone who needs help."

He looks down at me with a puzzled expression. "What do you mean?"

I suck in a deep breath, searching for the right words. "What if there's someone else out there, right now, about to be tortured by someone like Amelia? What if someone takes over and makes this entire system even more corrupt? What if we could change that?"

The weight on my shoulders feels even heavier now. But it's not just the weight of my parents' memories. It's the weight of responsibility, of destiny, of wanting to make things right.

"So you want to do it? Lead the authority?" he says.

I shake my head slightly. "I don't want to. But maybe I should. Maybe I could change it. Make it better. My father gave me some sort of power. I feel... I feel like I'm meant to do this. To make things better for others. Even if I have no idea where to start."

The room grows silent, except for our synchronized heartbeats.

Henry stares into my eyes. "Whatever you decide, I'm with you. Always." Drawing my hand to his lips, he presses a soft, lingering kiss on the back of it. Then, with a playful glint in his eyes, he goes down on one knee, bowing his head. "Should I address you as my queen now?"

Laughing, I tug on his arm, pulling him up. "Don't be ridiculous. We are equals, always have been, always will be. If we're going to reshape this world, change the authority, it will be *together*, side by side."

I look around the room, the enormity of the task looming, my mind racing, searching for a starting point. I've already stood up to Amelia, even if I had help. If I could confront someone as twisted and powerful as her, then I must have the strength to lead, to make a difference.

"I can do this," I whisper, more to myself than to Henry, a personal affirmation. "I can."

᰾

This bedroom is unfamiliar, not the place of my earlier confinement with Wes. It's a simple guest room with muted tones and feels somehow less tainted. Even though the guards, Elara, and Torin haven't shown any hostility, a sense of unease lingers in the air. Every fiber of me knows I'm an outsider here, in uncharted territory.

I curl into the bed, cocooned by the soft sheets, but my thoughts whirl uncontrollably. I've been thrust into a situation much bigger than me and I'm crumbling under the weight. How did I end up in the center of this chaos? In *charge* of this?

In every story I've ever read, the hero is nearly flawless, the epitome of strength and wisdom. Yet here I am, with a lifetime's worth of mistakes and imperfections. I'm not that gleaming protagonist who swoops in to save the day. I'm a mess.

I barely notice Henry at first, as he leans against the doorframe. It's only when I see the gentle concern in his eyes that I realize he's been watching me. Wordlessly, he approaches, fingers brushing softly against my face, grounding me. "You're not alone in this."

"And what if I screw it all up? Make things worse?"

"We all make mistakes. They say that's what makes people human, right? And maybe that sense of humanity is exactly what's needed when ruling those like us." He moves closer, kneeling by the bed's edge. The sincerity in his gaze is unwavering, and for a moment, the world shrinks to just the two of us. "Everything that's happened, it led to this. To us. And I believe in us, in you. I love you."

I draw him into an embrace, my heart syncing with his. "I love you too."

The world contracts to the two of us. A tug on Henry's shirt sends him hovering over me, our breaths mingling. My fingers stroke along the ridges of his back.

He moves, bringing me higher up on the bed. Our eyes lock, a silent promise between them. When his lips meet mine, it's with a tenderness that makes my heart throttle. I deepen the kiss, letting go of all the fear and uncertainty, getting lost in the whirlwind of emotions he always brings out in me.

Henry's fingers, warm and steady, glide under my shirt, yanking it off while I help him shrug out of his. Each piece of clothing removed feels like shedding what we've been through. With a gentle insistence, he pushes my arms above my head, his fingers intertwining with mine. A soft gasp escapes me, and our eyes meet again as my body arches up to meet his.

He glides inside of me and our bodies move in sync, intense, heated—until everything builds up to a crest and I finally lose all control. Henry's pleasure matches my own. We shudder together, Henry sighing into my neck.

Lying there, wrapped up in the comforting tangle of limbs and sheets, my fingers lazily dance across Henry's skin until they find that all-too-familiar marking—the psi symbol on his forearm. An outdated badge of compliance—a branding to show your submission.

And now that I'm in charge, it's time for this symbol, and so many other archaic rules, to become a thing of the past.

CHAPTER FORTY-FIVE

NATALIE

I JOLT AWAKE, my heart pounding. As I turn, expecting to find Henry beside me, I'm instead met with Wes's chilling gaze.

My instincts kick into overdrive; my heart beats wildly against my ribcage, my muscles tensing, ready to flee. But to my horror, I can't move. An invisible weight holds me down, cementing me in place.

Though it's clearly Wes, he looks different—less tangible, more like a shadow, a wisp. The contours of his face are familiar yet distorted, giving him some bizarre otherworldly quality. His signature smirk, however, remains.

"Did you think you wouldn't see me again?" His voice is almost amused, dripping with a sort of dark delight.

Every fiber of my being wants to scream and run, but instead, I find my shaky voice. "I hoped not, but I knew better. Especially now that I'm in charge."

His hollow laugh sends shivers down my immobile spine. "You might be in charge, Covington, but you don't control me."

"Don't you get sick of this, Wes? Sick of the games, the

manipulation, the deceit? Not just the lies you feed to others, but the ones you feed to yourself?"

For a moment, I see a glimmer of something in his eyes. Regret? Pain? But it's quickly replaced by his typical steely resolve. "Sometimes. But it's the only way I know how to exist. It's how I've always been."

"Is it because you're a fallen angel?" I counter.

A shadow passes over his face, and his smirk softens into something more melancholic. "I know what I am now. I'm no longer in your world. I'm home."

Confusion clouds my mind. "Then how are you here with me? How can you be in two realms at once?"

He sighs, weary, like I should know. "You're asleep, Covington. And I'm not physically with you. I'm dream-walking. And yes, I can traverse between realms in dreams. Apparently, a fallen angel perk."

A million questions flood my brain, but one pushes its way to the front. "Did you always know? Know what you truly are? Did you lie the whole time about being a precog…Cambion…whatever?"

"No, I didn't always know. But after Amelia played with time, in the middle of everyone's countless attempts to get rid of me, I did my research—found out what I am. And now I wear it as armor and albatross."

"Albatross?"

"Sailors once believed seeing an albatross was a good omen, but killing one was a curse—a reminder of your sins. The poet Samuel Taylor Coleridge wrote about it, about a sailor forced to wear the dead bird around his neck so he'd never forget the awful thing he did." I watch as his gaze turns inward, lost in thought. "Being a fallen angel is my albatross. It's the weight around my neck, a constant reminder of my fall from grace."

I can't help but challenge him. "After everything you've done, do you really think you're just…destined to be this way? That you have no choice but to be obsessive and compulsive, to lie and hurt people?"

He pauses, his eyes distant. "Somewhat," he says. "But I'm trying to be better. I showed you my journal, didn't I?"

"You've shown me a lot of things, including a hellish display of cruelty."

Wes nods slowly, his form appearing to flicker, reinforcing the fact that he isn't really here. "Being on a different plane from you has given me some clarity. And while I originally thought we were destined to be together, that our goals were aligned, now they seem… different."

"Different how?"

"You're now in charge of the authority, and I can predict the changes you'll make. I've watched you, Covington. Obsessed over you. Fixated on your every move. I know precisely how you think. I know you inside and out."

"You don't know everything about me."

"No," he says, "but I can read you well enough. And let's be honest—while you're smart, you'll face a lot of resistance. You can't expect everyone to just roll over and follow your lead."

I narrow my gaze, a thought sparking in my mind. "What about the blood bond?"

"Resurrection was only possible with magic. That no longer exits, so neither does any bond."

"You mean since I destroyed Amelia's device?"

"Exactly," he says. "When you crushed that thing, its magical influence died along with it. The blood bond was only a product of that magic."

"So it's just gone?" I probe, wanting to be sure. "Just like that?"

He nods, a glimmer of regret in his eyes. "Yes, just like that. Free from that tie."

I exhale, a mixture of relief and unease filling me. Knowing that bond was truly severed, in any timeline, is liberating.

Wes watches me, his lips splitting into a grin. "It's a good thing, Covington. For both of us."

His assurance feels off. After being at the center of his intense fixation for so long, his sudden indifference is jarring. While a huge part of me is relieved, another part can't shake the feeling that something is very wrong.

"Elara said you have a tendency to fixate. It's in your nature. If it's not me, then who? Or *what* … has caught your interest now?"

Wes's grin fades, replaced by a more sincere expression. "There's something new, something that's demanding my attention. A purpose that goes beyond you."

I swallow, unease bubbling within me. "So what does this mean for us? Are we going to be enemies across realms? Every decision I make, every move, you'll fight?"

"I don't want to fight. And with you guarding things, I suspect my visits will be few and far between. If they happen at all. I can't just hop between realms, only in your dreams."

"So, what? You'll just be my reoccurring nightmare now?"

His expression flattens, as if all emotion has been sucked out. "No, my fixation on you has run its course. I wish you luck, Covington. You're gonna need it."

The certainty in his words is like a punch to the face. Just as I'm about to respond, he fades.

My eyes snap open from the dream and I feel the cool, damp blanket wrapped tightly around my form, my heart still racing from the confrontation. I turn, practically throwing myself toward Henry's side of the bed, my fingers gripping his arm urgently, shaking him awake.

"Henry!"

His deep, steady breaths falter, and his eyelids flutter open. "What's going on?" He sits up, ruffling his tousled hair, immediately sensing my distress.

"Wes. He… he walked into my dream."

Henry's face contorts, caught between disbelief and growing concern. "That's not possible… is it?"

"He did it before. It's some ability he has as a fallen angel. Supposedly, he's not here anymore, not in our realm. When that portal was opened—the one my dad came through? Wes went back to wherever he's from. But he can still get to me, in my dreams at least."

Henry pulls me close, his embrace warm and comforting against the cold dread coursing through me.

"So he's trapped, away from this world, unless the portal opens again?" he murmurs into my hair. "That sounds like a good thing."

"Only guardian angels can bridge the gap." My eyes drift to the door, beyond which a world of responsibilities and dangers lie, thinking about the only guardian angel we know of—Adip. Who doesn't want to see me again.

Henry holds me tighter. "Adip…and his father."

If Wes wants back in our world, Adip or his father could be manipulated, threatened, or worse. And if they aren't the only guardian angels out there, the potential danger is multiplied.

Wes might have said he was done with me, but there's a nagging feeling in the pit of my stomach that tells me it's not as simple as that.

As if reading my thoughts, Henry whispers, "We should warn Adip. And we need to find out more about these guardian angels. If there are others, Wes could use one of them to get back."

I nod, my resolve hardening.

Henry brushes a stray hair behind my ear, his gaze intense. "We've come this far. We can handle whatever the universe throws at us."

His confidence is infectious, but the weight of responsibility still presses down on me. The emotions, the revelations, the threats—they're not going away.

But as I melt into Henry's embrace, one thing becomes clear: I don't have to face this madness alone. I've got him right beside me.

CHAPTER FORTY-SIX

HENRY

WEEKS AND MONTHS blur together, and the pace with which Natalie begins reshaping the supernatural world is staggering. Amelia, with her ability to warp time and space, might have twisted reality in a lot of ways, but now? Now, everything feels grounded.

Together, we comb through every inch of the authority that once was Amelia's. The rehabilitation centers, the dark, silent places where people were imprisoned for disobeying, are now empty. In their place, Natalie's set up counseling groups. People are healing, reconnecting with loved ones, rebuilding their lives.

The Armory's arsenal—both the weapons and the people—have been fully integrated into the authority—not as instruments of force, but of protection. Old rules? Scrapped. New ones, crafted by Natalie, now dictate the order of things.

At the center of it all, Lockwood remains a place of memories— not all good. With Amelia gone, those connected to the authority, like Ms. Whitney, are being flushed out. Natalie chooses to keep Lockwood open, at least until the current class graduates. After that, she's set on shutting its doors, maybe for good.

And with everything constantly changing, Natalie keeps an unwavering focus on us—supernatural beings. Her plan is to train them, make them aware of their powers at a young age, make sure it's no longer a forbidden act. There are no more acts of coercion or control, like branding marks on our arms.

But not all transformations are smooth. Adip vanishes without a trace. It feels like he just erases himself from our lives, or even this plane of existence.

Ciel also vanishes. She doesn't return any of our calls, doesn't return to Lockwood. When Natalie finally manages to get ahold of Ciel's mom, she acts cold, short—claiming Ciel is taking time for herself, healing. Understandable, really.

On one of our more introspective days, we visit Lockwood, not daring to enter the iron gates. Students wander the grounds, seemingly unaffected by our absence. Maybe they genuinely don't notice. Maybe Lockwood is right about one thing—its students often live in their own bubbles, blissfully or willfully ignorant of the chaos beyond their manicured lawns. Or maybe the reality is too dark, too overwhelming to acknowledge. These are students cushioned by wealth and opportunity—high school's a fleeting chapter for them. They'll move on, find new lives that aren't impaled with danger like ours.

And then, there's Natalie's father—the fake one, anyway. In a previous timeline, he was killed by Amelia, but because things were reset, he is now back—alive. He has a wife, a child, a life that doesn't include Natalie. Driving past his home, seeing that alternate reality, hits her hard. But she says nothing. Her now-blue eyes glitter with emotions, but her face is stoic. I know that look, and it's better not to ask.

The chaotic months leave both of us drained, with a need to find solace. We discuss it at length, weighing our options, until one place becomes the obvious choice.

"We could go to the cabin," I suggest one night as we lay

entwined on a hotel bed. It's becoming a habit—a new city, a new hotel nearly every night.

Natalie looks up at me, her blue eyes clouded with thought. "The cabin where you took me before?"

I nod. "Yeah. It's secluded, away from all of this. It'll give us a moment to breathe, to plan our next steps."

She pauses, a playful challenge in her eyes. "That's when you rescued me from Wes… and everything else. And when I was still figuring out whether to trust you. You were such an asshole back then."

In a swift move, I pin her down on the bed, hands pressed above her head. "Admit it, you loved every minute of it."

Her laughter bubbles up, a sound I never tire of. This routine, this push and pull, has become our ritual. Every night, we scheme, strategize, and play our parts in trying to set things right. Then we look back, teasing each other about our past mistakes, our wrong turns, all the secrets we hid, the feelings we refused to share. Every night ends by getting lost in each other, in every possible way. Then we wake up, do it all over again, always side by side.

We know the cabin won't be a permanent solution, but it's the breather we desperately need. A place where we can refocus and remember why we're doing all of this in the first place.

Now that we're here, with every passing moment inside this place, it feels more and more like a sanctuary. Memories, both bitter and sweet, resurface. It's off the beaten path, hidden by ancient pine trees. If it wasn't for the worn wooden swing outside, you might miss its existence altogether. Perfect for us.

"Feels different, doesn't it?" Natalie says, snuggling closer to me on the bed. "Being here, without danger breathing down our necks."

I nod, kissing her forehead. "It does. It feels…warm. Like home."

She looks up, eyes lighting. "Maybe it can be. Someday."

I have to admit, the idea of setting roots here, even if temporary, is pretty enticing.

But our peaceful night is shattered the moment Natalie's gaze locks on to an uneven floorboard. "What's that over there?" she asks, wriggling free from my arms. I try drawing her close again, but when she's curious about something, there's no holding her back.

I shift her attention to the present, to us, to the bed. "Nat, this cabin's ancient. It's bound to have a fucked-up floor."

But it's too late, She's already fixated. Snatching a hammer from a kitchen drawer, she pries up the floorboard. "There's something hidden here…"

From the concealed space, she retrieves a photo album—it's water-damaged, its edges frayed from age and weather.

She joins me on the bed, hands over a photo to me, and then another. The woman in the photo, barely older than us, is cuddled against a guy with intense, shadowy eyes. Their happiness is obvious, even in this faded image.

I squint, getting a better look at the familiar face of the woman— long, raven-black hair framing violet eyes. *Effie.*

"That's your aunt. Effie. The one who rescued your mom."

Natalie gently runs her finger over the photos. "This guy must be my dad's brother." She points at a handwritten caption on the back. "This one says, 'Hayden and Effie,' but this photo says, 'Hades and Persephone.' Are these pet names?"

"Could be their real names," I say, caught up in the mystery.

Natalie carefully flips through more dated photos: month after month… it's like a timeline.

Then, the trail grows cold, abruptly ending.

I search for a logical explanation. "Maybe they just moved away, left this album behind."

But Natalie's eyes, troubled and deep in thought, remain on the album. "My dad said something about past mistakes, destroyed relationships. He mentioned his brother. The timelines match. I was born not long after this date. Maybe whatever happened to my dad happened to them too.

Before either of us can voice more thoughts, Natalie shuts the album with a soft thud, and a sealed letter slips out from the back. The envelope is yellowed and brittle, untouched for decades. She takes a deep breath, tearing the seal, carefully unfolding the aged letter.

"What does it say?"

Natalie swallows hard, her eyes glistening with emotion, combing her eyes over the paper. "This… is from Effie. Addressed to my dad." She hesitates, looking at me.

The history between her family of Gods is layered with secrets and hurt, and this letter could unravel another chapter.

"Do you want to read it to me?" I ask, wanting to give her the choice.

She nods, takes a deep breath to steady herself.

Cy,

It feels weird writing to you, especially after everything that's happened, but there are things you should know. First, about Hayden—God, where do I even start?

Hayden's been… different. Haunted. He's discovered some stuff about your family, things he was never meant to find out. All these years, he thought he was protecting you, doing right by you. He couldn't have been more wrong.

He's learned more about your dad. About the things you went through when you were separated from him. The idea that your father played any role in your mom's death, and the way your dad treated you while Hayden was locked up, has nearly broken him. He believed he was protecting you, and realizing that he might have inadvertently hurt you even more? It's tearing him up inside.

Hayden is spiraling. He's drowning in responsibilities he never asked for, obligations to a realm he's not sure he even wants. But he's also rebelling against it, in his own way. He's conflicted about where he belongs: with me, here and now, or the underworld.

I've heard that you've fallen in love, and that the person you've fallen for is off-limits, forbidden. You're sworn to Amelia and I can understand the horrors of that. And now, learning that you've been separated from Madeline, especially when she's carrying your child? I can't even imagine the pain. It's got me thinking. If anyone would understand the anguish of loving someone who's hurting, it'd be you. I've tried reaching Hayden, but he's shutting me out. I believe—I have to believe—that you're the one who can get through to him.

Maybe you two, with your shared destinies, could come together, lean on each other. Change the narrative? Find a better path forward? I don't know.

He's your brother, Cy. Maybe, just maybe, you can bring him back from hell.

Hoping for better days,

Effie

I see a tear glistening at the corner of Natalie's eye, the stories of her family's past pulling at her heart.

"If the letter is here, sealed, that means it never reached my father."

CHAPTER FORTY-SEVEN

NATALIE

THE COOL BREEZE from the ocean brushes my cheeks as I settle alone on the dock, nursing a mug of my favorite cinnamon tea. This spot, right here, has become my favorite, a place to clear my mind.

I think back to a time when life felt simple, almost predictable. Days of making choices about which outfit to wear to an event or what subject to study next. How naïve was I to think my biggest decision would be which college to attend, based on my not-even-real-dad's wishes, or which guy he thought was my ideal match.

Then Henry stormed into my life, spinning everything out of control. His presence ignited my passion, confusion, and a chaos that was as exciting as it was terrifying.

So much of our story is littered with mistrust and miscommunication. Secrets and hidden feelings. The pieces of the puzzle never seemed to fit. Henry, who I once believed had turned against me, was, in truth, always on my side.

And me? I spent a month—regrettably—manipulating Wes, using his twisted affection to extract what I needed. The taste of that decision, bitter and cold, still lingers. Even with Henry back by my side, our reunion wasn't immediate sunshine. With each challenge, another layer of my life got stripped away, especially when Amelia's intentions became all too clear.

In those more difficult hours, hope sometimes felt like a distant star, twinkling but unreachable. The weight of isolation, the sting of betrayal, the cold clutches of captivity. Yet every setback, every heartbreak, carved out a new piece of the fighter in me. Discovering my true ancestry, confronting the reality of my parents, and embracing my new role—each was a lesson in resilience and purpose.

But victories come at a price. The absence of Mom, the lost opportunities with a father I barely got to know, Adip's sudden disappearance, and Ciel distancing herself—each loss rings in the silent corners of my heart.

Thankfully, in the midst of all this mess, there's Henry. His presence, his love, acts like a balm, soothing the raw wounds.

A sigh escapes me as I take another sip of my tea, its warmth spreading through my bones. Life is unpredictable, and while I can't change the past, I can shape the future. And with Henry by my side, I know I'm not facing it alone.

The gentle lapping of the waves pairs well with my mood. My thoughts inevitably drift back to Henry. They always do. Our relationship has been a roller coaster of emotions, riddled with detours and pitfalls. The beginning? It was challenging, to put it mildly. We were like two forces, colliding, clashing, yet also inexplicably drawn to each other. There were times I wasn't sure if we were each other's salvation or undoing.

As I roll over our countless confrontations and misunderstandings, mixed with more tender moments and shared dreams, one thing remains—our love for each other. Love became our compass, guiding us back no matter how far we strayed. It's a love that grounds me, that provides an anchor in the rockiest of seas. It's my safe harbor, my sanctuary.

With Henry at my side, I'm on a new chapter: leading the authority. The memories of what the authority once represented, the atrocities it committed, are reminders of the heavy responsibility I now shoulder. But it's a challenge I willingly accept.

My goal is to create an authority that stands for justice, for unity. An organization that ensures that the cruelties of the past aren't replicated. That supernaturals of all kinds and humans can one day coexist harmoniously.

Taking on this effort is daunting. I understand the magnitude of the responsibility—the hope for a brighter, inclusive future rests heavily on my shoulders. There will always be those resistant to change, challenges that threaten to derail my ambitions, and the inescapable reality of my own imperfections. I will stumble, make mistakes, but I've come to realize that's okay. Mistakes are the stepping stones of experience, and I'm no longer that naïve girl who thought life was black and white. Sure, I'm still a bit messy, but aren't we all? Whether you're human, supernatural, or somewhere in between, life is just a tangled web of emotions and decisions.

I've faced down enemies, traveled time, and survived the worst challenges. Each experience has left a gash on my soul, sculpting me into who I am today. With every tragedy, I've evolved, emerged stronger, more resilient. I'm ready to face whatever comes my way.

Taking a deep breath and letting the ocean breeze play with my hair, I consider the wild ride I've been on. It's amazing how life schools you in ways you never see coming.

For starters, I've got a whole new definition of control. It's not about having a tight grip on every aspect of life or asserting dominance. It's not about the thrill of wielding power or the intoxication of having everyone dance to your beat. It's about the silent strength of knowing what that power truly means and carrying the weight of its responsibility. It's like realizing you're the captain of the ship—it's not about shouting orders, but about guiding it safely through storms.

And life, with all its unpredictability, will inevitably unravel. It's not always going to be neat, linear, or within the confines of our expectations. But it's in those chaotic moments, in the scattered threads of events and choices, that the real patterns of our existence emerge. Every setback, every heartbreak, every twist I didn't see coming? They were lessons, guiding me, refining me. It's the detours that teach us resilience, that show us who we truly are and what we're capable of.

And finally, I've embraced the concept of being undone. It used to terrify me—the thought of losing myself, of becoming vulnerable, of letting people in, worrying who was judging me. But now, I see it differently. Being undone is not an ending—it's a new beginning.

The wooden boards of the dock creak under my feet as I make my way back to the cabin. The early morning mist is lifting, revealing the world in soft hues of dawn.

As I enter the cabin, a familiar warmth wraps around me from behind. I twirl around in Henry's arms. We exchange a glance, and in his eyes, I see the same fire, the same determination. No words are needed. Our bond speaks for itself. We've been through hell and back, and this silent gesture says it all—we're in this together. Forever.

BONUS CHAPTER

NATALIE

Three Months Later…

ANOTHER NIGHT. ANOTHER hotel. The past few months have been a blur of unfamiliar rooms and transient lobbies. We left behind the safety and solitude of the cabin, diving back into the chaos of running the authority.

I'm sprawled on the bed, flipping through authority documents, when Henry's voice cuts through my thoughts.

"Look at this," he calls over to me. He's hunched over his phone, fingers rapidly tapping and swiping.

I shuffle over, my eyes settling on the video playing on his screen. It's nighttime in the video, but streetlights illuminate a chaotic scene on a bustling New York City sidewalk. At its center, a guy, clearly intoxicated, is making a commotion. He's flailing his arms and yelling, his speech slurred. The camera pans and zooms in, and that's when we hear it—Adip's unmistakable voice.

"Fuck," Henry says, pointing to a blurry section of the screen.

As the video quality momentarily sharpens, a glimpse of what appears to be wings is visible on Adip's back. My heart throttles into my stomach.

Henry pauses the video and runs a hand through his hair. "It's already going viral. Luckily, most of the commenters seem to think he's wearing some fake, costume wings."

The stakes here are enormous. Humans don't know about supernatural beings, at least not yet. And we certainly can't let them find out about us like this.

"I need to go to New York, talk to him."

Henry hesitates, torn. "Are you sure?"

I meet his eyes, determination swelling inside me. "I can't have him exposing his wings in the middle of Manhattan. Besides, he's my friend. Or was. I owe it to him to try and help. He's clearly struggling."

⌘

New York's iconic skyline pierces the horizon, skyscrapers sending shafts of light into the darkened streets below. But away from the glitz and the glamour, in the older parts of the city, old bars sit with their secrets.

It's in one of these bars that I track down Adip. The atmosphere inside is thick with the scent of aged wood and stale beer. Flickering bulbs cast a dim yellow light, and the low hum of conversations provides a haunting soundtrack, every so often punctuated by the clink of a glass or the soft music from an old jukebox playing songs from decades ago.

Finding Adip was an experience in itself. As I scoured the neighborhood from his unfortunate viral video, each person I spoke to had a different story to share—about the "winged guy" who'd made a spectacle of himself, getting drunk and ranting. He'd been kicked out of several bars, becoming almost legendary—in this neighborhood, at least—and not in a good way. Every pointed finger, every whispered tale led me here…to this bar.

And there he is, seated at a table, nursing what looks to be his tenth drink of the night. The amber glow of whiskey in his glass casts a glow onto his frown.

Approaching him with cautious steps, my shoes sticking slightly to the floor, I take in the sight of him. This isn't the Adip I knew, not entirely. This version is frayed at the edges, coming apart at the seams.

My presence barely registers to him until I'm almost at his side, my reflection ghosting beside his in the mirror on the wall. Taking a deep breath, I prepare myself to bridge the gap that seems to have opened up between us.

"Fake ID, huh?" I gesture to his drink.

Adip glances up, not exactly happy to see me. He takes a long, lazy slip before bothering to speak. "Does this look like a place that gives a shit if you're of age?"

Looking around, I can't help but agree. The walls are worn, and the customers look even more so.

He finally acknowledges my presence with a tired glance. "What are you doing here, Natalie?"

I gesture to the seat across from him. "Can I sit?" I ask tentatively, not wanting to push him too much.

He gives a long, contemplative pause as if weighing his options, then reluctantly motions for me to join him.

I sink into the leather bench, feeling the worn cracks and creases beneath my fingers. "Can we talk?"

His eyes, slightly bloodshot from the alcohol, flit to his nearly empty glass. "You've got until I finish this drink."

I guess our window for conversation is as limited as the dwindling contents of that glass.

Choosing my words carefully, I begin. "I realize things haven't been easy for you. Discovering that you're not…"

"Human?" he interrupts sharply, his voice dripping with bitterness. "Save your sympathy, Natalie. I don't need it."

I keep treading on thin ice. "We can't be reckless, Adip. The wings…in the middle of the city… it's not safe."

With a visible effort to keep his temper in check, Adip spits back at me. "You may lead the authority, but don't forget, guardian angels like me don't fall under your jurisdiction."

I nod, acknowledging his point. "I'm aware that you don't answer to me. But you must answer to someone. And I'm sure they've told you—"

His scoff cuts me off mid-sentence, a mixture of humor and exasperation. "Hmmm, who do I answer to? The Gods? My father? Some asshole lurking in the shadows that I've yet to meet?" He takes a swig from his glass, his face twisted in a grimace. "To be honest, I don't have a fucking clue who I answer to. And I really don't care."

The low hum of the bar seems to fade into the background, and for a moment, it feels like there's only the two of us in this worn-out room.

"Adip, we used to be friends," I say, my voice quivering just slightly, betraying the emotion I'm trying so hard to keep together. "You were like a brother to me. What happened?"

His gaze, once filled with warmth and concern when directed at me, is now cold and distant. "What happened? You really want to know? Maybe you should talk to your father."

I swallow the lump in my throat. "You know I can't do that. That's not possible."

He leans in closer, his voice low and strained. "Then maybe you'll just have to take my word for it when I say your family—not just your father, but you too—ruined my life."

I'm taken aback, reeling from his words. "How can you blame me for my father's actions? For the choices he made?"

Adip's anger is palpable, his fingers gripping the whiskey glass so tightly, I fear it might shatter. With a forceful motion, he slams it down on the table, the sound echoing loudly in the tense silence. "It's not just about your father. It's about you. How *you* acted, the choices *you* made. I used to defend you, feel sorry for you. But the more I think about it, the more I realize how willfully ignorant you were. You wrapped yourself up in this victim narrative, never taking responsibility for your actions. Just like your father, making choices without considering the consequences."

His words are a dagger to my heart, each syllable a twist of the blade. I can barely breathe, struggling to comprehend his anger towards me.

And he just continues twisting that blade, over and over. "You were busy playing puppet to everyone who pulled your strings— your dad, Jack, even that maniac Wes. You think you can lead the authority?"

"I'm trying my best," I say defensively. "Of course, I'm going to mess up sometimes, but I want to make things right."

Adip's voice is hollow. "It's because of *your* family that we're in this mess to begin with. Your father, your parents, their recklessness… They ruined everything."

My heart races, but I keep my tone even. "I don't have the whole story. All I know is that I want to make amends."

"Your father has caused nothing but pain, even to my dad."

Confusion twists through my mind. "Then why did your dad help him get through the portal?"

Adip looks away, a shadow crossing his face. "Cy's apparently got a way of getting into your head. Making you believe in things, even if they're against your better judgment."

I try to process that, linking together the fragments of stories I've been told. "Did your dad share this with you? About mine?"

He just stares at his now-empty glass, not meeting my eyes.

When he stands to leave, I reach out, placing my hand over his. "Wait. I just… I want to understand."

Adip lets out a bitter chuckle. "I think we're past understanding."

"But you were estranged from your dad, too, weren't you?" I proceed carefully, choosing each word. "Maybe he thought, in his twisted way, he was doing the right thing. That by helping me, and by extension, my father, he was fixing things with you."

"You think this was about father-son bonding? That he was trying to make up for lost time? My dad is *gone*, Natalie. All his problems, his power, his obligations—they're on me now. I didn't ask for any of this, yet here I am, drowning in a legacy I never wanted and no guide on how to navigate it."

I try wrapping my head around the concept. "Gone? But I thought guardian angels were… immortal. Eternal."

His gaze hardens, eyes glinting with something raw. "Eternity doesn't just mean living. In other realms, with different rules, 'gone' takes on a different meaning. It's not as binary as human life. It isn't just dead and alive."

I grimace, the weight of the conversation ripping at my heart. "My father acted out of love, saved me out of love, Adip. Misguided, maybe, but it was love."

"And look where that got him. Look where it got me. My dad. Look where it's getting you and Henry. Drowning in each other, in some fantasy land, losing sight of the bigger picture. The world is not happy, Natalie. And you being in charge? There are plenty who aren't fans."

The iciness in his voice chills me to the core. "But I'm trying to help—"

His voice cuts through my words. "The portal was opened. Your dad and mine are gone. Amelia is gone. Wes is gone. But others have come in. And trust me, they aren't here for a friendly visit." He stands, his silhouette imposing against the dim light.

"Adip, wait. Don't leave."

He turns to me. "There's nothing more to say. Every decision you make, every choice, it's always been about you and Henry. Everyone else is just collateral damage."

I shake my head, desperately trying to convey my sincerity. "It's not like that."

"Isn't it? Time and again, I've watched you prioritize your own needs, your own wants. And in my experience, history tends to repeat itself."

His accusations weigh on my chest, challenging my every intention and motive. I watch him take a step towards the exit, but then he pauses, turning slightly. There's a hint of the old Adip I once knew, the warmth beneath the hardness.

"I'll try to keep a low profile. Control the wings, lay low," he mutters. "But you? You really need to watch your back."

And with that, he's gone, leaving behind an unsettling silence.

The Adip I remember was caring, selfless. Now? He's transformed, shadows of bitterness swallowing him whole. But then, haven't we all changed in some way or another? Been molded by our experiences, the good and the bad?

Despite everything, despite his anger, deep down, I know Adip's concern is genuine. And he's right to an extent—the toughest battles are still ahead of us.

But he's wrong about one thing: I do care. Deeply.

My heart has space for me, for Henry, and for others. And I will rise to the occasion, always striving to make the best choices, not just for myself, but for everyone.

THE END

NOTE TO READERS

Dear Reader,

Thank you so much for following along with Henry, Natalie, and Wes's story in The Lockwood Trilogy. As you can see, Natalie has some big shoes to fill. And, as I'm sure you've guessed, this won't be the last time you'll see Natalie & Henry.

But it's time for other characters to get the spotlight. As the stories unfold, you'll discover more answers, more secrets, and more twists you never saw coming.

If you'd like a sneak peek at the next book, *Of Stars and Tides*, which features Cy and Madeline's backstory, keep reading.

Here's a snapshot of the other books out now and coming soon to the Lockwood Metaverse:

BLACK SEA - Read Now

This prequel novella to *Control* tells the love story of Effie (Perse-phone) and Hayden (Hades). As their paths first cross at Lockwood, tensions flare with Hayden's enigmatic brother, Cy, and Effie's tormentor, Amelia. Follow them to hell and back in this haunting, fated mates love story.

OF STARS & TIDES (June 2024)

Following *Black Sea*, this heart-wrenching reimagining of Romeo & Juliet charts the doomed romance of Madeline (Natalie's mother) and Cy (Natalie's father). Their illicit love, shadowed by Cy's fateful obligations and Amelia's revenge, is a twisted story of passion and tragedy.

GUARDED (November 2024)

Two years after the tumultuous events in *Undone*, Adip is transformed—a tough figure haunting the streets of New York City, rebelling against his fate as a guardian angel. When Ciel seeks him out, his past comes rushing back and his fate refuses to be sidelined. As looming threats converge, only Adip holds the power to restore balance. His choices might just tear apart all that Natalie has painstakingly built as the head of the authority.

SYMPHONY OF ICE & ILLUSION (December 2025)

In a shadowy, twisted rendition of *The Nutcracker*, Wes reemerges in our world, masterfully concealing his true identity. Infiltrating Lockwood—now an academy for the supernatural—he finds a new obsession, one that exposes his deepest weaknesses. Yet, in this story, the most menacing villain isn't Wes himself.

20 Years Earlier...

OF STARS AND TIDES

CY

WHAT A POMPOUS piece of garbage this party is.

I straighten the suit jacket that used to fit me, but after lifting weights twice a day for the past six months, I'm bulging out of it. The thing is like a fucking corset at this point.

Working out obsessively is the only way to keep my other impulses in check. Maybe if I'd figured this out months ago, I wouldn't have destroyed my relationship with my brother. My hands twitch in rage as the fractured memories loop around my mind.

Fuck this. Fuck Hayden.

I peer up at the gaudy chandeliers that hang from the ceiling, lighting up this sea of small talk, fake smiles, and other bullshit.

I catch a whiff of sickly-sweet perfume as an older woman slinks past, grazing her arm against mine and casting a glance in my direction to indicate that she's open to fucking me tonight. Or right now.

Maybe. I'll see what my tastes are like later.

Amelia makes her way over to me. She teeters on her high heels, indicating she's already a few too many glasses of champagne deep. After we graduated from Lockwood, my father practically locked me up in this monstrous compound in Istanbul for the summer, one of his many properties across the world. He set me up with some important internship, making sure I keep up mortal appearances while I begin dealing with the real cards I've been dealt as an immortal God.

"Wanna play a game?" Amelia asks.

"Sure." Why the hell not? Might as well have some fun at this party if I'm stuck here.

"I pick someone in this room and you have until the end of the night to fuck them," she says.

Amusement coats my expression. "Every woman in this room would say yes to me. What kind of game is that?"

"You'll see." Darkness gleams in Amelia's green eyes as she floats past.

Another one of my father's bright ideas was for me to date a "normal" girl, and he chose Amelia Collins. Not the worst choice. Amelia has some darker tastes in the bedroom that bode well with mine. She also doesn't mind if I fuck anyone else, nor do I care who she brings to her bed.

But she's a complete psychopath and I don't particularly like who I become when I'm around her.

I also don't believe for a second that she's normal, or even human. But my father forbade me to spill the truth about what I am, and I've spent enough of my life enduring his wrath that I know never to disobey him.

I'll never forget when my father revealed to me that I'm an immortal God. It was right after Hayden was locked up at Iron Rose. I was sixteen years old and he swore me to secrecy, said the time wasn't right to tell my brother because Hayden wouldn't "react so well." I was so fucking shell-shocked I never even wrote Hayden a letter, called, or visited the entire time he was locked up. I didn't know how I was supposed to speak to my brother and not tell him *that* truth.

My father also dropped this news on me right after my mother died, or rather right after she was killed by my father's hand.

Hayden doesn't know our father killed our mother, just like he didn't know he was an immortal God until I told him. My brother believes he was protecting me, when the reality is, I was always protecting him. I'm *still* protecting him.

I know he's hiding away in that cabin with Effie, but I haven't told my father. I won't tell him. He doesn't know about that place and if I have anything to do with it, he never will.

All those years enduring my father's abuse and I didn't realize I was turning into him. I got angry with my brother when he was released, envious that he doesn't bear the weight of these secrets, jealous that he got the girl I wanted, and it incited such rage inside of me that I nearly killed both of them.

Just like the night my father killed my mother.

Guilt snaps against my chest. *I will not turn into my father.*

A few times, I swam over to the cabin at night to check on Hayden, watching him sleep next to Effie. My talent for swimming extremely far distances in even the most treacherous waters is apparently one of my gifts as a God.

I could practically feel Hayden's happiness sleeping next to Effie, and it made me sick with envy. I don't have a desire for Effie any longer, just a desire for the affection they have. When will it be my turn? Will it ever be?

My gut twists as I catch a glimpse of my face in the reflection—the faint mark left on my cheek by my brother. He burned me with his fucking hand. But I tried to drown him and his girlfriend, so I suppose we're even now.

My father enters the room and everyone circles around him like compliant minions. He gives a speech and his words sound good on the surface, but I can see through them, right to the bitter poison of his manipulation.

Once he's finished, the crowd explodes into applause. I swipe a whiskey off a waiter's tray and suck it down.

My father makes his way over to me. My body straightens in his presence, a physical reaction that I fucking hate. I don't like that he has so much control over me and I look forward to the day when that won't be the case. Since he's immortal, I don't know how that works, and he refuses to give me any information. At what point does he stop aging? He's fifty-two right now, tall, broad, imposing, with chilling blue eyes like mine and dark hair like Hayden, streaked with gray.

"Ease up on the drinks, son. There's someone I'd like you to meet."

I slam down the empty glass and follow my father to the woman who was eye-fucking me just moments ago.

"Cy, this is Vivian. She works at GlobalCorp and will be your direct boss when you start your internship next week."

Vivian beams, extending her hand out to mine. "A pleasure to finally meet you, Cy. You come highly recommended."

That means my father blackmailed my way into the position.

I play the role of the polite son, planting a kiss on her hand. "The pleasure is all mine."

She crosses one leg over the other, squeezing her thighs together, and I can already tell that I'll have her bent over her desk on my first day. Though, to be frank, I'm a bit bored by that prospect already.

As my future fuck-buddy keeps chatting with my father, I'm able to excuse myself, grabbing yet another whiskey off the tray.

The centerpiece of this tacky party is an expansive fish tank, a wall of glass that my father considers a liquid masterpiece. It divides the room in half, flooded with vibrant fish that dart among coral and seaweed. Fish are supposed to have a calming effect, and I have to admit they sort of do. For a moment, I become mesmerized—the annoying laughter and clanking glasses blur and fade away. I'm not sure if the fish are bringing me peace, or if I'm just getting drunk. Either way, I feel better than I have all night.

As a group of fish part, my eyes latch onto a girl on the other side of the glass. She's striking, fucking gorgeous—her long, dark, chestnut hair draping over a golden dress with thin straps. Her expression sparkles with innocence as she watches the fish, captivating me even more.

A thrill chases up my spine, lodging in my throat, my attention completely hijacked by this girl. I circle around the tank, my heart drumming against my chest with every footstep. The anticipation of closing in on her, a lion after his prey, and tugging that dress from her pretty shoulders later has just made this night fucking magical.

As soon as I'm around the other side of the tank, I'm staring at the back of her, drifting to the right, moving to where I was just standing. My stomach clenches with excitement. Was she coming over to me? Or avoiding me?

To be honest, I'm not sure which turns me on more.

I move ahead, ducking around the corner of the tank, only to find her walking away, across the room. My gaze clings to her perfect figure, the golden silk dress hugging every inch, leaving nothing to my imagination. While her dress is revealing, there's a palpable mystery to her—a mystery that I personally need to unravel. Tonight, preferably.

Desire surges through my bones as I push through the crowd after her, ignoring Amelia along the way. I'm sure she's picked someone out for me to play with, but I've got eyes for only one girl tonight… and she's getting away.

The stranger moves into the hallway and up the winding staircase, her dress trailing behind her on the marble steps. She's several paces ahead of me and I don't want to startle her, so I wait until she's out of view before climbing the stairs after her.

Once I hit the landing, I notice a door wedged open at the end of the dark hall—my father's home office. A chill runs down my spine as I creep closer.

I push the door open a fraction and a surge of emotions boil over—confusion, suspicion, *jealousy*. Why is she in here? Does she know my father? Is she here for him?

She's alone, which somewhat alleviates my jealousy. Her finger loops around the handle of his desk drawer and she pulls it open, digging through the contents, face etched with determination. Her fingers clasp a piece of paper.

What is she looking for? Her poking around into my father's private things gives me another unexpected thrill.

Moving swiftly, I dip inside the office, closing the door behind me. The soft click of the lock startles her and she glances up at me with that gorgeous, now terrified gaze.

Catching her stirs something deep and primal inside of me and I stride towards her, each footstep an unspoken challenge. In one move, I have her pinned against the desk, my arms caging her in from behind.

"Looking for something?" I sound so much like my father in this moment, and that bothers me.

I instantly feel better watching this girl's hands clench the sides of the desk, fear radiating off her perfect skin. "Your father sent me up here to get something for him."

I know she's lying, I can practically smell it. But her words do reveal something—that she knows I'm his son. Has she been watching me too?

I lean into her neck, causing her body to tense even harder. "I'm supposed to believe you work for him?"

"I don't really care what you believe."

Defiant girl, isn't she? It takes every shred of my willpower not to bend her over this desk right now and coax the truth out of her.

"Tell me your name."

"I'll give you a name, but you know it won't be the truth, Cy."

Fuck. She's challenging me. She knows my name, but I don't know hers. The power here is far too imbalanced for my liking.

I grip her by the arm and whirl her around, pressing my body against hers so she has no choice but to lean back on the desk. "I'm not playing games."

She holds my gaze, her defiance appearing to melt into something more vulnerable.

There we go. That's a good girl. Just how I imagined you'd be.

"Maybe you should," she says.

I have no time to process her words when her knee crashes into my groin. I double over in pain as she slips away and reaches the doorway with inhuman speed. I also notice she's still holding a piece of paper. How did she manage to grab that from the desk so fast? Or at all?

She twists around to face me. "My name is Madeline."

"Madeline what?"

Her lips split into a grin. "Nice meeting you, Cy." She glances down at the paper she stole from my father's desk. "Or should I say, *Poseidon.*"

My mind twists in confusion as she races off, her name—and the name she called me—hanging in the air between us. A thread of truth or a bold lie? I have no idea.

But I sure as fuck am going to find out.

ENJOYED THIS BOOK?

Please leave a review on Amazon. I greatly appreciate any support!

ALSO BY MELISSA CASSERA

Books in THE LOCKWOOD TRILOGY:
CONTROL - Book One
UNRAVEL - Book Two
UNDONE - Book Three

Other books in the LOCKWOOD MULTIVERSE:
BLACK SEA
OF STARS AND TIDES (Coming Soon)
GUARDED (Coming Soon)
SYMPHONY OF ICE & ILLUSION (Coming Soon)

ACKNOWLEDGMENTS

To everyone who took the time to read *The Lockwood Trilogy*, THANK YOU, THANK YOU, THANK YOU. I am forever grateful that you took time out of your world to read my words. *Sobs in happiness.*

To my Lockwood Elites street team and my ARC readers. Thank you from the bottom of my twisted little heart for all of your support, shares, and sweet reviews.

To my husband, Gary, thank you for always supporting my writing and encouraging me through all my wild ideas and writerly mood swings. None of this would be possible without you.

To Susan Hyatt for getting this series out of a sad desk basket and encouraging me to put it out into the world. Look at us now!

To Dawn Ius, my incredible developmental editor, who always pushes me and cheers me on, no matter what new twist I throw out. I'm so grateful to have you in my corner.

To Jessica McKelden, the most badass line editor/proofreader in the whole world. Your attention to detail is truly mind-blowing.

To my alpha and beta readers, thank you for your invaluable, honest feedback.

To the team at Damonza, my cover designers, who create the most gorgeous designs. I would never have sold this many books without you!

To my friends Alexandra Franzen, Shenee Howard, Lisa Fabrega, Nicole Antoinette, Jessie Rosen, Shelley Cohen, and everyone else who supported and encouraged me along this wild ride. I'm forever grateful.

To my mom for always taking me to the library as a kid, letting me watch soap operas, and for not noticing when I stole your romance novels. Ha!

To Washington state, my beautiful home that partially inspired this story.

To anyone who writes/creates Turkish dizis (quite literally the best TV shows out there).

To everyone who makes unapologetic, obsession-worthy entertainment. I'm obsessed with you.

CONTACT THE AUTHOR

Thank you so much for giving *Undone*, book three of The Lockwood Trilogy, a chance! If you enjoyed following the twists and turns of this story, I'd be so grateful if you could rate and review the book.

Join Melissa Cassera's author mailing list for exclusive sneak peeks and giveaways: https://melissacassera.com/control/

Instagram: https://www.instagram.com/melissa.cassera/

TikTok: https://www.tiktok.com/@melissacassera

ABOUT THE AUTHOR

Melissa Cassera is a professional screenwriter and the bestselling author of angsty, twisty romances with a soft spot for the morally gray. She is also the writer of 11 movies for *Lifetime Network*, including "The Obsession Thrillogy," the network's first trilogy of movies.

When Melissa isn't writing twists you won't see coming, she can be found drinking too much coffee, playing at the lake with her dogs, or getting lost in the romance section of a bookstore. You can sign up for her author newsletter *HERE*.